BRINDLEY, LOUISE

WINTER SOLSTICE

70044227

Dosbarth Class No.	F	Rhif Acc. No.	

AC

WINTER SOLSTICE

WINTER SOLSTICE

Louise Brindley

This first world edition published in Great Britain 1995 by
SEVERN HOUSE PUBLISHERS LTD of
9–15 High Street, Sutton, Surrey SM1 1DF.
First published in the USA 1995 by
SEVERN HOUSE PUBLISHERS INC., of
595 Madison Avenue, New York, NY 10022.

British Library Cataloguing in Publication Data

Brindley, Louise
  Winter Solstice
  I. Title
  823.914 [F]

  ISBN 0-7278-4864-X

Typeset by Palimpsest Book Production Limited,
Polmont, Stirlingshire
Printed and bound in Great Britain by
T J Press (Padstow) Ltd, Padstow, Cornwall.

For Grace and Kathleen

Chapter One

Christmas lights spilled on to wet pavements, shoppers hurried along, heads bent. The Salvation Army band, grouped together near Woolworths, played 'Away in a Manger'.

Searching in her pocket for a coin, Catherine popped it into the collecting box, smiled, and hastened towards a little café overlooking the sea, her favourite Saturday afternoon refuge.

Turning the corner, the wind came at her like a battering ram. In the gathering dusk of a December afternoon, the sea was scarcely visible, but it was there right enough, crashing in on the shore, thundering against the rocks of the Marine Drive, its continuous roar reminiscent of a stampede of buffalo.

Desperately in need of a cup of tea, she found herself a table near the window, stacked her shopping bags out of harm's way, noticed with pleasure that the shore-lights outlining the bay had been switched on, and saw the intermittent beam from the lighthouse illuminating the dark, heaving mass of water beyond the harbour mouth.

The waitress, a plump motherly woman whom she knew well by sight, came up to the table. "The usual, dear?" she asked. "A pot of tea and a scone?" Glancing at the shopping bags she said, "A right carry on, this Christmas shopping lark, isn't it? I'll be glad when it's all over and done with, and that's a fact." She sighed deeply. "Funny, I used to love Christmas as a kid, an' I try to make it special for my grandchildren, but it doesn't seem the same anymore. Little 'uns want so much nowadays, an' they're still not satisfied. I dunno!"

Catherine knew what she meant. The magic was

missing. In her case the sense of security she had known as a child, at home with her parents and her sister Mavis; the hanging up of their stockings on Christmas Eve; awaking at the crack of dawn to find that Father Christmas had been in the night, leaving a pile of presents stacked at the end of their beds; filling their stockings with oranges, nuts and chocolate doubloons in gold paper wrapping.

Sipping her tea, she thought about past Christmases and the one facing her. Before the deadline of Christmas Eve, clients would arrive at quarter hour intervals to have their hair done in readiness for the family reunions and parties they had planned. A daunting prospect, but she had worked hard to make a success of her business, so why complain at being 'rushed off her feet'?

The door opened suddenly to admit a group of laughing teenagers. Paper serviettes scattered like leaves in an autumn gale as they trooped into the café, the girls as skinny as beanpoles in their jeans, boots and thigh-length sweaters, hair tangled by the wind, seemingly impervious to the cold.

Rescuing her serviette, Catherine wondered if they realized how lucky they were, these kids of a younger generation who had been spared the horror of the war years. Hopefully they would never experience, as she had done, the bitter ending of a wartime marriage.

Finishing her tea, she paid the bill and wished her friendly waitress a Merry Christmas. Facing the icy wind once more, joining the throng of shoppers in the main street, what had possessed her to start thinking of the war years, she wondered. But Christmas was like that, a rattle-bag of memories good and bad. She didn't want to dredge up the bad times. What would be the point? She preferred to remember that during her short-lived marriage to Nicholas Willard, there had been times when she had believed that he loved her.

In any event, she was a different person now from the vulnerable girl she had been then. Crossing the road to the car park, she smiled inwardly remembering how, at fifteen, shy beyond belief, she would dart into a shop doorway rather than come face to face with that grammar school boy she had admired from a distance, afraid that she would blush crimson if he spoke to her. Not that he had ever done so. In retrospect, she doubted if he had even noticed her.

Shyness had continued to plague her throughout the war years, despite her smart Wren uniform. What a naïve little fool she'd been in those days; wearing her heart on her sleeve. No wonder she had fallen in love so quickly, so easily, at that RAF Officers' Mess dance in the summertime of 1944, when she was eighteen.

Starry-eyed from her first encounter with Flying Officer Willard, she had been unprepared for the verbal attack of a fellow Wren, Heather Harper.

"Look here, Cathy Mitchell," Harper said brutally, "If you think Nicholas Willard is interested in you – forget it! The bastard danced with you all evening to make me jealous! That's the way he operates, and you'd better believe it!"

"I'm sorry. I didn't ask him to dance with me, that was his idea. In any case, he's asked me to have dinner with him tomorrow night, and I've said yes."

"Huh," Harper snorted, "knowing him, you'll end up paying the bill! Well, just you wait and see, my girl! You'll live to regret the day you met him!"

Finding her car in the crowded parking lot, Catherine opened the boot and stowed away her shopping bags and parcels. Christmas imposed endless lists of jobs to be done, food and presents to buy, cards to be written and posted before the final shut down of shops and post offices in readiness for the three-day Christmas holidays.

Desperately tired after a busy week at the salon, the last thing she felt like at the moment was cooking an evening meal, but Adam was coming to dinner.

Switching on the ignition, driving home, she thought about Adam – the antithesis of her ex-husband. Nick had been weak, charmingly indolent, unreliable. Adam, on the other hand, was strong, reliable and kind – very kind. A friend worth having: basically a lonely person, as she herself had been until their meeting six months

3

ago. Not that she was in love with him, and the distance between them precluded frequent meetings.

Adam's home was in York, forty miles from Scarborough, and they had their own lives to lead. Nor had she any desire to allow their relationship to develop beyond the bounds of friendship. In a sense, she regarded the forty miles between them as a safety barrier. But there were deeper underlying reasons why she preferred to keep their friendship on an even keel.

She was no longer a starry-eyed girl but a mature woman of thirty-four. No longer Cathy but Catherine. A world of difference lay between the two.

Parking her car beneath a street lamp, she opened the boot and carried her various items of shopping to the front door. Searching in her shoulder-bag for her latchkey, she felt the soft brush of snowflakes against her cheek – flakes as soft and white as goose feathers; as if the 'old woman in the sky', of her childhood imagination, had begun plucking her geese in readiness for Christmas. Not that she minded. She had always loved snow for its whiteness, its essential purity; the hand of the Master Craftsman in fashioning each flake uniquely, so that no two, in the millions that fell, were ever the same.

Climbing the forty-odd stairs to her flat, entering the long, angle-ceilinged drawing room, she saw as if for the first time the smooth moss-green carpet and matching velvet curtains, the circular mahogany table with its centrepiece of gold and white chrysanthemums, the deep, comfortable settee and armchairs grouped about the fireplace.

Nothing ever detracted from her joy in homecoming. This was her sanctuary from the storms of life. Each item of furniture had been chosen to complement the Victorian dimensions of the rooms, in which modern furnishings would have been out of place, and she had taken her time in choosing; picking up pieces from country house sales and village salerooms.

The carved oak chest, for instance, had once graced the hall of a country mansion, the settee and armchairs had

4

been among the effects of a gentlewoman about to move into an old people's home, and Catherine loved the blurred colours of the chintz covers and cushions, the feeling she had of guardianship of the treasured possessions of others, people she would never know, who had once taken pride in their homes just as she derived pleasure from hers.

As time went on, she had added softly shaded lamps here and there; gilt-framed mirrors, a few original oil paintings by unknown artists, a richly-patterned Persian rug to lay in front of the fireplace; bowls of flowers; bookshelves; blending in modern touches with the traditional where necessary – a television set, an electric fire beneath the long white, china-decorated shelf which served as a mantelpiece.

Crossing the room to the kitchen, she dumped her shopping bags on the table. Adam was due at seven o'clock, which meant she had time for a leisurely bath before making a start on dinner – her own version of *Coq au vin*.

Running the bath water, she switched on the radio to listen to the weather forecast for the north-east of England. Many of the minor roads were already impassable, the weather man said, and accidents, in blizzard conditions, were causing problems on the major roads. Travellers whose journeys were not strictly necessary were advised to stay at home. Surely Adam wouldn't venture the forty mile journey from York to Scarborough on a night like this?

The phone in the drawing room rang suddenly, and kept on ringing until, enveloped in a towelling bathrobe, her feet bare, she hurried from the bathroom to pick up the receiver.

Adam's voice came on the line. "Just to let you know I'll be with you as soon as possible," he said. "In an hour or so, I imagine."

"But Adam, is that wise? The forecast is dreadful. Why risk ending up in a snowdrift?"

"Rather that than risk disappointing you, my dear. Not to worry, I'll make it somehow, come hell or high water." The line went dead.

5

Replacing the receiver, Catherine went back to the bathroom, her mind in a turmoil.

"My dear," Adam had called her, a no-nonsense term of endearment sincerely meant, unlike Nick who had called most women 'darling' – flung to the wind like chaff.

A train of thought once embarked upon could not be easily discarded. Nick had entered her mind earlier that day. Now it seemed there was no getting rid of him. Every way she turned, he was there, laughing at her down the corridor of the years, haunting her with memories of a past best forgotten.

Dried and dressed, looking out of the drawing room window, she saw that the roofs of the houses on the other side of the road were thick with snow, the street below seamed with the tyre tracks of passing cars. How still, how silent everything was. Her hand on the curtain, she remembered those winter Saturday nights of her girlhood, before the war, when she had walked alone in the snow, rejoicing in the silence.

Daft, her mother had called her, wanting to walk in the snow when she'd be far better off indoors. "Do you want to catch your death of cold?"

"I'll be all right, Mum."

"Well, don't blame me if you end up with pneumonia!"

How could she have explained to her mother her need to get out of the house for a while – away from the rexine-covered chairs in front of the sitting room fire; the oak sideboard bristling with family photographs, those of her Dad in his First World War uniform; of her sister Mavis' wedding; snapshots of her two children in various stages of development from nappies to rompers.

Seven years her senior, sensible Mavis had married an equally sensible young man, and gone away to live in a modern brick bungalow on the outskirts of Darlington. Ten months later, she had given birth to twins. Now aged forty-one, she had moved with her family to a house of sizeable proportions near Croft Spa, from which her rapidly balding husband, aptly named Ernest, ran his lucrative accountancy business.

6

Her hand on the curtain, Catherine deeply regretted the loss of her father who had died when she was six years old, leaving her widowed mother to bring up Mavis and herself on the slender means available to her, making her seem old before her time. Poor Mum. And yet she had continued to cling to the family home in Sussex Street, as a limpet to a rock.

Drawing the curtains, Catherine went through to the kitchen to prepare the vegetables for the *coq au vin*, worrying about Adam as she did so, wishing he had decided not to drive from York on a night like this. He was an excellent driver, she knew, but what if his car skidded off the road? "In an hour or so," he had said on the phone, but it was now eight o'clock, and still no sign of him.

At least the chicken stew was safely in the oven, and what, after all, was *coq au vin* except a stew with a pinch of herbs, a clove of garlic, and a soupçon of white wine thrown into the pot for good measure?

Nick had told her she was a rotten cook, and she had believed him. She could almost see him now, leaning against the kitchen door, saying in that bored, bantering tone of voice she had known so well. "Why not stick to bangers and mash or fish and chips, Cathy, my love? The kind of grub well within your scope, given your upbringing."

Constantly, during her short-lived marriage to Nicholas Willard, had occurred similar reminders of his superior education and intellect, so that no matter how hard she tried to please him, she had failed.

Fluent in French, he had poured scorn on her feeble attempts to master the language. Somehow she had never been able to get the hang of the various genders. As for the pronunciation, well! Least said about that, the better.

Setting the table, Catherine remembered her first meeting with Adam, when she had gone to The Crown Hotel to wash and set a client's hair.

7

"Let me help," he said, relieving her of her portable hair-dryer and case of equipment, and ringing for the lift.

"Thank you very much."

"My pleasure entirely. My name is Adam Jesson, by the way. I'm staying here at The Crown . . . If you'd care to have a drink with me later, I'll be in the bar." He'd sounded diffident, as if anticipating a refusal.

His diffidence had won the day. Here, she had realized, was a shy person, unsure of himself and his surroundings. A brash, self-assured approach would have sent her running for cover.

Later, she had gone down to the bar to find him sitting alone at a table overlooking the Esplanade, apparently deep in thought. Then, catching sight of her, he rose quickly to his feet, pulled back a chair for her, and asked her what she would like to drink.

"Gin and tonic, please. I feel I've earned it."

"Do you do this kind of thing very often?" he asked.

"Meet strange men in public bars, you mean? No, hardly ever."

"That's not what I meant."

"I know. I'm sorry, I was teasing you."

"What a relief. Being teased, I mean. I'd forgotten what it felt like. I'm afraid I take myself too seriously at times."

And that had been the beginning of their friendship. When he returned from the bar, she explained that she did sometimes visit clients after business hours when called upon to do so, as a matter of goodwill. The elderly lady she had attended earlier, for instance, had a badly sprained ankle, and so Mohammed had come to the Mountain, or was it the other way round?

It had struck her, at the time, a little odd that an attractive man should find it necessary to invite a complete stranger to have a drink with him. Why, she wondered. Later, she had discovered the reason.

His mother had died recently after a long and painful illness. This holiday in Scarborough was, in essence, a 'think tank', a period of reflection to take stock of his

8

life, to come to terms with the past and decide what to do about the future.

"I have a brother in Australia," he said, "my one and only relative. Chances are I'll end up there in the long run. On the other hand, my business partner, Barry Fuller and I, have been together a long time now, and I'd hate to leave him in the lurch, especially now we've landed a franchise for the sale and maintenance of Bentleys and Rovers in the York area. Quite a feather in our cap after the years we've spent trying to put our garage on a sound footing. Besides which, Barry has a wife and children to support. But here am I doing all the talking. Tell me about yourself, Miss . . . I'm sorry, I don't know your name."

"It's Catherine. Mrs Catherine Willard, and there isn't much to tell. I own a small hairdressing salon in Falsgrave. I live alone, and like it. I have a sister, married with children. Thankfully my mother is still alive, and I make it my business to visit her as often as possible. I married during the war. It didn't work out, I'm afraid. Fairly dull, wouldn't you say?"

"I'm sure there's more to it than that."

"Possibly, but I won't bore you with the details. In any case, it's time I was leaving. Thank you again for your kindness."

Escorting her to the foyer, "I just wondered," he said haltingly, "if you would care to have lunch with me tomorrow?"

"I'm sorry, I can't. Friday is my busiest day of the week."

"Dinner, then? Please say you will. I could book a table for two here, or we could drive into the country, if you'd prefer."

"No, here will be fine. Shall we say eight o'clock?"

She had known by the look on his face that, had she suggested midnight, he could not have been more delighted that she had accepted his invitation.

The table set, she went through to the kitchen to see to

the casserole, glanced again at her watch, and returned to the drawing room to look out of the window.

At last! Greatly relieved, she saw Adam getting out of his car, and ran downstairs to let him in. His face lit up when he saw her. Bending down, he kissed her cheek.

"I was beginning to think you'd had an accident," Catherine said, as they went up to her flat.

"No, fortunately I made it in one piece, but there'd been a crash near Whitwell Hill. A car had skidded and turned on its side. The police were there, and an ambulance."

"I hope no one was seriously hurt?"

"I'm not sure. It was difficult to see what was happening, the snow was coming down so fast." He shivered slightly.

"Let me take your coat and get you a drink," Catherine said. "You look half frozen. Sit near the fire." Hanging his coat in the hall cupboard, she led the way into the drawing room. "What would you like? Whisky? Sherry? G and T?"

"I'd love a cup of coffee, if you don't mind."

"Of course not. Why didn't I think of that? It won't take a minute." She went through to the kitchen.

Sitting near the fire, warming his hands, Adam glanced round the room, noticing the little feminine touches which told him that Catherine was a born home-maker; the trailing ivies flanking the mantelpiece, the warm pools of light, the bowls of flowers on polished surfaces. Suddenly he remembered . . . How could he have forgotten the flowers on the back seat of the car? Quite easily, the state he was in, his mind centred on the very special gift he had bought in York earlier that day, wondering how Catherine would react to the important question he intended to ask her.

"Adam?" Setting down the tray of coffee on a low table near the fire, Catherine noticed that the door was slightly ajar. "Oh, I wondered where you'd got to." She laughed as he came into the room holding the flowers and a carrier bag.

"I left these in the car," he explained, breathless from

10

his two stairs at a time dash. "They're for you." He handed her the bouquet.

"Oh, they're lovely! Red roses! At this time of year! How extravagant of you!" Her cheeks flushed with pleasure. "I'll put them in water. Help yourself to coffee. I'll be back in a minute."

"I've brought some wine, too, and chocolates," he said, proffering the carrier bag.

"Really, Adam, you shouldn't have. You are far too generous."

"Just my way of thanking you for everything you have done for me these past six months," he said huskily. "For breathing new life into me. I can't begin to tell you how much our friendship has meant to me."

"It hasn't been one sided," she reminded him. "Now, drink your coffee before it goes cold."

Finding a large enamel jug, she unwrapped the flowers and plunged them deep in water to refresh them, surprised to find that her hands were trembling slightly. Why, she wasn't quite sure, except that she wished Adam hadn't thanked her for breathing new life into him. She didn't want their friendship to get out of hand, to become emotional, imperfectly balanced. Too soon for that. She liked him enormously, but she was not in love with him the way she had been with Nick. But then, would she ever love any man again the way she had loved that charming, feckless ex-husband of hers?

At dinner, she asked Adam where he would be spending Christmas. After telling her he would be with his partner, Barry Fuller, and his wife and children at their cottage at Stockton-on-Forest, he asked her, "More to the point, where will *you* be?"

"Here," she replied lightly, "with my mother for company; cooking the traditional Christmas lunch of turkey and plum pudding."

"I'm glad," he said simply, "no one should be alone at Christmas."

"Oh, I don't know," she answered, gazing into the past. "I've never quite seen loneliness as a disease in need of a cure. But then, I've always been a – loner. Ask my mother if you don't believe me."

Thinking how lovely she looked in the softly draped hostess gown she was wearing, deeply in love with her, forgetful of the speech he had been mentally rehearsing for the past fortnight, knowing it was now or never, a case of do or die, plucking up courage, Adam said simply and directly: "Cathy, darling, I love you. I want you for my wife. Please say you'll marry me!"

She looked at him, appalled. He had called her Cathy, something he had never done before. Why now? Tonight of all nights? Was she the destined to live forever in the shadow of the past?

"What is it, Cathy? What's wrong?" Laying aside his serviette, Adam rose to his feet, stunned by her reaction to his proposal, the stricken look on her face, as if the woman he loved had gone away from him and a stranger had taken her place. "I didn't mean to shock you. I thought, presumptuously perhaps, that you knew how I felt about you.

"For me it was love at first sight, the night we met. I was lonely, at a low ebb. You took the trouble to talk to me. I felt then that there was some purpose in life, after all."

Pushing back her chair, she crossed the room, standing with her back to him. "I'm sorry, Adam," she said, "I'm fond of you, I like and admire you more than words can express. But marriage?" She shivered slightly, hugging her arms about her slender, upright body. "To marry again is out of the question. I made such a hash of my first attempt."

"But Cathy . . ." He strode swiftly towards her. Laying his hands on her shoulders, he turned her to face him.

"Please don't call me that," she said hoarsely, close to tears. "My name is Catherine, not Cathy!"

Puzzled he said, "What difference does it make?"

"A great deal of difference! Only one man ever called me that. I grew to loathe the name, the way I loathed being treated as a child, a stupid little fool without a brain in her head, a mind of her own!"

12

Drawing her down beside him on the couch in front of the fire, speaking gently, "Why haven't you told me this before?"

"The subject never arose. I never intended that it should! All I wanted was friendship. No emotional hang-ups, no digging and delving into the past, no uncovering of old bones . . . I'm sorry, I never meant to hurt or deceive you in any way."

"You haven't deceived me, Catherine. I took too much for granted, that's all. I should have waited, given our friendship time to develop before rushing in where angels might fear to tread. I should have known it was far too soon to ask you to marry me."

He added wryly, "Blame the time of year, the so-called Christmas feeling when one believes that miracles might just still happen."

"It was the same in wartime," she said, "in a different context perhaps, but there was that same sense of urgency, the need to make every moment count, the belief that, miraculously, all would turn out right in the end."

She smiled sadly. "How does the saying go? 'Marry in haste, repent at leisure'? I went into marriage without thinking twice about the future: what might happen when the war was over; if love would prove strong enough to endure through the years ahead."

"And yours didn't – is that it?"

"Not at all," she said wistfully, "I loved Nick when I married him. I went through the divorce trauma still loving him."

"Then – why?"

"Why the divorce?" With a proud uplift of her head. "Because of another woman. Can I put it plainer than that? Because my husband wanted rid of me. Perhaps because, for the first time, I thought about myself and my own future; what *I* wanted from life. Nick had made it perfectly clear there could be no future for us together. I had no choice other than to believe that what he said was true. It came as no surprise to me. I had known for some time that the end was near."

13

"Oh, my dear, I'm so sorry," Adam said compassionately. "And now?"

"Now, I can't get over the feeling that I gave in too easily. If only I had tried a little harder, been more understanding, more forebearing, things might have worked out right in the end."

Her eyes filled with tears. "The most dreadful thing of all; wondering what became of Nick after the divorce . . . I still love him, you see. I'm sorry, Adam, but that's the way it is."

"Yes, I see. Thank you for telling me. Well, I'd best be going now," he said, rising to his feet.

Alarmed, she said, "You're not driving back to York tonight, are you?"

"No. I'll find myself a hotel room somewhere; drive back tomorrow, weather permitting."

She said quietly, "I have a spare bedroom. You are welcome to stay here, if you like."

He smiled briefly. "I don't think so, but thanks for the offer."

Feeling in his jacket pocket, he handed her a small morocco leather box. "This is your Christmas present, by the way," he said. "Please accept it. No strings attached. And remember I meant what I said. I do love you, Catherine, and I shall go on loving you – 'till all the seas gang dry'."

"Adam!"

"No, stay where you are. I'll see myself out. Goodbye, my dear."

When he had gone, she opened the box. It was a lovely ring, a diamond and sapphire cluster.

Looking at it, she thought what a fool she'd been to turn her back on future happiness. And yet she knew, deep in her heart, that there could be no settled future for her until she had come to terms with the past.

Chapter Two

Sunday had always been a difficult day for Catherine to live through. She preferred the streets to be busy, shops open not locked; life, movement. Living was easier in summertime when the seafront and the sands were crowded with holidaymakers, and the ice-cream parlours and cafés open for business.

Today, she felt trapped by Sunday; the weight of snow which had fallen during the night, memories of last evening's dinner for two which had ended so painfully, opening the floodgates on the past she had tried so hard to forget.

Moving about the flat, doing her normal Sunday chores; dusting, polishing, vacuuming, doing the washing, she remembered how, in the old flat which had been their first home, Nick would lie in bed late on Sundays, reading the Sunday papers, scattering the pages untidily on the candlewick spread, wanting endless cups of black coffee; smoking cigarette after cigarette, filling the room with a blue haze, the ashtray beside the bed with burnt out stubs.

Sometimes, when she brought him the coffee, he would pull her down beside him, aware of her not as his wife but a body he happened to desire at that moment, a fact she had begun to realize with a feeling of humiliation; using her as if she were a woman of the street.

Nick. The name conjured up a deep sense of frustration, an emptiness, a piece of unfinished business, a phase of her life which had created feelings of continuing uncertainty, edginess, and insecurity.

Arranging the red roses in a slender Chinese vase, she placed them on the oak chest, and thought about Adam.

Where had he spent the night? she wondered. Had he set off on his return journey to York? Would he telephone later? Had she any reason to think that he might?

At least it had stopped snowing for the time being, but the sky was overcast, and the wind was rising, moaning about the eaves, rattling the windows.

Two o'clock. In urgent need of movement, of fresh air, finding her oldest raincoat and a scarf for her head, she hurried down to the street and crossed the road, picking her way through the snowdrifts.

Walking quickly, she began the ascent of Oliver's Mount. Panting hard with exertion, doing battle with the wind, she reached the summit of the hill crowned with a slim grey obelisk honouring the dead of two world wars.

Thrusting her gloved hands into the pockets of her raincoat, standing near the parapet overlooking the town below, she saw the familiar streets of home, in miniature, looking for all the world like crisscross threads in a tangled skein of wool; the grey sea beyond.

Regaining her breath, she picked out first one landmark, then another – the bridge spanning the valley which cut the town from east to west, church spires, the main street, the cream blocks of the Odeon Cinema, its red neon sign emblazoned against the dusk of a winter afternoon.

Street lamps, she saw, were springing to life like blossoms, a reminder of the passage of time, the ritual of Sunday afternoon tea with her mother.

Turning, she hurried back the way she had come, not wanting to keep her mother waiting.

Her car wouldn't start. The leads must be damp – or frozen. Try as hard as she might, the engine failed to emit anything other than a dull coughing sound. Giving up the unequal struggle, she hastened to the nearest bus-stop.

Sitting on the top deck, she glimpsed, briefly, other people's lives through undrawn curtains; Christmas trees in front room windows, the 'iced-lolly' lights of the Valley Bridge; fairy lights threaded between the branches of the trees in the main street; the pale blobs of the station's Janus clock-faces.

16

Alighting from the bus, she hurried along Aberdeen Walk and turned right into Sussex Street, to the house in which she had spent the formative years of her life before the outbreak of war and just after, until she had joined the Women's Royal Naval Service.

Ringing the front door bell, she awaited the usual unlocking and unchaining of the door, the chink of light on the doorstep heralding the arrival of her mother from the fastness of her cluttered back parlour.

Summoning a bright smile, "Hello, Mother," she said. "Sorry I'm late. The car wouldn't start."

"Humph! Cars, a waste of money, if you ask me," Mrs Mitchell muttered, leading the way along the passage to the back room. "Your Dad an' I never had one, nor felt the need neither. Shanks' pony was good enough for us."

"I daresay, but that's going back a bit, isn't it?" Catherine's heart sank. Mother was in one of her argumentative moods.

"That's right. Rub it in that I'm getting old."

"I wasn't. In any case, you're not old. Sixty-three isn't considered old nowadays."

"That's as may be, but I feel old, especially in this weather. I don't know where the draughts come from. I have to wear a shawl when I'm watching telly."

"Why don't you turn the fire up a bit?" Catherine glanced at the old-fashioned gas fire in the hearth.

"Because I can't afford the bills, that's why." Mrs Mitchell opened a drawer of the sideboard and got out the tablecloth.

"You don't need to worry about that, Mum. Just give the bills to me, I'll take care of them. Perhaps you should have a new fire. I'll call in at the Gas showroom tomorrow, see what's on offer, ask their advice about central heating."

"You needn't bother, I'm not having the floorboards ripped up at my time of life. In any case . . ."

"In any case, what?"

"I may not be here for very much longer." Mrs Mitchell

17

got out the cups, saucers and plates from the sideboard cupboard.

"Oh, for heaven's sake, Mother, what a morbid thing to say. You're not going to die for a very long time yet."

"Die? Who said anything about dying? No, that's not what I meant. If you must know, Mavis wants me to live with her. She wrote me a letter; says there's plenty of room in the new house."

Catherine looked at her mother, aghast. "Sell up here, you mean? Leave Scarborough? Give up your independence?"

"Yes. Why not? Independence is just another word for loneliness at my age. The house is far too big for me now. Besides, I miss the children."

"I think Mavis might have discussed it with me first."

"Why? It has nowt to do with you, has it? Not really. In any case, Mavis said in her letter she'll come to see you in the New Year to talk things over, if I agree to move. You don't think straight at times, our Cath. Not much use discussing it with you until she'd asked me how I felt about it, that's just plain common sense."

The time had come, Catherine thought, to redeem her sin of past selfishness; turning a blind eye to her mother's loneliness, not even realizing that her mother was lonely. She said quietly, "You are welcome to live with me, if you want to."

Mrs Mitchell shook her head. "Nay, it's good of you to offer, but it wouldn't do. You have your own way of going on. I wouldn't fit in. Your place isn't big enough for one thing. You only have that one spare room. I'd have nowhere to put my own furniture, and you wouldn't want my bits and pieces cluttering up that fancy lounge of yours, now would you?"

Catherine made no reply. Tears filled her eyes. All this had come as a shock to her. She had taken for granted that her mother would always be here, in this house, her childhood home, along with the photographs on the sideboard, the ritual of Sunday afternoon tea.

Mrs Mitchell went through to the kitchen to fill the kettle, Catherine followed to cut and butter the bread, to

18

open the tins of salmon and fruit salad whilst her mother got out the cakes and buns she had baked earlier that day, at the same time as her Sunday dinner.

"Look, Cath love," she said matter-of-factly, "no use upsetting yourself. Whatever happens will take time. I'll have to sell the house first if I decide to move, and I haven't made my mind up yet. In any case, I have Christmas to look forward to – only don't give me any fakey foreign food, will you? It upsets my stomach."

"As if I would," Catherine said.

"And don't put that electric blanket in my bed. I don't trust those things. I'd rather stick to my hot-water bottle."

"No, Mother."

At eight o'clock she excused herself, said good-night, and walked home, buffeted by the searching December wind. Crossing the Valley Bridge, she heard the tumult of the sea crashing in on the shore; saw, as she crested the rise to the South Cliff, the winking lights of the Methodist Church Christmas tree; heard the straining of its wires; the creaking of shop signs in Ramshill Road, saw lights shining in upper windows above the shops.

Hastening her footsteps, she hurried home to the safety of her flat, and switched on the lamps and the electric fire, willing the telephone to ring . . .

On Christmas Day, seated in the armchair nearest the fire, "That was a grand dinner, Cath," Mrs Mitchell said appreciatively, "the turkey was nice and tender."

"Yes. Mr Henderson always does well for me, because I'm a regular customer, I suppose."

"It's nearly time for that film you wanted to watch. Shall I switch on the telly?"

"No, Mum. You sit still. I'll do it. Meanwhile, I'd better clear the table and do the washing-up."

"And miss the film?"

"I'll listen to some music on the radio. Don't worry about me, Mum. I have things to see to in the kitchen."

It was over at last, the meal she had dreaded. Plunging

19

her hands into the washing-up water, a web of memories drew Catherine back to the Christmases of long ago when, as a child, she had awakened to discover the doll she had longed for in a cardboard box at the end of her bed.

How lovely and uncomplicated life had been then, when the house in Sussex Street was filled with the scent of roast goose, plum pudding and hot mince pies; when at breakfast, sitting on her father's lap, she had dipped bread 'soldiers' into his boiled egg, and they had laughed together as the yolk ran down the sides of the shell.

Memories. So many memories . . . That Christmas, for instance, when Nick had come home from the Middle East.

She had expected him at eight o'clock in the morning; had gone to bed the night before, her hair in curlers, her face smothered in skin cream. But Nick, the unpredictable, had arrived three hours earlier than expected, having caught the milk-train from York. Stumbling downstairs at the urgent ringing of the doorbell, mazed with sleep, she had opened the door to discover him standing there, smoking a cigarette, an amused smile lighting up his thin, quizzical face as she threw herself into his arms, sobbing with joy because he was safely home again.

"Hey, mind my cigarette," he said. Then, throwing it aside, holding her at arm's length, "What the hell have you done to yourself, Cathy, my love? Is this the end for which we twain are met? A returning hero and a wife with a greasy face and her hair in curlers? I take it that I have come to the right address, that you are my wife? Or are you an imposter?"

"I didn't mean you to see me like this. I was coming to the station to meet you. I'd saved a good pair of stockings and bought a new lipstick."

"The ship docked earlier than expected. We were carted off to the nearest demob centre, counted like a lot of ruddy sheep, and told to hop-it. God, those pork pies they served at King's Cross. Made from decayed horse flesh, I shouldn't wonder."

"Nick! How horrible!"

He laughed. "Have you anything decent to eat? And

what about coffee? No? I might have known it. It'll have to be tea, then. A good old English cuppa and – pork pie? Are you sure it's fit for human consumption? Well, I'll have to take your word for it, but you might have sported a bit of rump steak and several pounds of mushrooms."

Upstairs in the flat, she had hurried to the bathroom and washed the grease off her face, removed the curlers and brushed her hair.

"Ah, that's better. Come here."

He had kissed her then with the air of someone bestowing a favour – akin to patting a child on the head and telling it to be good. His brief, nonchalant embrace had come as a bitter disappointment to her after all the waiting.

"I'm comotose." He yawned deeply. "Haven't slept for twenty-four hours. Where's the bedroom?"

So that was it. He was tired. She smiled. "Over there." She'd experienced a sudden feeling of shyness. "What about the tea?"

"Bring it to me, like a good girl."

When she had taken in the tea, he was fast asleep, his dark hair straying on to his forehead. Sitting beside him, she experienced a surge of tenderness towards him, a feeling of love impossible to express when his mocking eyes were upon her.

He was still asleep when she left the flat to go to work. She had hated leaving him, but what else could she do? The salon would be packed solid with clients all day. Besides, she liked her job, her employer, and she needed the money to buy the small luxuries that Nick would expect. Decent coffee, for one thing, the mushrooms he'd mentioned, with luck, a piece of rump steak, a chicken for their Christmas dinner. She knew that her boss, Mrs Maitland, would allow her a half-hour off to dash to the shops between clients.

All had gone as planned until, hurrying home after the shop closed, she had found the flat empty. "Nick? Where are you?" she'd called out. There was no reply. Where on earth had he got to?

21

Going through to the tiny kitchen, she'd unloaded her shopping basket, pleased with her purchases – the chicken and the small piece of steak, the mushrooms, coffee, sprouts, chipolata sausages, and the wedge of Cheddar cheese she'd brought home with her.

How surprised and delighted Nick would be when he came in to find a meal of steak, chips and mushrooms awaiting him. Eagerly, she had set about peeling potatoes at the kitchen sink. Afterwards, she had gone into the bedroom to make the bed, to the bathroom to tidy up his shaving gear and pick up the towels he had left in a heap on the floor, wondering if she should start cooking the steak now, or wait a while?

She'd decided to wait. After all, he couldn't have gone far. He'd be home any minute now. Setting the table in the cramped living room, perhaps he'd gone out to buy her a Christmas present, she thought. Yes, of course, that would be it – a bottle of perfume, a scarf, or a box of chocolates. She had already bought his present, a green wool sweater and a matching Paisley tie.

The war was over, true enough, but luxuries and food were still hard to come by. It had taken her ages to save up enough fruit, butter and sugar for a Christmas cake and plum pudding.

Eight o'clock, and still no sign of him! Perhaps he'd met with an accident? Seriously worried, she'd considered rushing to the box on the corner to phone the Police. But no, Nick would never forgive her for causing a rumpus. Possibly he had just gone for a walk in the fresh air? A stranger in a strange town, he might easily have lost all sense of direction.

The next three hours had seemed like a nightmare; not knowing what to do, what to think, how to act. Her nerves were stretched to breaking point when, at eleven o'clock, he had appeared, on the doorstep, a little dishevelled, more than a little drunk.

"Nick! I've been out of my mind with worry," she cried. "Where on earth have you been?" A foolish question. Where he had been was obvious.

He said thickly, "You mushn't make noishes like a

22

wife. I like my wives to be unnershanding. In any cashe, what the hell? Thish is Chrishtmas Eve."

"Nick, you're drunk!" Taking hold of his arm, she half dragged him upstairs, deeply shocked at the state he was in. Closing the door behind them, she said, "Why, Nick? Why have you done this? Our first evening at home?"

Collapsing into a chair, "Home? Waddayo mean – home? Thish – dump?"

"How can you say such a thing? If you knew how hard I've worked to buy the furniture; the suite, the tables and chairs. Everything!" She'd burst into tears.

"You mean you've acshually paid good money for all this junk? Wha' the hell possessed you to do that?" He had slumped further down in the chair then, eyes closed, mouth open, snoring slightly.

Sick at heart, she had left him where he was and gone to bed to cry herself to sleep. Next morning, she had wakened to remember that this was Christmas Day.

At seven o'clock, bleary-eyed, but sober, he had come into the room.

"I'm sorry about last night, Cathy my love," he said quietly. "I behaved badly and I know it. Please forgive me."

"Of course I forgive you." Loving him so much, how could she have not forgiven him?

"Move over," he said, undressing, "let me hold you in my arms, make love to you. After all, you are my wife, remember?"

The hour of lovemaking that followed would remain branded in her memory, for all time, as the sweetest she had ever known, or would know ever again. It had seemed to her, in that intensity of passion, that their separate identities had fused suddenly to become one whole and utterly complete human being.

Lying flat on his back when the loving was over, Nick said, bunching up his pillows, lighting a cigarette, "About this place, Cathy, I was shattered, to put it mildly, when you told me that this is Home, Sweet Home! What on earth possessed you to buy all this furniture?"

23

"Because you said in your last letter that I had to find a flat, so I did. I thought you'd be pleased."

"I meant a furnished flat, you simpleton. Somewhere to stay for the time being. You didn't seriously imagine that I would want to be tied down here indefinitely, did you?"

"I didn't know what you wanted. How could I? You never said exactly, so I just went ahead and did the best I could. I suppose all I really wanted was to make you happy, to make a home for you."

She added wistfully, "We had so little time together before you were posted abroad, I felt I scarcely knew you at all. Truth to tell, I've often wondered why you married me in the first place – it was such a rushed affair – that registry office wedding, the briefest of honeymoons, and then you were gone. I thought, afterwards, that I must have dreamt the whole thing, except for the wedding ring on my finger, the changing of my name from Mitchell to Willard in my pay-book."

Puckering her forehead, she ventured the question that had puzzled her all along. "Why did you marry me, Nick? I'd really like to know."

Stubbing out his cigarette, unbunching his pillows, drawing her into his arms, "Because I happen to like stupid women with fair hair and nicely rounded bodies," he said flippantly, "or hadn't you noticed?"

"That's all very well, but about last night—"

"Oh, for God's sake, Cathy, so I had a drop too much to drink? What of it? How would you have felt if you were me? No sleep for twenty-four hours, dumped in this God-forsaken hole on Christmas Eve. Left on my own all day. You might have stayed with me; rung your boss and told her you were feeling off-colour."

"I couldn't have done that! It wouldn't have been fair on her. I like Mrs Maitland. She's been good to me. It never occurred to me to leave her in the lurch on one of the busiest days of the year."

"My, aren't you the prissy one? I think I'll start calling you 'Goody Two-Shoes'." Rolling away from her, swinging his legs out of bed, "What I need is a

24

hair of the dog," he said, rummaging in his duffle-bag. "Hang on! Salvation is at hand!"

She saw that he was holding a full bottle of whisky. "You're not going to start drinking that now, are you?"

"Why not? Oh, for God's sake don't look so shocked. I need it!" Unscrewing the top, he tilted the bottle to his lips.

In a shaking voice, appalled by his action, she said, "What has happened to you, Nick? You never used to drink like this."

He laughed shortly. "Let's just say I picked up the habit in the Persian Gulf. For one thing there was damn all else to do. It was a case of drink or go mad."

"But you're not in the Persian Gulf now, are you?"

"You know what?" he said bitterly, "I wish I were!"

"You can't mean that?" Tears rolled down her cheeks. "How could you be so cruel? If you knew how much I've missed you, how much I looked forward to seeing you again – how much I love you."

Putting down the bottle, he said softly, "I believe you really mean it. Why, God alone knows. I'm not a very lovable person, am I?"

"You are to me."

"Poor little Cathy," he murmured, gathering her into his arms, smoothing her hair, "come on, now, dry your eyes, get up and make me a cuppa. Let's make the best of a bad job, eh?"

She said shyly, "I bought you some coffee yesterday, and some steak and mushrooms."

"You did? Who's a clever wife, then? Tell you what, we'll have a slap-up breakfast, get ready and take a nice brisk walk, tire ourselves out, then come back to bed. How does that strike you?"

"Fine, except, I have the dinner to cook, and, well, please don't be angry, but we're invited to my mother's for tea. I said we'd go. After all, it's time you two met."

"Oh, Christ," Nick said bleakly.

The film was now over. Catherine had not seen any of it.

She had done the washing-up automatically, reliving that past Christmas.

Returning to the drawing room, she saw that a cartoon was now filling the TV screen and her mother was sitting with her hands folded in her lap, smiling.

The telephone had rung that morning when Catherine was preparing lunch. She had hurried to answer, hoping it would be Adam. Instead, Mavis' voice had replied. She and the children were ringing to wish Gran a Merry Christmas, to Mrs Mitchell's delight. "Oh, bless them," she said. "Did they like the jumpers I knitted for them? Yes, put them on . . . Hello Jamie, Teddy. Are you having a nice time?" Talking to them as if they were still toddlers, Catherine thought wryly, going back to the kitchen. "And how's Ernie?" Mrs Mitchell asked. She was fond of her industrious son-in-law, unlike Nick, to whom she had taken an instant dislike that Christmas Day in 1945.

"Jumped up," she'd called him afterwards. "Mark my words, our Cath, he'll neither work nor want, that 'un!"

The rift between Catherine and her mother, begun that day, had never quite healed.

26

Chapter Three

It was over at last, the Christmas that Catherine had dreaded. She sensed her mother's relief when it was time to go home, her bits and pieces of luggage stowed beside her on the back seat of the taxi.

Getting into the car, Annie Mitchell breathed on more freely. Cath's flat overwhelmed her. It was too posh – all that expensive furniture and soft lighting. Give her a good central light any day of the week, with a sensible 100 watt bulb.

Not that she could fault her daughter's generosity or kindness of heart, but something was wrong with the lass, anyone could see that; fairly jumping out of her skin when the phone rang, looking out of the window every five minutes, getting up in the middle of the night to wander about the lounge. Annie knew this much because she had heard her with her own ears. Not that she'd dared get up to ask what was the matter, and Cath wouldn't have told her anyway, even if she had.

The way she was carrying on, she'd end up having a nervous breakdown, Annie thought, and she'd said as much on Boxing Day afternoon. "The trouble with you, our Cath, you're working too hard, not getting out enough. When you're not working, you're stuck in here by yourself listening to high-brow music on the wireless. That's no life for a young woman."

"Please, Mum, I'd rather not discuss it if you don't mind."

Pursing her lips Annie continued, "It's all *his* fault, that man you married. Dragged you down, he did! Changed you entirely. You were happy enough till *he* came along to fill your head with his fancy ideas. Worse still, he made you look down on your own kind, him an' his blooming university education. And where did that get him in the end? Nowhere!"

"Stop it, Mother! I don't want to listen."

"No, I reckon not. You never would listen to a word against him, even when you knew what he was up to."

"He was my husband!"

"Yes, well you're not married to him now, thank God, though you often act as if you were. Seems to me you're hoping that one day the door will open and he'll walk into the room as if he'd never been away. Is that what you want? To get on that merry-go-round all over again?"

Her car still out of action, Catherine decided to walk to work, the day after Boxing Day. The exercise would do her good.

The ground was icy. Trees flung gnarled branches to the cold grey sky. Her breath whirled away like cigarette smoke. Taking a short cut to the salon, she hurried downhill, past a church, beneath a railway arch, and came at last to a main shopping thoroughfare.

How odd to see Christmas goods still in the shop windows, reminders of the pre-holiday stampede. Christmas now seemed to be a distant memory not only two days ago. Soon, sale notices would go up in the dress shops and the haberdashers, creating a small increase in custom during the lean months ahead.

The salon would be comparatively quiet now and in the New Year, business almost at a standstill, especially if the weather was bad. January and February brought a kind of hibernation of clients. Hoteliers and boarding house keepers would be busy spring cleaning in readiness for the Easter influx of visitors. This was the pattern of life in a seaside resort.

June, the senior assistant, and Esme the apprentice, were dusting and cleaning the shampoo basins when Catherine entered. "Good-morning, Mrs Willard," June, a buxom, dark-haired girl said with a twinkle, looking rather like a puss with a saucer of cream. "You'll never guess what! I'm engaged!"

28

"Engaged?" Until that moment, Catherine had no idea that June's affections were seriously in jeopardy. There had been a succession of young men, the last being a commercial traveller who had made improper suggestions about a dirty weekend – or so she had thought – obviously an outsider had come up on the rails. "What a surprise! May I look at your ring?"

Extending her left hand, "Gorgeous, isn't it?" June smirked, exhibiting a galaxy of diamond chippings set in platinum. "Course we shan't be getting married till we've saved the deposit for a house, but Pete's got a real good job on that new building development at Weststead. Oooh, those houses are really smashing. All mod cons. Great big picture windows, tiled bathrooms and coloured – er – suites. I've told Pete that's what I want. Not any old-fashioned dump."

Catherine remembered Bridie's cottage at Cloud Merridon. A Georgian gem; the curved fanlight above the front door, the delicately spindled staircase, panelled wainscoting . . . A perfect setting for her charming, unorthodox mother-in-law. The loveliest house she had ever seen.

But Nick had never wanted a house. Never could she recall him saying, "When we settle down," or "when we find a place of our own."

The telephone rang suddenly. June answered it. The door opened, Catherine's first client of the day bounced in. "Ugh, what a dreadful day!" she cried in a high, clear voice.

This was a wealthy woman who lived in one of the detached houses on the road leading to Oliver's Mount, whose husband had made his fortune from government contracts during the war.

Placing a pink nylon cape about the woman's shoulders, "Did you have a good Christmas?" Catherine asked.

"My dear, simply hectic! I'm *exhausted*!"

Mrs Hobart's carefully made-up face belied her statement. She looked radiantly plump and well manicured. Her coat was ocelot, her shoes crocodile, the diamond in her engagement ring the size of a peanut.

What constituted exhaustion to a woman like this? Catherine wondered. Planning the day's menus? Giving orders to the cook, attending too many coffee mornings?

Mrs Hobart chattered unceasingly as Catherine washed and set her hair. "I'm at my wit's end," she wailed. "The mayoress's coffee morning clashes with the Masonic affair, and I can't be in two places at once."

"How unfortunate," Catherine commiserated, wishing she dare tell the woman what she really thought, to stop acting like a spoilt child.

Her hair done up in pink rollers, Mrs Hobart tripped across to the drying-area. Safely ensconced, she lit a cigarette and opened the latest copy of *Vogue* which she had brought with her.

Looking out of the window, Catherine saw a tired-looking woman wheeling a push chair, to which clung two older children. Her heart went out to the young mother whose life must be spent washing and ironing, cooking and cleaning; providing food for herself and her family; worrying, by the look of her, how to make ends meet. And yet the children seemed happy enough; clean and well-fed.

Suddenly it began to snow. Flakes descended thickly, whirling and fluttering. Catherine smiled, touched by a stirring of old delight, remembering how she had loved snow, as a child – laughing at the absurdity of snowflakes clinging to her lashes, turning her head to see her own footsteps imprinted in the snow before it became churned up with other people's footprints.

Esme was ushering Mrs Hobart back to the cubicle for the dressing-out process.

"Oh lord, no!" the woman cried in alarm. "Don't tell me it's snowing again! What a bore! I promised to go to Stoneby for sherry, but I simply can't go in this! I must ring Sheila at once! I simply daren't risk being late for lunch! May I use your phone?"

"Of course."

"How sweet of you." Mrs Hobart picked up the receiver, dialled the number she wanted. "Hello? Sheila, is that you? Anthea here. Darling, I simply can't come.

Have you seen the weather? The thing is, we're having Monty for lunch, and Caro's latest boyfriend. All very serious, I gather. I really am most frightfully sorry . . . Hmm? Oh yes, of course, the Latimer's party at The Crown! You and George will come to us for drinks first, won't you? Yes. Lovely. 'Bye, darling."

Mrs Hobart hung up, her world put to rights. She was free to go home now, Catherine thought, to oversee the setting of the luncheon table, and worry the cook.

When her hair had been moulded into a smooth, shining cap, she consulted her diary. "I'll come again, let me see, Friday week, I think," Mrs Hobart said. "About ten o'clock if you can manage it. Yes? That's fine, then. 'Bye."

Mrs Hobart teetered across the pavement to her Mini. As she drew away from the kerb, another car drew up, the driver of which got out and hurried, head bent, towards the shop door.

"Adam! What are you doing here?" Catherine said in a low voice, knowing that June and Esme were listening intently.

"I just had to see you," he murmured. "Please, can we talk?"

"Not here," she replied. "Not now."

"Then may we meet somewhere for lunch?"

"Very well, then, I'll be free around one o'clock. Wait in the car, if you don't mind."

"Of course, dear. Just as you wish."

Adam's car ground to a halt on the roughly pebbled car park of The Ploughboy, three miles out of town.

They ran, heads bent, to the door of the inn, from which patches of light shone out on the snow. Entering the bar, they saw that it was crowded despite the weather. Fumes of tobacco and beer thickened the air. The buzz of conversation, a crackling log fire imparted a conviviality reminiscent of Charles Dicken's 'Pickwick Papers'.

"Sit by the fire, love," Adam suggested. "What would you like to drink?"

"Sherry, please." She warmed her hands at the blaze.

31

Adam returned, carrying two glasses. "I've enquired about lunch," he said. "Someone will be along presently to take our order."

Raising his glass, "Cheers," he murmured. She replied the same, remembering Nick, thinking how easily drink might become the cure for all ills, especially in an atmosphere like this, warm and heady, surrounded with humanity in a state of intoxication to a greater or lesser degree, oblivious to the world outside – the steadily falling snow, the enervating chill of winter.

The sherry was potent, the fire warm. Looking up at him she said, "You still haven't told me why you came to see me."

"Because I love you."

"In spite of what I said?"

"In spite of everything. I've been through hell, this Christmas, I don't mind telling you."

"It wasn't easy for me, either." She paused. "Why didn't you 'phone?"

"I wanted to. I just wasn't sure how you'd react."

"I haven't changed my mind, if that's what you're thinking."

"As long as I haven't forfeited your friendship. I can't bear the thought of losing you. Is there any reason why we can't stay friends?"

"No." She smiled and held out her hand to him. "I hated the thought of losing you, too."

"Your table's ready, sir." The waitress bustled up, breaking the tension.

The dining room was small, very bright and cheerful with red tablecloths and trailing greenery. Adam felt they should have wine to celebrate their reunion, and food as far removed from poultry as possible. Studying the wine list, he suggested Beaujolais, admitting frankly that wine was a mystery to him, a subject he knew little about.

"As long as I'm not expected to pronounce judgement beforehand," he laughed. "The tasting ritual seems a bit absurd to a novice like me."

Nick had taught Catherine a great deal about wine. His knowledge garnered from tours abroad, before the war, when he had shepherded parties of tourists to the bistros and night-clubs of Paris and chosen the wine for them.

"Chablis is best with shell fish," he'd told her, "and Grands Cechezeaux is a wonderful red burgundy to complement red meat. I'll take you to France one day, Cathy. I'll take you to Rheims and show you the cathedral and the champagne cellars." And she had been carried away by his description of the cold, dank cellars where the champagne was stored.

She remembered the first time she had dined out with him, she in her Wren uniform. He had taken her to dinner at an expensive hotel to 'impress' her, he'd confessed carelessly. He'd certainly impressed the wine waiter.

Later, he had winked and borrowed a pound from her to help pay the bill, explaining that he had forgotten to pick up his other wallet. And if she had seen through the lie, his wink had minimized the offence. Nothing had mattered to her except being alive in the same world together.

"Are you all right, dear?" Adam's voice cut into her reverie.

"Yes, of course. Why do you ask?" How long had she been lost to her present surroundings?

"Forgive me for saying this, but I'm worried about you, Catherine. You seem so – distant, so preoccupied."

The food had arrived, and she hadn't even noticed – a heaped plateful of roast beef, Yorkshire pudding and vegetables, the sight of which made her feel physically sick. "It's nothing," she said, "I'm a bit tired, that's all, after the Christmas rush, and . . ."

"And?" he prompted gently.

She shook her head. "I'm sorry, Adam. You'll think it dreadful of me, but do you mind if we leave now?" She rose unsteadily to her feet with one thought in mind, to go outside as quickly as possible, to breathe in the cold fresh air, to feel the wind on her face.

"Of course not!" Concernedly, he helped her out to the car before going back to pay for the food they had not eaten, the wine they had not tasted.

Returning to the car, "Look, Catherine," he said quietly, "you can't go on like this. What you need is a break, a change of scenery." Taking the plunge he continued, "Let's go away somewhere together, shall we? Let the rest of the world go by!"

"But I have my business to think of."

"So have I, but Barry will be delighted to see the back of me, I reckon, and you appear to have someone to take over for the time being."

"June? Oh yes, she's very good at her job. I trained her myself and the clients are used to her." Catherine experienced a frisson of pleasure at the thought of a change of scenery. She had been static far too long. She asked, "Have you anywhere special in mind?"

Scarcely believing his luck, "How about London?" Adam suggested. "Plenty to do there even if the weather's bad. We could go by rail, take in a show or two, or just feast our eyes on the greatest city in the world. Who was it who said: 'When you're tired of London, you're tired of life' – or words to that effect?"

"Samuel Johnson, I believe," she replied with a smile.

"You mean you'll come with me?"

"Yes, Adam, you're right, I do need a change of scene."

She spent the evening packing. Adam had gone back to York to make the necessary arrangements and to pick up his things. They would meet at York Station tomorrow morning at ten o'clock; travel to London together.

Earlier that evening, she had called in at the house in Sussex Street to tell her mother that she was going away for a few days.

"Oh? Where to?"

"To London, Mother. I'm going to London! I thought you'd be pleased."

"What? All alone?"

"No, Mum. I'm going with a friend, Adam Jesson."

Annie Mitchell's eyes opened wide in surprise. "Well, you're a dark horse an' no mistake. Who is this man? Why haven't you mentioned him before? Is there something wrong with him?"

The catechism had continued.

*　　*　　*

34

When she had finished packing, Catherine cooked herself a simple meal of scrambled eggs. Waiting for the coffee to percolate, she looked out of the window. How lovely, how diamond-clear the stars were. The same stars that had shone down that night during the war when she and her special friend, Maisie Foster, had put on their nylon stockings and twisted them round to make sure the seams were straight before hurrying out to the transport.

What a magical evening it had been, filled with the scent of wildflowers from the hedgerows. It had seemed a pity to go indoors, into the Officers' Mess quarters where the dance was being held.

"I wish I hadn't come," she'd told Maisie.

"Oh, don't be daft, Cathy, you'll enjoy it once you're inside. These RAF dos are great as a rule. Plenty to eat and drink, an' lots of smashing blokes."

"I'm not a very good dancer."

"Who cares? There probably won't be room to swing a cat anyway."

The room was long and low ceilinged, she recalled, dimly lit, with tables and chairs around the dance floor, music played on a radiogram, the murmur of voices, laughter, the scrape of shoes, bunting and fairylights, a diamond-faceted witchball.

The group of girls she was with were welcomed jovially by the officer in charge of the entertainment who found them a table, offered them drinks, and introduced them to the group of people at the nearest table, not that she had caught any of their names.

Suddenly, Maisie had nudged her. "Look at Heather Harper," she murmured, "showing off, as usual. Trust her to shove her nose in!" Glancing over her shoulder, Catherine saw Heather Harper talking to a dark-haired man at the next table; accepting a light for her cigarette, flirting with him outrageously, fluttering her eyelashes. "The silly bitch," Maisie snorted. "Mind you, he ain't half dishy! I'd let him light my cigarette any old time of the day! Hi-up! He's coming over to us!"

*   *   *

35

Sipping her coffee, Catherine remembered that night as a replay of an old movie; *Casablanca* or *Brief Encounter*, seen so many times that one knew the dialogue, the music, by heart.

"May I introduce you?" Nick had said. "This is Estelle Winter, her husband Frank, Richard Henry, George Robinson, Blackie Phillips, Guy Flint. Heather Harper you already know."

Somehow, she and Maisie had found themselves moving to the next table. There had been the scraping of chairs as the men rose to their feet. Heather Harper had glared at them jealously. Guy Flint went to the bar for drinks. Maisie and Richard Henry had got up to dance.

"This is my favourite tune," Heather said, looking at Nick.

"In which case, may I?" George Robinson had led Heather Harper on to the dance floor.

"Come on, old girl, you like this tune too, don't you?" Frank Winter said cheerfully to his wife Estelle.

"Not particularly. In any case, I'd rather finish my drink, if you have no objection."

"No, of course not. I just thought. I mean, you never stop playing the damn record."

It had crossed Catherine's mind that the woman called Estelle was deeply unhappy. She looked strained, ill even. It had been a momentary thought at the time, easily dismissed as unimportant when Nick had asked her to dance with him.

Taking her hand, he had led her on to the dance floor. Silver flecks of light had spun and whirled about them, they had moved as one person to 'Begin the Beguine'.

Dancing in a trance-like state of happiness, Nick's arm about her, she had known that the words of the song were true; that she was in heaven now, in danger of falling in love.

Afterwards, taking her arm, he had led her outdoors for a breath of air. Standing beneath the stars, looking down at her, he'd said softly, "You're a very pretty girl, Cathy." And then he had kissed her.

It had taken a long time to realize that his kiss, which

36

had meant the world to her, meant less than nothing to him, that it wasn't Heather Harper he wished to punish, to make jealous, but another woman. The woman he was really in love with.

Chapter Four

They emerged from the creaking lift at Lancaster Gate and walked, arm in arm, along the gusty underground passages until they reached the busy Bayswater Road. Turning right, they battled, eyes watering from the wind blowing against them, in the direction of Devonshire Terrace.

The hotel Adam had chosen was small by London standards, the windows muffled with heavy brocade curtains, draped with ruched Austrian blinds. The carpets were thick, richly patterned, well worn. The reception desk was presided over by a tired-faced Cockney who had brushed up his accent but failed to obliterate its origin. Urbane, wearing an immaculately tailored grey suit and a pink shirt with matching tie, he consulted the ledger and said, "Ah yes, sir. Two singles with barfs. If you'd care to sign the register, I'll 'ave your luggage sent up right away."

Their rooms were on the same landing. Catherine's, heavily curtained, overlooked a small square. London soot and sunshine had long since faded the original pink of the curtains to an indefinite shade of peach, which blended admirably with the blurred markings of the walnut furniture.

Unpacking her suitcase, she recalled Adam's look of surprise when she had elected to travel to the hotel by means of the Underground instead of hiring a taxi from the forecourt of King's Cross Station.

"But *why?*" he'd asked. And, somehow, she had found herself incapable of explaining that she was sick and tired of the obvious behavioural patterns of life, that she wanted to experience something new and different for a change.

The basement dining room had emptied when they went down for lunch at half-past one. The waiter, richly Irish, served them with remarkable speed and dexterity.

Glancing round the room at the white-clothed tables and the red-shaded lamps, the ornate iron grille concealing the kitchen door, Catherine remembered another hotel, long ago, very similar to this, not in London, but Paris . . .

Nick, she recalled, had been moody and irritable most of the time because Frank and Estelle Winter had cried off at the last moment from that weekend break in Paris, she had then become the butt of his irritability and frustration. Alone, she realized, she was not enough for him. He needed the company of others to bolster his ego.

There had been a chocolate stall across the road from the hotel. She remembered the sickly sweet smell mingled with that of dust and petrol fumes. The woman tending the stall had shouted her wares in a hoarse patois. She had been thrilled, at first, when Nick had bought her six huge bonbons wrapped in silver paper, until, thrusting them at her, "Here, ma petite cochon," he said cruelly, "an extra pound of flesh won't make that much difference to your waistline. You're not pregnant, are you? No? Thank God for small mercies!"

After lunch, turning up their mackintosh collars against the knife-thrust of the wind, they had gone out to explore the neighbourhood. Adam tucked his hand into the crook of Catherine's arm, a protective gesture which she found irritating. Why, she couldn't explain even to herself, except that protectiveness implied possession, and she didn't want to be possessed by any one man ever again. Her memories of Nick were still too painfully etched in her mind, her feelings for him far too strong to admit Adam into the deep, inner circle of her life.

They caught a tube train to Tottenham Court Road, and headed in the direction of Covent Garden, not that walking was particularly pleasant, and the roar of the traffic was horrendous. Lighted buses lumbered past them, cars and taxis. People were hurrying along the pavement, heads bent, not looking where they were going. Catherine felt uneasy; lost, vulnerable, a stranger in a strange place, dwarfed by the crush of humanity flowing towards her.

"Let's have a cup of tea, shall we?" Adam suggested, thinking how pale and tired she looked. "In here?"

The interior of the café was so dim they could scarcely see the other tables set deep in curtained recesses. Catherine's head began to throb. The place was oppressive, reminiscent of a magician's disappearing cabinet: black lacquered, scrolled with golden-scaled dragons. The waitress, a sloe-eyed Chinese girl brought their tea in an oriental pot. The tea-bowls were delicately fashioned, unsubstantial, like doll's house china. Adam apologized profusely, "I'm sorry, my dear, I expect you'd have preferred a less exotic atmosphere?"

"You weren't to know." Attempting a smile she said, "By the way, Adam, I wish you'd stop calling me 'my dear'. It makes me feel – old."

"I'm sorry, I had no idea."

"No need to apologize."

"I've felt tempted to call you 'my love' or 'my darling', from time to time," he confessed, "but I knew you'd object, the way you did when I called you Cathy. It's simply that Catherine sounds so – formal."

"Then why not call me Kate?"

"May I?" He drew in a deep breath.

"Why not? No one has ever called me that before."

Stepping from the plummy warmth of the café was like stepping into a cold shower after a steam-bath. Catherine's headache had increased in intensity. She shivered. The rising wind drove sleet against them as they stood on the pavement deciding what to do next.

A film seemed the only solution. "I'll flag down a taxi," Adam said optimistically. Easier said than done. Despite his frantic signalling, the cabs he hailed sped past without stopping.

"It's no use," Catherine said wearily, "we'd better start walking. We can't be far from Leicester Square."

40

The film showing at the Odeon was *Judgement at Nuremberg*, starring Burt Lancaster and Spencer Tracy.

It had been a far longer walk than she had expected, during which London had roared and thrust its way into her consciousness like a rapacious monster intent on swallowing whole the population of a city bemused by its glaring neon signs, its shady clubs and dance-halls, prostitutes and pimps. Even the elements seemed dwarfed by the explosion of lights and sounds – the churning of the traffic, honking of horns – a ceaseless, nerve-racking cacophony which ground deep into the heart and soul of her, increasing her feeling of isolation in this city of strangers; filling her with a strange, sick longing for home.

Home? But she had no real home any more since the man she loved had deserted her. If home was where the heart is, where did she truly belong? Nowhere at all . . .

In the powder room of the cinema, she twitched a strand of damp hair into place, and saw, looking into the mirror, that the sleet had taken her mascara, leaving a sooty line beneath her eyes; that her nose was shining.

Staring at her reflection in the glass, if age were a state of mind, she thought, then hers had begun to accept its limitations. How was it possible, she wondered, that the pretty, expectant girl she used to be, as smart as paint in her Wren uniform, had changed into the sad-eyed stranger in the mirror?

Wiping away the smudged mascara with a corner of her handkerchief, her mind shifted like the colours in a kaleidoscope, as busy as a bird pecking crumbs. Oh to be rid of self, as children playing on the sands with bucket and spade, the world no bigger or more complicated than a golden curve of beach against a summer sky; as young lovers are, walking hand in hand, their world a green park at dusk.

She had stayed too long in the powder room. Adam would be waiting. "Feeling better?" he asked, looking worried.

"Yes, the attendant gave me an asprin and a glass of

water," she said. Moving across the foyer, he handed her a box of chocolates. "Thank you," she smiled, preceding him into the darkened auditorium.

The film had just started. Praised to the skies by the critics, it was the fictionalized account of the trial of the Nazi leaders. There was nothing enlightening about it. The photography brilliant but sinister; shot in black and white. The screen seemed far too big, the characters blown to gigantic proportions. She felt that the churning, spinning world outside had followed her into the cinema.

Dreams of childhood, sweet and uncomplicated, of lovers at dusk, remembered earlier, seemed to dissolve like candyfloss, too light to hold its shape.

If only there had been a child, she thought, if Nick had cared enough to want children, but there had always been a barrier between them, something impenetrable. It was Estelle he had wanted, not her.

The figures on the screen ballooned grotesquely. She felt as if the world she knew had ceased to exist, as though she were being drawn into a dark vortex beyond her power to resist.

The sense of panic was unlike anything she had experienced before, an engulfment by slow waves of heat until her clothes clung to her body and beads of perspiration broke out on her forehead. Closing her eyes, she fought to master the horrifying fear that gripped her, the feeling of her own nonexistence, of unreality; akin to staring into an abyss, powerless to save herself from falling headlong into it.

There was some confusion. Voices.

"She's coming round."

"Poor dear."

She found herself lying on a couch in the manager's office. Two women were hovering over her. Adam was holding her hand. "What's happening?" She stared at them uncomprehendingly.

"You fainted," Adam told her quietly.

"Did I? I can't remember."

"Not to worry, dear. How are you feeling now?"

"I feel sick," she managed shakily.

"You'd better go, sir," one of the woman said. "We'll take care of her."

Sickness engulfed her, leaving her weak and shaken.

"We'd better call a doctor. I think she's got a temperature."

"Perhaps it's food poisoning. She must've eaten something that disagreed with her."

"I'll have a word with the manager, he'll know which doctor to send for. Where's he got to, by the way?"

"I think he's gone down to the foyer for the St John's Ambulance man. He'll know what to do."

"Please, no," Catherine said weakly, "just send for a taxi. I'm fine now. I want to go back to the hotel." She must get out of here, she thought desperately. There was something she wanted to think about, but she couldn't remember what it was.

"I'll tell the gentleman." One of the women went out, the other gave her a sip of water. "There, ducks," she said sympathetically, "is that better? My, you have been poorly."

She *was* ill. She knew that now. This breakdown had been coming on for some time, Catherine realized. An outward shell of calm; overwork, loneliness, responsibilities – longing for something over and done with forever. "Nick. Where are you?" she murmured.

"Who? Oh, the gentleman," the woman said, "I expect he's ringing up for a taxi."

Her hotel room seemed a haven, a refuge removed from well-meaning comforters. The women at the cinema, whoever they were, had been marvellously kind to her. Now, she felt calmer, but afraid. Afraid of that abyss she had fallen into – which might open up again at any moment to engulf her.

The day had been too much for her; the train journey, the masses of people surging about her on the escalators, the Underground platforms, the pavements, the teeming city, the roaring traffic, the spinning lights . . .

Adam knocked, and entered the room. Worried sick, yet

afraid to appear over-anxious, he sat on the bed beside her. "Kate, dear, is there anything I can do?" he asked gently.

"Just stay with me for a while," she murmured.

The texture of his tweed jacket brought back memories of her father, comforting her as he used to when she was a little girl. Then suddenly he had gone away, and she couldn't understand why he had left her. Her memories of him were few and fleeting; impressions rather than memories, apart from sharing his breakfast, dipping bread soldiers into his boiled egg; standing beside him near the kitchen sink when he was shaving, fascinated by the lather, the way he drew the razor over his chin and cheeks, removing the foam as if by magic; awaiting the moment when he would dot her nose with his shaving brush.

These were memories she treasured. Her impressions were of a different nature, to do with security, warmth and happiness whenever he was there, whether in the same room or not. Whenever her father came home after work, she would run to him, wanting to show him her toys or to read to her from the comic her mother had bought earlier to keep her quiet. And, "Don't pester your dad just now," Mum would say, "let him have his tea in peace, first."

She had not known at the time, how could she? that her father was a sick man, living on borrowed time, yet utterly refusing to give up working, to provide for his wife and children as long as he had breath left in his body.

Now, feeling Adam's hand smoothing her hair, the texture of his tweed jacket against her cheek, she knew that she was no longer capable of resisting her need to be held, to derive comfort and strength from another human being.

She had been alone too long, struggling against the current, like a salmon fighting its way upstream. She longed for her father, and Nick. But her father was dead. And Nick? Where was Nick?

Adam continued stroking her hair. Her eyelids closed . . .

"Bitch! You did it on purpose to humiliate me. Little Miss Purity! Butter wouldn't melt in your mouth, would it? Pah, you make me sick, Cathy Mitchell! And what the hell chance do you think you've got of keeping a man like Nick Willard? Don't you know, you bloody little fool, that he'll have you for breakfast and spit you out before lunch?

"Well, you needn't think I'll stay in this cabin a moment longer! I'll ask Chief for a transfer! And I hope to God I'll never set eyes on your silly simpering face again!"

"Heather, please listen to me. I never meant it to happen. I don't know how it happened. It just did, that's all. And you're wrong about Nick. He really cares for me, I know he does!"

Catherine stirred uneasily in her sleep, but the nightmare continued . . . Then came the banging of a door as Heather Harper, wild-eyed with jealousy, rushed from the cabin and clattered down the stairs of the Wren quarters.

Then, she herself was running, running, running away from the building, her feet pounding on the gravelled drive. But running where to? And why?

Suddenly the gravel gave way to turf, and she was in a wood, the trees of which threw long tentacles about her waist to impede her progress, and, "Let go of me! Please let go of me," she cried aloud to the trees. "You don't understand! I need my freedom! He won't wait for me if I'm late!"

Twisting and turning, she heard a voice calling her name: "Cathy", over and over again. And "Yes," she cried out, "I'm coming! Please wait for me! Don't go without me! Nick, darling, please wait for me! I'm coming!" . . .

Chapter Five

The events of the night remained unclear in her mind. There had been a nightmare which had made her cry out, a phantom figure ahead of her, always out of reach, an awareness of someone beside her, half sitting, half lying, murmuring softly when she opened her eyes, giving her sips of water.

Waking in the early hours of the morning, she found herself alone in the room. No stranger to disturbed nights, she recalled the endless hours she had lain awake before the divorce proceedings, dreading her appearance in the witness box. Despite Nick's admission of adultery, she, the petitioner, had been obliged to state her case in a Court of Law, under the watchful eyes of the presiding judge, a stern-faced man who appeared to view, with a certain air of mistrust, herself and everyone connected with the case. He had obviously not believed that a young, attractive woman had nothing to hide. His attitude conveyed that quite clearly; his manner suggested that she was to blame for her husband's misconduct.

Collusion, he'd reminded her, was a serious offence in the eyes of the Law. Also, it had weighed against her that she had been the person responsible for ending the marriage. She had had her clever, partisan solicitor to thank for the line of questioning which had finally convinced the judge of her veracity.

"Tell me, Mrs Willard, when did you decide to end the marriage?"

"When my husband admitted his adultery."

"How long had his affair been going on?"

"For several months, I believe."

"Had you questioned him regarding your suspicions?"

"Yes."

"What was his response?"

"He laughed and said I must draw my own conclusions."

"And your conclusions were?"

"That my husband no longer loved me."

"Did he say so?"

"Yes."

"Tell me, Mrs Willard, were you still in love with your husband?"

"Yes."

"So, am I right in thinking that you did not seek the discretion of this Court, because your own conscience was clear?"

"I'm sorry, I don't quite understand."

"In simpler terms, Mrs Willard, had you been entirely faithful to your husband?"

"Yes, of course. I still loved him."

"Then why did you ask him to leave the marital home?"

"It was an intolerable situation to be in."

"How so? What do you mean by 'intolerable'?"

"I felt I was fighting a losing battle."

"I see. And had you sought medical advice at the time?"

"Yes."

"Have we conclusive evidence on that point?"

"I believe so. My doctor came with me today, to speak on my behalf."

"And is this doctor a qualified member of the Medical fraternity?"

Gripping the edge of the witness box, her mouth dry with tension, she said, "I believe him to be so. I'd be surprised if he were not, he has been our family doctor for as far back as I can remember."

"Then may I suggest, m'lud," Mr Pardoe, the solicitor, enquired of the bench, "that this witness be excused and Doctor James Stuart be called upon to give evidence on the petitioner's behalf?"

"That will not be necessary," the judge said coldly.

47

"Obviously, a long-standing member of the Medical profession would not have risked his reputation to come here today to tell the Court a pack of lies. I therefore grant the petitioner a Decree Nisi."

In his own room, Adam moved stiffly, like an automaton. Flexing cramped muscles, he rubbed the back of his neck which ached abominably, after which he ran a bathful of hot water, shaved, put on a clean shirt, brushed his suit, and returned to Kate's room along the landing.

She appeared to be fast asleep, or at least resting more comfortably than she had been the night before.

Silently entering her room, he saw with infinite pity her clenched hands on the coverlet, her nimbus of fair hair against the pillows, the slender line of her throat; dark eyelashes fanning her cheeks, the lace edging of the nightdress she was wearing, and knew, beyond a shadow of doubt, that this was the only woman in the world for him, that he would love her till the end of time and beyond, whether or not she loved him in return.

Covering her more closely with the eiderdown, common sense warned him that he should call a doctor to discover the underlying reason for her collapse.

Reaching a decision, he went downstairs to the manager's office. The Cockney receptionist appeared, wearing a navy suit, blue shirt and a red bow tie. "Wanting the manager, sir?" He sounded faintly disapproving – at this hour? his manner implied. "Sorry, but he's not come down yet. He don't live in his office. He has an apartment on the top floor. What would you be wanting him for, if you don't mind my asking?"

"It's about Mrs Willard. She's not well. She needs a doctor," Adam explained. "I thought the manager would know who to send for. It is rather urgent."

"Oh, well, in that case, sir, I'll give Dr Ellerby a ring. He's the one we usually send for. Very obliging, is Dr Ellerby."

Adam waited impatiently until the call had been made, worrying in case he had made a wrong decision. What if Kate saw his action as interference? In her present nervous state she may well do so. On the other hand, he was the one responsible for bringing her to London in the first place, the one responsible for her welfare.

Hanging up the receiver, "The doctor will be here about eleven o'clock," the receptionist told him. "May I suggest, sir, that you have breakfast while you're waiting? The dining room will be open in a few minutes." He added helpfully, "We could send up a tray to Mrs Willard's room, if you wish. Toast, and a pot of tea, perhaps?"

"No, I think not. She was asleep when I saw her a few minutes ago. I'd rather she wasn't disturbed."

"Just so, sir." Adam knew what the man was thinking, that he and Kate were having an affair. If only that were true, he thought wryly, going down to the dining room, ashamed that he felt hungry. With good reason, he supposed. He'd had nothing substantial to eat since yesterday lunchtime.

At eleven o'clock, he was on the landing, awaiting the arrival of the doctor. Thankfully, Kate had not demurred when he told her a doctor had been sent for. On the contrary, she had seemed not to take it in. She had simply looked up at him and smiled faintly, then drifted back to sleep.

When Dr Ellerby, a small, brisk man, came upstairs he asked, "Are you the patient's husband?"

"No, just a friend." Adam liked the look of the man, noticing the shrewd eyes behind the horn-rimmed glasses which, despite the brusqueness of his approach, betokened a sense of humour allied to a wealth of experience of sick people and their problems. He would be in his late fifties or early sixties, Adam surmised. Certainly he was no fool.

"My name is Jesson, Adam Jesson, Mrs Willard and I came to London yesterday, at my suggestion, I'm afraid."

"Why 'afraid'? Mr Jesson," Ellerby enquired.

"I thought a change would do her good. Apparently I was wrong," Adam admitted. "She – Mrs Willard – fainted last night in the cinema. I should have known

49

better than to take her there in the first place. I could see she was tired."

"Come now, Mr Jesson, no need to blame yourself," Ellerby said briskly. "We are all wiser after the event." He added kindly, "I suggest you wait here until I have examined my patient."

"Of course, Doctor."

The waiting had seemed an eternity.

When the doctor emerged from Catherine's room, he said, "I've prescribed tranquillizers for Mrs Willard as a temporary measure, to calm her down a little for the time being. She has, I believe, been overworking for some time now, and there appears to be some deep emotional stress involved in her condition, which only a qualified psychotherapist could adequately come to grips with and treat successfully."

"Oh, God," Adam said bleakly, "is there nothing I can do to help?"

"Most certainly there is," Ellerby declared firmly. "First and foremost, you may battle your way to the nearest chemist, pick up the tranquillizers, and make sure that Mrs Willard takes them according to my instructions."

"Yes, of course. Is that *all*?" The mood he was in, Adam felt like a latter-day Don Quixote devoid of windmills. A Knight of The Round Table robbed of shining armour, a poor excuse for the man he wished himself to be in the service of the woman he loved.

"For the time being, yes," Ellerby said quietly. "Just remember, 'They also serve who only stand and wait'. That is my best advice to you, Mr Jesson, be patient. What Mrs Willard needs most, right now, is peace of mind, someone strong and trustworthy to lean on. I think that person is you."

Catherine thought about Ellerby's advice to her: "You must do some straight thinking, Mrs Willard, and find some answers." Scribbling down the prescription he said, "There is nothing physically wrong with you – apart

50

from weakness; dehydration caused through vomiting. You should remain in bed for the next twenty-four hours, take plenty of liquids – fruit juice, weak tea, water – no coffee, and the pills I have prescribed for you."

He added kindly, "Most people come to a crossroads once in a while. I think that you have reached such a crossroads. When that happens, we should pause for a moment to ask ourselves in which direction we should go next. Try and solve whatever is worrying you; reach some firm decisions."

Food for thought. Make some decisions? It seemed that every decision of her life had, in some sense or other, been made for her. War came, and so she had joined the Wrens. Forced to earn a living, she had set up in business. In need of a home, she had bought a flat. Marriage? Nick had decided that in 1945, when she was just nineteen. He had not even asked her.

They had been with the usual crowd, Dick Henry, George Robinson, Blackie Phillips, Guy Flint, Maisie Foster, at Frank and Estelle Winters' flat, when out of the blue, Nick had said suddenly, light-heartedly, "By the way, folks, Cathy and I are getting married! What do you think of that?"

There had been a stunned silence followed by a chorus of congratulations. Only Estelle had not joined in. Standing on the edge of the crowd, she looked as if she had been hit in the face.

"Why on earth didn't you give us an inkling? Secretive bastard," Frank roared, slapping Nick's shoulder. "Never thought I'd see the day! God, this calls for a drink! Several drinks! A full-scale celebration! And how does the bride to be feel about it? Come on, Cathy darling, give us a smile! That's better!"

Suddenly, Maisie was hugging her, the men clamouring to kiss her, and she was standing there, her heart beating fast with excitement, cheeks flushed, eyes shining. Then Nick's arm was round her waist, and he was laughing, his face – triumphant. But why had he done this thing? He had never even mentioned marriage, much less proposed to her. *Why*? There must be a reason.

51

Despite her excitement, the feeling of being swept off her feet in the best Hollywood tradition, she could not help wishing that Nick had told her first how he felt about her, had proposed marriage in the accepted way; given her an engagement ring. At least given her the chance to say yes. This way, he had simply taken for granted that she wanted to marry him. Of course she did, and she would have said yes in any case. Even so, she had felt a fool when he had announced their engagement so blatantly at a Saturday night get-together in front of a roomful of people.

Searching back painfully, she recalled that night; remembered the worn armchairs drawn up to form a semicircle round the hearth; lounging figures in RAF uniform, the inevitable haze of cigarette smoke. How easy it had been to forget about the war in the company of Nick's friends, listening to music on the radiogram in a corner of the room. The people present had been Nick's colleagues, fellow officers, apart from Maisie, herself and Estelle, in the Winters' flat in the married quarters, near Rington airfield, a home from home for off-duty aircrew, where they could relax, take hot baths, drink beer or coffee, listen to Glenn Miller records, and smoke endless cigarettes.

And yet she had never felt entirely at ease in Estelle's company. When the others were laughing and talking, glancing at Frank's wife, she would find Estelle's dark brown eyes fixed upon her with an expression of – what? Pity? Dislike? She couldn't be sure which. But that look had unnerved her.

A tall, slender woman in her mid-twenties, about Nick's age, Estelle Winter moved with the innate grace of a trained dancer.

She had, Frank had once confided tipsily, wanted to make ballet-dancing her career, then the war had happened, putting an end to that particular ambition, and so she had joined the Women's Auxiliary Air Force. Luckily for him, they had met at a Mess dance twelve months ago. Later, he had proposed, she had accepted, and they had married. As simple as that. It had been love at first sight so far as he was concerned. But was it really that simple?

Estelle was not beautiful in the accepted sense of the word, Catherine had thought at the time, unless one saw beauty in high-planed cheekbones, a high forehead framed with burnt-sienna hair, brushed back and cropped short at the nape of her neck; skin the colour of ivory, the kind of skin that would become dry and wrinkled in time, like parchment, in decided contrast to the bright lipstick she wore, almost defiantly, as if afraid to reveal to the world the pale unsmiling lips beneath that covering of make-up.

Poor Frank, Catherine thought, forever smiling, crinkling his eyes against the rising smoke of a cigarette; coughing his deep, ingrained smoker's cough; nursing his whisky and soda, knowing, deep in his heart, that his wife was not, and never had been in love with him. So why had Estelle married him, not loving him?

It had seemed to her, when the laughing crowd departed in the early hours of the morning, that Frank should have left also, calling 'good-night' over his shoulder as the rest of them did. Never had she been able to visualize them sitting together when their guests had gone, talking over the events of the evening, enjoying a final cigarette, a companionable last drink together.

More likely Estelle would move restlessly about the flat, clearing away the clutter of empty glasses, emptying ashtrays, and Frank would follow her from room to room, watching and waiting, longing, perhaps, for a crack in his wife's cool façade, a smile, a warm, spontaneous gesture of love – a hug, a kiss – which never came.

She couldn't help noticing the hungry expression on Frank's face when he looked at his wife, the hurt expression in his eyes at her indifference towards him, and yet he managed to maintain his hail-fellow-well-met attitude to life. Dear Frank, warm-hearted, kind, affectionate, how sad that, drinking too much, too often, to drown his sorrows, he had appeared as a court-jester in cap and bells, playing the fool to capture the attention of the woman he loved.

When Adam returned to her room with the tranquillizers,

Catherine said, "I must get up. I feel so selfish lying here, spoiling your holiday."

"That's nonsense, and you know it. The doctor said you must stay where you are for the time being. Please, Kate, you mustn't worry about me, just concentrate on yourself for a change. In any case, it's wicked out, snowing like hell!" He smiled at the solecism. "Well, you know what I mean?"

"Yes, Adam, I know. And thank you."

"For what?"

"For being so kind to me. For your patience and understanding."

He went through to the tiny adjoining bathroom to fetch her a glass of water, glad of the excuse to hide his emotion, the tears in his eyes.

When she had swallowed the pill she said, "Please promise me you'll go down for lunch, I'd hate you to starve to death on my account."

"If that's what you want. But how about you? Shall I have a tray sent up to you?"

"No, I'm not hungry, just tired. But perhaps a cup of tea around four o'clock would be nice."

"Your wish is my command," he said, pressing her hands to his lips. "Remember, my love, 'till all the seas gang dry'."

The four o'clock cup of tea had tasted good, and she had managed to swallow a thinly cut egg and cress sandwich before taking the next tranquillizer, after which she had fallen into a deep sleep, so profound that she had slept until the early hours of next morning, awakened by the revving of a car engine in the square outside.

Glancing at her bedside clock, she saw that the time was three in the morning. Getting out of bed, she crossed to the window. Drawing back the curtains, she saw the car she had heard drawing away from the kerb; imagined some faithless husband going home to his wife, thinking up excuses to account for his lateness, should she still be awake, awaiting the stealthy turning of his key in the lock, the sound of his tiptoeing footsteps on the stairs.

This had happened so often to herself, the nerve-stretching waiting for the sound of a key in the door, the furtive footfall on the stairs. She imagined some woman in the Greater London area awaiting the sound of a car engine, as women the world over waited for some man to come home to them. But never again would she do it. Never again wait for Nick to come home to her with his lies and excuses.

Three o'clock. Now there was absolute silence. No sound, no movement, just gently falling snow, the trees in the square garden starred with white snow blossoms.

Try and make some decisions, Dr Ellerby had said. We all reach a crossroads from time to time – decide which way to go next.

Getting back into bed, she lay in a pool of light from her bedside lamp, remembering the letter Nick had received from his mother saying she wanted to meet the girl he intended to marry. And so she had gone with him to Wiltshire, terrified at the prospect of meeting her future mother-in-law.

Nick had laughed at her fear. "If you're worrying about Bridie, forget it!" he said. "As long as you fall in with what she wants to do, she'll love you. My dear mama is as selfish as hell – like me!"

Whatever motivated Bridie Willard's attitude to life, Catherine had fallen immediately under the spell of her strong, unorthodox personality.

Bridie was in the kitchen when they had arrived at the cottage, making sandwiches, listening to Vivaldi on the wireless. It was a tiny kitchen, cluttered with the paraphernalia of cooking. Copper pots and pans were suspended from hooks on the walls. A row of well-thumbed cookery books leaned next to a row of blue and white Cornish jars. Bunches of herbs and dried flowers decorated the beamed ceiling. Gingham-curtained windows looked out on a small orchard of apple trees set among imperfectly scythed grass. A crooked row of dainty lace pants, bras and stockings hung on a washing line strung between branches, the sight of which would have shocked her own mother, Cathy thought, pretending not to notice.

Bridie, apparently, harboured no such inhibitions. She flaunted her pretty garments as she flaunted her pots of cyclamen in the loggia beyond the kitchen, indeed all her possessions – not in an aggressive way, Cathy realized, simply because she treasured her belongings – so that everything she owned bloomed and shone and blossomed as if by magic.

Entering the kitchen, Nick had scooped his mother into his arms and kissed her. Bridie merely smiled and said, "When you've stopped behaving like an overgrown schoolboy, you'd better take Cathy upstairs and show her her room." Then, holding out her hands to her future daughter-in-law she said to Catherine, "Nick told me you were pretty." She laughed, "But not this pretty. How do you do, my dear? And please call me Bridie, everyone else does."

Turning suddenly, she had dashed out into the garden to shoo away a young cat from the herb-bed near the back door. "She's in kitten," Bridie explained, "so we mustn't be too hard on her. She's only doing what comes naturally to cats and humans." She added, returning to her sandwich making, "Jimmy will be in soon. He went for a walk in the fresh air before tea." Smiling at Cathy, "Come down to the drawing room when you're ready," she said. "And you, Nick, can set the table when you've shown Cathy her room."

"Well, what do you think of it?" he'd asked, depositing her suitcase.

Gazing about the room, starry eyed, noticing the glowing antique furniture, the tester bed, the rose-patterned curtains, the bowl of spring flowers on the dressing table, the pink-shaded lamp on the bedside cabinet. "Oh, Nick, it's lovely," she breathed ecstatically, holding up her face to be kissed. Suddenly, a door had banged shut downstairs.

Brushing her cheek with his lips, he turned away from her. "That'll be Jimmy," Nick said, hurrying on to the landing.

56

"Jimmy? Who's Jimmy?" Trying her best not to feel jealous of the individual who had taken Nick's mind off kissing her.

"Jimmy? Oh, he's a lodger of sorts. He had a nasty smash-up a few months ago. Bridie's nursing him back to health as only Bridie can." Leaning over the banister, "Hello there, Jimmy," he called out, "I'll be down in a sec!" And then he was gone, calling over his shoulder, "See you in the drawing room, Cathy."

She had entered the drawing room nervously, having exchanged her Wren uniform for a cotton dress and a hand-knitted cardigan. "Come in, my dear," Bridie said warmly, "come and sit near the fire."

It was the loveliest room she had ever seen, a blend of restful colours, antique furniture, lovely objects, gleaming silver in elegant cabinets, Chinese bowls, original oil paintings in heavy gilt frames, masses of spring flowers growing in profusion in Spode containers.

And yet it was a home, warm and lived in. She'd noticed a bag of knitting on a blue brocade armchair, library books on a Georgian side-table, letters pushed behind the white Staffordshire dogs on the mantelpiece; the low table in front of the fire, delicate china cups and saucers on a gadrooned silver tray, a fluted silver Georgian teapot, milk jug and sugar basin.

Bridie, she realized, was the kind of woman who lives and breathes what she is. Fearlessly, impervious to what the world thinks or says.

"Come and meet Jimmy," Bridie said. A tall individual in faded corduroy trousers and a tweed jacket rose to his feet to shake hands with her. He was lean and handsome with a charming smile, obviously more than a lodger, and yet Nick had never mentioned him. She wondered why not.

After tea, they went out into the garden – herself, Jimmy and Nick – while Bridie was busy in the kitchen preparing dinner – and strolled there until the light began to fade. Jimmy, Cathy noticed, carried a stick and walked with a limp. She had offered to help Bridie with the vegetables, but her hostess had shooed her away in much the same way that she had shooed the cat from the herb-bed. "There's really no need," she'd said lightheartedly, "I adore cooking, in any case it's nothing spectacular we're having, just curried beef, rice, fresh fruit salad, cheese and biscuits."

They had eaten what Bridie termed 'supper', in the exquisitely furnished dining room adjoining the kitchen, at a long Regency table with a centrepiece of hyacinths; rush tablemats, gleaming silver cutlery and starched damask napkins. Jimmy had drawn the curtains and lighted the tall red candles in the silver candelabrum on the Regency sideboard, so that the room, dimly lit, heavy with the fragrance of the hyacinths, had seemed to Cathy a world far removed from her mother's house in Sussex Street, an experience which marked the glaring difference between Nick's upbringing and her own.

After supper, they had returned to the drawing room for coffee, Jimmy had stirred the fire and thrown on more wood to create a warm and welcoming blaze, then limped across to the radiogram to put on a record – Debussy's 'Clair-de-Lune'.

When the coffee had been drunk, and Nick had carried the tray to the kitchen Bridie asked, "Now, Cathy dear, which would you prefer? Beaujolais or Sauterne?" She was seated in the deepest armchair at the time, smiling and flicking ash from her cigarette with a quick movement of her supple wrist, wearing a low-necked blouse, her long ash-blonde hair scraped back into a becoming knot tied with black velvet ribbon, looking rather like a gypsy.

"Neither, thank you," Cathy had replied, "I-I don't drink. That is, I'm not used to it."

Bridie raised her eyebrows. "It's quite innocuous, I assure you," she said with an amused smile. "I made it myself. A kind of local witch's brew, though the beastly stuff took ages to make, didn't it, Jimmy? I had buckets of fermenting liquid all over the place."

"Don't I know it," Jimmy responded, "I kept on tripping over the damned things! The reason why I'm still limping, if you must know."

And so Cathy had accepted a glass of home-brewed

58

Sauterne, not that she liked it entirely, she had simply wished to become an integral member of Nick's family circle, to join in their laughter, to feel the warmth of his body next to hers on the settee in front of the fire, the touch of his hand on her shoulder, to marvel at the fact that they would soon be man and wife. And yet she had known that, despite her efforts at integration, she had scarcely understood a word of their conversation, the reason for their laughter, based on topics which had meant less than nothing to her.

Later, Bridie had come up to her room to ask if she had everything she needed. Sitting on the edge of the bed, she had pulled a feather from the eiderdown and idly picked it to pieces.

"You love Nick very much, don't you?" she asked.

"Oh yes, of course I do," Cathy replied quickly, a shade too quickly perhaps, unnerved by his mother's dissection of the feather.

"Tell me, Cathy, have you ever been in love before?"

"No."

"Then how can you be sure that you are in love now?"

"I *do* know, that's all! I've never felt like this before. I can't think of anything or anyone else except Nick. Nothing else matters . . ." Tears sprang to her eyes.

"I didn't mean to upset you. It's simply that Nick isn't an easy person to understand. He's moody, and he can be utterly selfish. So am I. I've been alone too long. My husband left me when Nick was a baby – left me for a woman who would tie his shoelaces before they came undone, give him an aspirin before he had a headache." She smiled ruefully, and shrugged.

"Fortunately he was a rich man, so money was not a problem. He was happy to give me this cottage and a lump sum to salve his conscience and pay for Nick's education. Am I boring you with all this?"

"Oh no. Please go on."

Bridie had taken a cigarette case and lighter from her skirt pocket. Lighting a cigarette, she inhaled deeply, and continued, "I've never tried to stop him doing anything he wanted, quite the opposite. I taught him to be independent, and I vowed never to interfere in his life – a two-edged sword, at times. Perhaps I was too lenient with him, allowing him to twist me round his little finger."

She sighed and flicked the ash from her cigarette. "He might have gone to university had I taken the trouble to . . . Well, I won't go into that."

"But I thought . . ." Cathy frowned. Surely Nick had been at Queen's College, Oxford?

"What did you think?"

"Oh, nothing. It doesn't matter."

"In the event," Bridie went on, "when he left school at seventeen, he found himself a job with a travel agency. His French was superb, and his work as a courier suited him down to the ground. The old ladies loved him, so did the young ones come to that. Then, when war came, he joined the Royal Air Force. You probably know all this anyway."

"No, not really. Nick doesn't talk about himself very much." Older and wiser than she was then, Cathy might have asked Bridie what she was driving at. But she had been neither old nor wise at the time.

Bridie changed the subject. "I take it you've met Frank and Estelle Winter?" she asked, stubbing out her cigarette.

"Yes, of course."

"What do you think of them?"

"I don't know. What I mean is, I like Frank. He's funny. Nice. He makes me laugh. I'm not sure about Estelle. I don't know if I like her or not. I just think she doesn't like me very much."

"They are Nick's friends," Bridie reminded her. "Basically, they are his kind of people."

"I know. At least I suppose they must be." She had stared unhappily at Bridie.

Getting up from the bed, "I've upset you a great deal, my dear, haven't I?" Bridie said, returning the cigarette case and lighter to her pocket. "You're a nice girl, Cathy. As Nick's mother, I felt it my duty to play the devil's advocate. Still, I'm a great believer in 'che sarà sarà' – whatever will be will be. If Nick loves you as much as you love him, you should be blissfully happy together." Turning at the door she said, "Sleep well, my dear."

It had been a disturbing conversation. And there were other disturbing elements too. She had not, at first, been able to fit Jimmy into the picture. Gradually, during that long weekend, it had dawned on her that he was more than just a paying guest, had realized why Bridie's delicate undergarments, strung on a washing line to dry, had reminded her of a bride's trousseau. Early one morning, on her way to the bathroom, she had bumped into Jimmy emerging from Bridie's bedroom in his dressing gown and slippers, and known that they were lovers.

The discovery had shocked her.

Later that day, about to enter the kitchen, she had heard Nick and Bridies' voices raised in argument. Bridie said heatedly, "You are being grossly unfair to her, you know that, don't you?"

"My darling hypocrite of a mother, who the hell are you to judge? You brought me up in your own image, remember?"

Remember, remember, remember . . .

Catherine was standing near the window when Adam entered her hotel room at eight o'clock in the morning.

Aware of his presence, not turning her head to look at him, she said softly, "Look, Adam, look at the square. Isn't it lovely? It reminds me of an Impressionist painting I once saw, by Pissaro or Monet, I forget which."

Standing beside her, looking down at the square with its soft covering of newly-fallen snow, "Yes," he said, "it *is* lovely, and so are you."

Glancing up at him, recalling Dr Ellerby's advice, filled with a sudden overwhelming desire for peace and understanding – belonging – she said quietly, "I will marry you, Adam, if you still want me."

"Want you? Oh, Kate!"

He had never kissed her on the mouth before. As she might have expected, his lips were firm and gentle, like the man himself.

Chapter Six

New Year's Eve.

Seated at the dressing table, Catherine thought about the step she had taken, and what it might entail. Almost certainly she would be giving up her independence. Married to Adam, she would have to sell her home and her business, move away from Scarborough, the town she loved. So be it.

In future she would settle for what most women wanted from life, a house on a pleasantly wooded estate, a husband incapable of cruelty, holidays abroad, Sunday afternoon outings in the car, evenings spent with friends or watching television. Why fight it? She would join some women's organization or other, shop in York city centre, have coffee and toasted teacakes at Betty's Café near Stonegate. Everything would be new and different. She might even have children. A consummation devoutly to be wished.

Consummation? She had longed for children – Nick's children, borne of her love for him. That dream had never come true. His fault or hers? How could she be sure? Inhibited by her upbringing, her mother's stringent views on modesty as a becoming asset in young women, had she ever fulfilled Nick's sexual appetite? His often careless, unorthodox approach to lovemaking had shocked her at times – a girl brought up in the belief that physical intimacy between man and wife occurred only in the marriage bed, with the lights out.

Her mind skirted round the inevitability of an intimate relationship with Adam. It had been hard enough, at times, to give herself unreservedly to Nicholas, hedged about as she had been by the shibboleths of her mother's dogmatic opinions of what was right and proper. But she had loved Nick with all her heart. How, then, would she fare with Adam, a man she was not in love with?

What did other women do under such circumstances? Did they cheat a little? Had she cheated Nick? Was she about to cheat Adam?

She had finished dressing when he came to escort her down to the dining room. "Are you sure you feel well enough?" he asked her.

She smiled and said, "Yes, I'll be fine," knowing she must make the effort, not give way to foolish fears and fancies.

"You look lovely," he told her. "But are you sure you're all right? You're trembling."

"It's nothing. I'm a bit cold, that's all."

"You're quite sure that's all? We needn't go down if you don't want to."

"Oh, for God's sake, Adam! I wish you'd stop fussing!" She hadn't meant to snap at him. "I'm sorry." She sank down on the dressing stool. "Please forgive me. I don't know what came over me."

"If only I knew what you're afraid of."

"It's hard to explain."

"Please try. I'd like to help." He sat down on the end of the bed. She could see by his face that she had hurt him, that what she saw as fussiness sprang from a very deep and real concern for her welfare. How could she have thought otherwise after all he had done for her?

She said, "Before you came in, I'd been thinking how easy it is to cheat even the people one loves most. Are you sure you want to hear this?"

"I'm sure. Whatever is worrying you, I need to know. It's about Nick, isn't it?"

"Yes." She paused to frame her words. "After the war, he wanted to go to New Zealand; make a fresh start, but I wouldn't even listen. All I wanted was to stay in the place I loved among the people I loved. I didn't trust him, you see."

"That was understandable."

"I went to see the bank manager, to ask for a loan to buy

64

into my own business. I thought if I could make enough money, Nick would forget about New Zealand, and I was right, but I knew at the time that I had taken an unfair advantage. Oh, I daresay the bank manager would have turned me down flat except that the business I wanted was well established and I had worked there for some time. The owner, Mrs Maitland, wished to retire, and she had given me the first refusal."

"Nothing wrong with that," Adam said quietly, "knowing you wouldn't be happy in New Zealand."

"But Nick might have been. That's the point I'm trying to make, don't you see?"

"Yes, of course. But the past is over and done with now, darling. Why torture yourself? You did what seemed right at the time, and you have made a success of your business."

He leaned forward. Holding her hand, he said, "You are still very weak, love, but try not to dwell on the past too much. Think about the future. We have so much to look forward to."

Saying what lay uppermost in his mind, "I know you are not in love with me, but I think that we can build a good life together." Looking into his own past he said, "First love happens only once in a lifetime. I know what it feels like, believe me." He paused. "There was this girl, you see. Her name was Margaret. We bumped into each other, quite literally, in the blackout, during the war.

"She was young, very pretty, bright and intelligent. I bought her a cup of coffee by way of an apology for having crashed into her so carelessly. She laughed and said it didn't matter, she was glad it had been me she'd collided with and not a lamppost.

"We met quite often afterwards. We would go to the cinema, occasionally for a quiet drink or a meal. I'd never had a girlfriend before. I found myself looking forward to seeing her . . ."

"What happened?" Kate asked.

"Nothing happened. That is, my mother didn't approve of the friendship. I made the mistake of taking Margaret home to meet her. I suppose jealousy entered into it,

Mother was rather possessive where I was concerned. My brother had left home some time before, so Mother had come to rely on me to take care of her. She saw Margaret as a threat to her security."

"And so you ended the friendship?"

"No, not really. It simply died a natural death. When Margaret joined the ATS, she promised to write to me every day, and she kept that promise for a week or two. Afterwards, she wrote less frequently until finally she sent me a 'Dear John' letter saying she'd met someone else."

"I'm so sorry," Catherine said compassionately.

"So was I at the time. But it wouldn't have worked out, I know that now. Mother hadn't a good word to say for her."

Catherine imagined the set-up – a narrow-minded old woman intent on destroying her son's happiness – an insidious form of emotional blackmail based on her dislike of the girl he was in love with.

Much the same thing had happened between herself and her own mother, she reflected, after that fraught Christmas Day tea-party in 1945, when Annie Mitchell had condemned Nick as a snob and a ne'er-do-well – a sponger who would neither work nor want. The difference being that she, Catherine, was married to the man on the receiving end of her mother's hostility.

"I'm glad you told me about Margaret," she said.

"I wanted you to understand that it is possible to love again in a different kind of way, Kate, darling. Nick was your husband. Margaret and I were never more than friends, two young people on a voyage of discovery of each other's needs, likes and dislikes. She wanted a home, children, a settled future, despite the war. That is to say, she needed the security of marriage, a cut and dried relationship to cling to."

He paused. "She begged me to marry her, secretly if necessary. That way we'd both know we'd have a future together after the war. It would be so romantic, she said. But I couldn't. I didn't want a hole-in-the-corner relationship, to build the future on a tissue of lies. I told her I loved her, that I'd work things out given time, and I meant what I said. Then she went away. The rest you know.

"What I'm trying to say, we are no longer in the first flush of youth, you and I. What was it Bette Davis said in *Now, Voyager*? 'Why ask for the moon, we have the stars'. I'll do everything in my power to make you happy, my love, when we are married. You know that, don't you?"

"Yes," she said softly, "I know."

Now, it seemed, she must drift along with the tide, abandon the wild sea-music of youth, settle for second best. The fight, the strength had gone out of her.

They walked slowly downstairs, past the reception desk to the cocktail lounge. The receptionist looked up from the hotel register and gave a funny, stiff little bow of acknowledgement. "I trust madam is feeling better? Well enough to join in our New Year's Eve celebration?"

"Yes, I'm much better, thank you."

In the cocktail lounge, a stout lady was reading a newspaper, flames licked greedily at the fresh logs a porter had just thrown on the fire. Reminders of Christmas were strongly in evidence, wilting a little by this time. The tree in the corner was shedding its needles; holly shrivelled from the heat of the fire.

Behind the bar, soft lights shone on rows of bottles, and the mirror behind the shelves floated mysteriously, aglow with all manner of reflections, as beautiful and dreamlike as an exotic sunset.

The room seemed to Catherine a cosily padded box insulated with red velvet curtains, a richly carpeted and curtained padded cell designed to keep safe the inmates from the harsh reality of the world outside.

The barmaid was the prototype for every barmaid that ever drew breath in comic pictures, with her carefully supported bosom, fashionably coiffed blonde hair and perfectly applied make-up. She was leaning on the bar talking earnestly to a young man, crested like a cockatoo and with tufts of hair on his cheeks.

She turned and smiled as Adam asked for sherry.

The pale young man got up and left, and the barmaid cast a swift, despairing glance at his retreating figure. Catherine sensed the drama of the situation – the older woman, the half-hearted lover glad of an excuse to make his getaway, the superficiality of the barmaid's smile, the little charade of friendliness necessary to keep her job.

Staring at her reflection in the mirror, Catherine saw there a woman she scarcely recognized as herself. How gaunt and strained she appeared – a stranger wearing her clothes. Her eyes seemed to have sunk, her hair to have faded, like wheat before harvesting when dust from the road has settled on it.

Adam raised his glass. "Here's to a happy New Year, darling." He was smiling, relaxed, optimistic about the future.

They went down to the dining room before it became too crowded. The Irish waiter ushered them to their table.

Strange, Catherine thought, the way good-looking young men loved to show off. The old primeval urge, like male peacocks spreading out their tail feathers to attract a mate.

He reminded her of someone – someone with the same kind of dark curly hair, that look, half insolent, half amused, which said more clearly than words: 'Watch me! I'm worth watching!' His handing of the menus was masterly – the flourish, the smile, the panache.

"We'd like a bottle of champagne," Adam said.

"Certainly, sir," the Irishman replied, "I'll send along the wine waiter directly. Would you care to order dinner first, or shall I come back later?"

"What do you think, darling?" Deferring to Kate's wishes in the matter, "Shall we order dinner first or wait awhile?" Adam asked.

"Oh, now, by all means." She consulted the menu, knowing that all she really wanted was a little soup and an omelette, that she could not possibly tackle *duck à l'orange*, loin of pork *Dijonnais*, *Boeuf Bourguignon*, or Lobster Thermidore. On the other hand, she had no wish to inhibit Adam's choice of food from her own lack of appetite. And so she ordered the same as he – prawn cocktail, and *coq au vin* – the way it should be made, with its full complement of herbs and spices, crushed garlic and red wine – a far cry from her own version of that particular dish.

Little wonder, she thought, when the wine waiter arrived, that Nick had poured scorn on her culinary efforts, which in no way matched those of his mother, Bridie, whose expertise in the kitchen possessed the power to change a few scraps of leftover meat, a handful of rice, a scattering of herbs and a soupçon of curry powder into a meal fit for an Eastern potentate . . .

Jolting back to the present, she heard Adam telling the wine waiter that the bottle of Veuve Cliquot he had ordered was to celebrate their engagement.

She was angry beyond belief, how dare he have done such a thing? Taking Adam to task when the waiter had gone, "You might at least have spared me the humiliation of broadcasting a very personal and private matter to a complete stranger," she said bitterly. "How could you? And *why*, for heaven's sake?"

"I'm sorry. It never occurred to me that you would mind. It seemed the most natural thing in the world . . . I'm afraid I have a lot to learn."

Her anger subsided as quickly as it had risen. "No, I'm the one with a lot to learn, the one who should apologize, and I do." Raising her glass of champagne she said, "Here's to you, Adam, whose kindness I have done nothing to deserve, and to the future – whatever it holds in store for us."

After dinner, they went upstairs to the lounge.

Music filtered through from the dance floor where couples were swaying together beneath a slowly revolving witchball. Adam asked her if she would care to dance. "I'm not very good," he said, "so be warned."

"Neither am I." She smiled, wanting to make the evening special for him – a new beginning for both of them.

69

Throughout her life she had felt the importance of new beginnings, self-imposing dares and conditions, thinking – in an hour from now – when I have counted to ten – when I reach the end of the street – tomorrow morning – or even – I shall start from now – mentally attuned like an athlete at the starting line.

Monday had always seemed a particularly good day for a fresh beginning, allowing her a whole week-end to indulge her vices; eat all the sweets she had bought with her pocket-money; tease her sister about Ernest; dawdle on her way to Sunday school. And she would think, snuggling down in bed on Sunday night, when I wake up, I'll be different. I'll never eat sweets again; never tease the life out of Mavis, never . . . Falling fast asleep before finishing her list of never agains.

At New Year, her list of Resolutions had included help-ing Mum with the washing-up, reading the entire output of Charles Dickens, starting with *David Copperfield*; taking her Saturday night libation of senna-tea without pulling a face or pouring it down the sink when Mum wasn't looking.

Now, here she was, years later, expecting the fresh white page of a new calendar to bring about some kind of miracle; forgetfulness of the past – the events of her life, so far, which had made her the person she was, not the person she wished to be.

The witchball sent diamond facets whirling about the room. Dancing with Adam, Catherine remembered a different witchball a long time ago, a laughing company of uniformed men and women who would never pass her way again.

One figure, dark-haired, with mocking eyes and a smile, seemed to stand at the end of a long, dimly-lit corridor, willing her to come back to him – and she fancied herself running, flying the corridor of time to follow where he led.

Adam found a table for them near the dance floor.

"May we join you?"

70

The man requesting the pleasure of their company was tall, portly, with greying hair, wearing executive-type glasses. His wife, a tiny blonde, was doing her best to sparkle. She wore a sequinned bodice and chiffon skirt, a paste-diamond choker to hide the crêpiness of her throat. Her lipstick had run into the creases on her top lip.

"My name's Vic," the man said, "and this is Marlene. Can't do with formality, it's the common touch that counts. People like it. I can mix with anybody; the secret of my success. What'll you have to drink?"

Edging onto the chair next to Catherine's, Marlene said, "We should be staying at The Savoy, by right, shouldn't we, Vic? I must say, I was a bit put out when they hadn't a room for us. I mean, a hotel of that size! So we had to make do with this. A bit disappointing, I must say. We wanted something a bit special, you see, to celebrate my hubby's promotion to the Board of Directors. Not before time, I must say. He's been with the firm nigh on twenty years now . . . Hmm? Oh, make mine a double gin and tonic."

"They seem a decent couple," Adam remarked, when Vic and Marlene got up to dance, wanting to get in a couple of demonstration whirls before the floor became silted up. "I wish I could dance properly. Perhaps we could take lessons, when we're married? What do you think of the idea?"

She could think of nothing she'd dislike more than walking into a dance studio in broad daylight, being taught how to position her feet, to see the dust on the coils of cable behind the radiogram.

Someone had switched on the television. Above the din of voices, the music and laughter, the commentator's voice was making solemn pronouncements on the cessation of the old year; recalling happenings of importance, uttering the inevitable clichés about the new year being the start of something better – as though, miraculously, at midnight, nations would cease to hate, to fight, to make war, as though amnesty would be declared for all political prisoners awaiting trial and execution; as though the hungry would be fed; poverty cease to exist, as if all the old and lonely people in the world would awake to find themselves young once more – and loved.

All one could hope for was the courage to face whatever lay ahead. She longed for a church, cold stone flags and ancient pews. A quiet place in which to pray; the lights of home strung against the darkness of the bay, the sound of the sea – the background music of her life.

Boom! Pandemonium ceased. For a moment in time the least enquiring minds sensed the drama, the underlying gravity of the booming of Big Ben, the inexorable movement of its hands gobbling up the minutes of one's life.

Ten, eleven, twelve!

"Happy New Year, Kate darling," Adam murmured, holding her close, kissing her lips.

"Should Auld Acquaintance be forgot, and never brought to mind . . ."

The dancers had formed a circle. Pandemonium had broken out once more. Round and round they went, hands clasped, singing the words of 'Auld Lang Syne'; half mad with excitement, befuddled with drink, drawing everyone within reach into the carousel, refusing to take no for an answer.

Drawn against her will into the mêlée, Catherine fought for release. Head spinning, so this, she thought, was the brave start to her New Year? Already the fabric seemed rotten, threadbare.

Breaking away from the merry-go-round, desperately in need of solitude, she stumbled blindly from the room to the foyer, and rang for the lift.

Adam came after her. "I'm so sorry, darling," he said hoarsely, "I never meant this to happen!"

"It doesn't matter!" The last thing she needed, at that moment, was sympathy, apology. All she needed was peace. "Please, Adam, leave me alone! For heaven's sake, leave me alone!"

Closing and locking her bedroom door, standing with her back to it, hands clenched, tears streaming down her face,

Catherine knew that *this* was the crossroads Dr Ellerby had meant; nothing whatever to do with her decision to marry Adam Jesson, but something far deeper, upon which the entire course of her life, and her reason, may well depend.

It seemed to her that two ghosts stood before her, her father and Nick. Her father was dead, but not Nick, the man she had met and married in the springtime of her life.

Sinking down on the bed, she remembered a church somewhere, long ago, and a very old man, so frail that he could not have climbed the steps to the pulpit without help. An old man with a luminous skin and the accumulated wisdom of age in his eyes.

"Behind the tumult, behind the violence of our times, behind the wars and rumours of wars," he had said, "lies the still small voice of God and of our own conscience, and it is this voice that tells us what we must do. It is *this* voice we must listen to above all else."

What he had said was true. Behind the long emptiness of her days and nights, her striving towards success, always, at the back of her mind had been a still small voice telling her what she must do. It was in the denial of that voice that she had foundered, she knew that now. Suppression of her desire to find Nick once more, to talk to him again, however fleetingly, had led to her breakdown.

Perhaps she was not thinking logically. She didn't know and she didn't care. She was desperate. She had never known desperation before. More than a word in the dictionary, desperation was a disease, an uncontrollable emotion leading, in some cases, to murder and violence.

Staring into the void of the future, she thought, desperation is the last-ditch stand of men facing death on a battlefield, the sword of cold, clear logic which substitutes heroism for blind panic. It is the unknown quantity which compels a person to act against his normal inclinations. It is the motivating force of a man trapped in a blazing building to jump from a high window into the safety-net below.

In her own case, it was the compelling force which would drive her to find Nicholas again. The still small voice had come to her amidst the tumult of her life, and she must follow where it led.

Chapter Seven

The station platform on which she stood had its counterparts all over the British Isles. There were sweet-kiosks, a cafeteria, newspaper-stand, racks of paperback novels.

It hadn't been like this during the war, apart from the paper-stand, and a refreshment room with a high counter – like the one in *Brief Encounter*; a smell of grease, steam-engines and trapped smoke beneath the station roof.

She had the feeling that if she waited long enough, the scene would change, that the sweet-kiosk and the cafeteria would disappear, and she would see Nick, in his airforce uniform, lifting their luggage from a corridor train.

She had come on a strange and frightening errand, to invoke the past. Yet, curiously, she was no longer afraid. It seemed that the past had been there all the time, an intrinsic part of her life, willing her to swim into its mysterious depths, to find the answers to questions whose roots lay buried there.

Carrying her case, she walked to the exit barrier. "Taxi, Miss?" a driver called out to her.

She shook her head. "No thanks. I haven't far to go." There was a small hotel near the station, she remembered, at least there used to be. She had noticed it that day she and Nick had hurried across the road from the station to catch the bus to Cloud Merridon.

"Come on, run, Cathy," he'd called to her over his shoulder. And, "I'm coming," she'd called back to him breathlessly, "I'm coming!"

The landlady showed her upstairs to her room.

There were folkweave curtains at the window, the

bed had a pink candlewick cover. There was an oak dressing table and wardrobe, a rexine armchair near a small gas fire; a print of 'The Light of the World' above the mantelpiece.

Catherine breathed a sigh of relief. No heavily-lined curtains, thank God, no embossed wallpaper, or thick carpets to deaden the sounds of living.

In retrospect, the London hotel seemed like something from a Gothic horror film, the people she had met there – the Cockney receptionist, Marlene and Vic, the blonde barmaid, the Irish waiter, the pallid young man with the cockatoo hairdo and the shaving brushes on his cheeks – as the unreal inmates of a well-upholstered asylum.

"If you'd like some tea," the landlady said pleasantly, "there's a nice fire in the lounge."

"Thank you. I'll be down in ten minutes."

The lounge of the Station Hotel at Lower Minter, contained a comfortable squash of armchairs, a roaring coal fire in a fawn-tiled fireplace, several occasional tables, and a flight of china ducks above the sideboard.

"Here we are." The landlady brought in a tray with tea and cakes, then poked the fire, sending a fresh blaze leaping up the chimney. "Give me a nice coal fire any day of the week."

Catherine couldn't have agreed more. "Tell me," she said, "have you been here long?"

"My hubby and I haven't, but his parents kept this hotel for years before they retired, then we took over."

"Were they here during the war?"

"The war? Yes, I suppose they must have been. Why? Did you know them?"

"No, but I stayed once with friends at Cloud Merridon during the war, and I remember that the bus stopped outside your front door."

"Is that so? Well, they don't stop here any more. They stop round the corner near the Zebra crossing. But that's the way it is nowadays, more's the pity! Progress, they call it! Things change so fast you don't know if you're on your head or your heels half the time!"

"Has Cloud Merridon changed very much?" Catherine asked wistfully.

"No, I don't think so, but that's only a village, isn't it, not a town? I know for a fact the National Trust has been busy in that area – preserving the environment, they call it. Still, Cloud Merridon's a pretty little place, with the duck pond and the village green, and those lovely Georgian cottages facing the common. A downright shame it would've been if the National Trust hadn't stepped in to prevent the village green being used as a car park! Well, enjoy your tea. Dinner's at half-past seven, so the cakes won't spoil your appetite. It's home-made steak and kidney pie tonight, with bread and butter pudding to follow." The landlady departed.

Alone, Catherine remembered Cloud Merridon: the duck pond on the village green, the row of Georgian houses facing the common, the Norman church nestling beneath its protective umbrella of giant elm trees, the ivied walls of the nearby vicarage, the gently curving main street leading up to the church; time weathered gravestones, their inscriptions indecipherable with age – apart from the later ones in a different area of the cemetery.

Overwhelmed with a sudden sense of foreboding: what if Bridie were dead? she thought. But no, not Bridie!

Never, under any circumstances whatsoever, would she have traded the life she loved for a plot of earth and a neatly engraved headstone, never again to smoke and stub out her cigarettes half finished, never again to peg out her lace underwear on the line strung between the apple trees, never more to lie naked and warm in the arms of a lover.

Bridie epitomized life, and the memory of her had remained vividly in Catherine's mind. Never had she blamed Bridie for the break-up of her marriage, she was not the kind to take sides. She had known her son's faults like the back of her hand. In any case, Bridie had been too involved in her own life, her creature comforts – wine, coffee, log fires, good food – to involve herself deeply in other people's affairs.

A family came into the lounge, a mother, father and three small children at the inquisitive stage. Mother, a faded cipher of a woman dressed in a baggy tweed skirt and a shapeless sweater which scarcely concealed the presence of child number four, fiddled with her wedding ring and left the endless queries of the other three to 'daddy', who seemed vaguely irritated by her presence.

Catherine went up to her room. She needed to be alone, to think about Adam. Day long she had pushed the thought of him to the back of her mind. Telling him that she was going to Wiltshire, leaving him alone in London, was one of the hardest things she had ever had to do.

She had lain awake till the early hours, worrying about what she would say to him. At eight o'clock in the morning, she had gone to his room fully dressed, and he had sensed what she had come to tell him.

"It's because of last night, isn't it?" he said harshly, "that stupid merry-go-round on the dance floor? I knew you were feeling ill, but I couldn't get to you for that damned woman – what's her name? Marlene, and her drunken sot of a husband. They wouldn't take no for an answer; just dragged me into the thick of things. And then you wouldn't let me near you."

He laughed bitterly. "No need to ask why. It's *him*, isn't it? Nicholas bloody Willard? You told me you still loved him. This I tried to accept and understand. I thought, mistakenly, that you meant you retained tender feelings towards him because he was once your husband, in much the same way that I remember Margaret, with a certain amount of regret because things didn't work out right in the long run. I never dreamt for one moment that you were still besotted by the man – obsessed by him. And that's what it amounts to, Kate – an obsession!"

"You are quite right, Adam," she said quietly, making allowances for his bitterness and anger. "That's why I'm going to Wiltshire, in the hope of finding him. I *have* to, Adam, don't you see?"

"Oh yes, I see right enough – to beg him to come back

to you, to make a fresh start? To throw yourself on his mercy; tell him how much you love him, that you can't live without him!"

"No, Adam, you're wrong if that's what you think. I don't want him back, just to set the record straight between us, not to go on wondering what became of him after the divorce, to heal all the wounds we inflicted on one another at the time. Then and only then can I get on with my life. The way things are now, I can't rest, eat or sleep properly, and it's getting worse, not better. If you knew how hard I've tried to put the past behind me. Then something happened . . ."

"What – happened?"

"Christmas," she said softly. "Christmas happened; a flood of memories I hadn't the strength to cope with. A bit like opening Pandora's Box. I've felt like a prisoner, not in body but spirit, lacking the courage to do what needs to be done to find peace of mind. Now, somehow, I've found that courage. Call it desperation, if you like – a last-ditch stand." She smiled sadly. "I'm sorry, Adam. Wish me luck?"

"And where do I fit into the picture?"

"I don't know right now. All I can possibly say is thank you for loving me, whether or not I deserve your love."

Waking in the early hours of the morning, she switched on the bed-side lamp. Someone had coughed on the landing outside her room – probably 'daddy' on his way to the bathroom.

Suddenly she remembered Frank Winter and his ingrained smoker's cough; that day in Scarborough when she had come home from the salon to hear voices, hearty male laughter from the sitting room of the flat.

Opening the door, she had seen Frank standing there on the hearthrug, nursing a glass of whisky, telling a funny story; his wife, Estelle, sitting in a chair near the fire; Nick's hands resting on the back of the chair.

"Well, look who's here! Cathy, my love, how are you? Surprise, surprise! Like old times, eh?" Frank laughed.

A fit of coughing had attacked him, from which he'd

79

emerged exhausted but still smiling. "This bloody cough of mine," he said, "can't shake the damned thing off! Not to worry, let's have another drink, Nick, old sport. You too, Cathy darling. This calls for a celebration!"

Whisky? Glancing at the half empty bottle on the sideboard, Cathy had wondered where it came from. Perhaps Frank had brought it with him? Then, catching Nick's eye, she knew instinctively that he had taken the five pounds she'd been saving, towards the rent, from the top drawer of her dressing table. How could he have done such a thing?

He'd said, at that moment, "Isn't it marvellous seeing Frank and Estelle again, out of the blue? Hadn't a clue they were coming! Well, go on, Cathy, get busy in the kitchen. Rustle up your *specialitié de la maison*, bangers and mash! How do I know? Because we always have bangers and mash on Thursdays. Part of our design for living!"

Hot colour had rushed to her cheeks. He was right. She had fallen into the habit of thinking sausages on Thursday, fish on Friday, meat and two veg on Sunday.

"Not on your life, old boy. You're to be my guests tonight," Frank had laughed. "Can't have Cathy slaving over a hot stove. Come on, you lazy bastard, let's sally forth to the metropolis, sample the night life. A few drinks first, then we'll have some grub at that hotel down the road. I'll fix up a room for Stell and me. What could be simpler?"

He spoke in a gruff, hearty 'uncle' voice. Poor Frank, so eager to please, impossibly extravagant and extrovert.

Parrying Estelle's cool, disdainful glance, saying the first thing that came into her head, "How long are you staying?" she blurted.

"Good God, girl, they've only just arrived," Nick said irritably.

"I know. I didn't mean—"

"Never mind that now. Shove some powder on your face, and let's get going."

He'd shooed her from the room as one might shoo a

recalcitrant child, making her appear more foolish than she already felt.

Washing quickly, she got soap in her eyes. Putting on a dress that needed airing, feeling the clamminess on her skin, she put on a skirt that needed cleaning; a blouse that needed ironing, flustered because Nick kept calling to her to hurry up.

Emerging from the bedroom, she saw that Nick was helping Estelle on with her coat, that the brown tweed matched the colour of her smartly cropped hair, and the elegant skirt and sweater she was wearing.

They had trooped downstairs, then, laughing and talking, the three of them — Nick, Frank and Estelle; talking a language she could not begin to understand as she followed in their wake, feeling expendable, out of place, an interloper incapable of adding anything at all to their conversation.

Later, seated on bar-stools, Frank, the raconteur, held sway as he had done all the way to the pub. "I mean to say, old boy," he guffawed, "what would you have done? The Winco on one hand, fuming, and that prime bastard Clegg bellowing that he wasn't about to be inspected by a bloody Yank!"

Cathy had squirmed uneasily on her stool, hating the sound of Frank's braying laughter as much as she had hated being seated next to Estelle, whose cool composure had accentuated her own lack of poise, of sophistication. Not that Estelle appeared to notice her discomfiture. And this, perhaps, had been the hardest thing of all to bear, the feeling that, in Estelle's eyes, she scarcely registered as a human being, simply a fat frump in a creased blouse and a crumpled skirt . . .

Suddenly, Frank had said, "Cathy, m'dear. Another drink? What'll it be?"

"No, thank you. No more for me."

"What? You must be kidding! The night is young and you're so beautiful. Got hours to go yet. You can't possibly say no after one piddling gin and orange! Gotta celebrate! Hell, yes! You and Nick never did have a real celebration party after the wedding, what with the pair of us being whipped off to foreign climes before we had time to say, 'Bob's your Uncle'! Know what? I still can't quite grasp it. I had Nick staked out as a confirmed bachelor. A womanizer, of course, wary of the old ball and chain. Then suddenly there he was, hog-tied and branded!"

"Frank! For God's sake!"

"Eh? What?" He looked at his wife with troubled eyes. "Sorry, m'dear. Not being offensive, am I? Never meant to be. Sorry, Nick, old chap, just trying to be funny!'

"Forget it!" Handing Frank his cigarette case, "Better ditch the one you're smoking before you set fire to your moustache," Nick said lazily.

Frank grinned broadly. "There, you see, all is well. Estelle's just feeling a bit jumpy at the moment, aren't you, m'dear? Christ, we really needed this weekend break. What a gesture from an old friend like you, Nick, asking us up here for a change of scenery. How bloody kind and generous of you."

And Nick had told her he hadn't a clue they were coming, Cathy thought bleakly. Why had he lied to her? Why? What was the point?

Frank had continued hazily, "You know, Nick old boy, can't help thinking, now the war's over, you and Cathy will be having kids; lots and lots of babies. Maybe even Stell and I will start a family one of these fine days."

His eyes filled suddenly with tears. "You know, Cathy love," he said emotionally, befuddled with drink, "I want Stell to get pregnant, I really do. She's got a crazy idea in her head that she can't have a baby, but that's all my eye and Fanny Martin! I mean, just look at her, as fit as a fiddle, the picture of health!"

Stone-faced, Estelle, quitting her bar-stool, had left the room without a word. With a murmured word of excuse, Nick had gone after her, to Cathy's distress. *Why*? Surely it was Frank who should have gone after her, not Nick?

Clasping her hand, his eyes dull and anguished, "You know what, Cathy," Frank said hoarsely, "I'm the bloodiest fool on the face of the earth, and I know it."

"Why? What do you mean?"

Leaning forward, he'd covered his face with his free

hand. Filled with pity, she had noticed the shaggy hairs of his moustache, the weakness of his mouth, his teeth, brown from too much smoking; the tired human being behind the hail-fellow-well-met image he presented to the world in general.

He said wearily, "I love Stell, you know, more than words can express. I don't really give a damn what she does, where she goes, just as long as she comes home to me at the end of the day.

"And, you know, Cathy, I think she loves me in a funny kind of way. That's the one thing I'm proud of, that she married me. *Me!* God alone knows why, but she did, and that's what I cling to; the only thing that makes life worth the living. The booze makes it a bit easier – the thought of dying, I mean: knowing it's something we all have to face sooner or later; just wondering how and when. The thing that frightens me most is leaving Stella; going out in the dark alone, not being with her anymore."

Then, smiling owlishly, he said, "Sorry, Cathy my love, I always talk this way when I'm pissed. Now, how about dinner? Where have your husband and my wife got to, by the way?"

They found an Italian restaurant near the pub. The hotel where Frank had booked a room, was unlicenced, and Frank wanted to celebrate a business venture he was about to embark on with an ex-RAF pal of his.

"The idea is this," he said at dinner, waxing lyrical as only Frank could, seeing the future through rose coloured glasses, "we're starting a first class employment bureau, cashing in on the manpower situation. Binky Charlton – you remember Binky, don't you Nick? Hell of a nice bloke, knows a hell of a lot of people. Well, he figured that, for a substantial fee of course, ex-majors, brigadiers and the like would be happy to stump up for intros to prospective employers – on a personal basis. All very discreet. What I mean is, can't have ex-Wincos and their ilk joining the flat-cap brigade at the local employment exchange, now can we?

"I mean, these blokes have their pride, and that's where

we'll come in. The old boy network. And that's not all. We're opening an exclusive little club where the old boys can meet for a game of squash, billards, or a quiet drink. Binky's supplying the bulk of the capital, and I'm sinking in a couple of grand. Well, what do you think?"

Nick stared moodily into his drink. Entering the restaurant, he had pulled her aside. "Look, Cathy," he'd said urgently, "lend me a fiver. I'm skint."

"Nick, I can't spare it!"

"Oh, for God's sake, girl, expand just for once, can't you? This is important. I don't want Frank and Estelle to think I'm a bloody pauper, even if I am."

"But what about the weekend groceries? And the rent? You've already had that money from my dressing table. I just can't earn it quickly enough!"

"To hell with the groceries. Look, do you want them to feel sorry for me?"

"No, of course not."

"Then stop arguing, for Christ's sake!"

Lying in bed at the Station Hotel, staring up at the ceiling, Catherine recalled, with a terrible clarity, the way Nick had turned on her after Frank and Estelle had said good-night.

His words: "I can't go on like this," muttered savagely as he paced the sitting room of the flat, had cut into her like a knife. But that was just the beginning.

"Frankly, Cathy, your mental processes are those of a ten-year-old child. You have no real concept of life as it should be lived. Your education began and ended in the one-and-nine's at the Odeon Cinema. That's all you understand, bloody make-believe! Nice love stories with a happy ending! That's meat and drink to you, isn't it? Well, I'm sick of it – and you!

"You are physically and mentally wet and soggy, like a sponge filled with lukewarm water! Have you looked at yourself recently? Well, go on – take a good look! Then tell me if you see any good reason why I should stay with you!"

Sobbing, she had run into the bedroom to fling herself

84

on the bed, face down, her tears wetting the candle-wick cover.

Later, she had got up to go to the bathroom. The flat was empty. And then she had seen the note Nick had left for her, propped up on the mantelpiece.

'*Cathy*,' she read, '*It has all been a filthy mistake, for you as well as me. I'll pick up my things later, when you are out of the way. Just make sure that you are. There is nothing further to discuss.*'

Just that, and nothing more. Not even a signature.

Chapter Eight

She breakfasted early, and went back to her room to light the gas fire and make her plans for the day. She would catch a bus to the town centre, look round the shops, have coffee, then lunch – after which she would take either a bus or a taxi to Cloud Merridon.

Gripped by a curious feeling of objectivity, she saw herself as a lost, possibly foolish, mature woman, attempting to prove to herself – the quiet, observant, critical and ever-present watcher – that she was the Captain of her soul, Master of her fate.

What she would say to Bridie she had no idea, or how she would feel at seeing Cloud Merridon again. Suppose that the village had changed beyond recognition? What if Bridie no longer lived there? These were the chances she had to take.

It was so nearly the same that she almost wept. And yet there were subtle differences. Or could it be that memory had kept Cloud Merridon leafy with an eternal springtime of the heart? But it was winter, now, not spring, and a world of difference lay between the girl she used to be, and the woman she now was.

The village duck pond was filmed with ice, the colour of pewter beneath a leaden sky, and where were the ducks?

Walking slowly up the hill to the church, she saw that scaffolding had been erected about the Norman tower, and there were notices warning the public to keep away while work was in progress.

Standing there, buffeted by the wind, she remembered the day she and Nick had visited the church together: how, emerging from its portals, she couldn't help pretending that they had just been married, that she was a bride on her wedding day, wearing a white dress and veil and carrying a bouquet of roses.

Then he, with one of his more charming gestures, had taken her hand and led her down the path to the lych-gate, pausing to gather a few daffodils growing in the long grass near the grey stone wall, which he had given to her with a smile and a kiss.

Turning away from the church, walking down the hill to Bridie's cottage facing the village green, heart pounding, eyes blurred with tears, she saw the white gate, the garden path, the fanlight above the front door – everything that she had remembered and loved for such a long, weary time.

Now the time had come, she felt inclined to turn back. But what would be the point or purpose in turning back now?

Grasping the iron bell-pull, she stood there on the doorstep and waited, hearing the faint clamour of the bell behind the front door of the cottage.

At first there was no reply to her summons. She rang again.

Slowly, the door opened.

Then Bridie stood before her. "Yes, who is it? What do you want?" the woman asked testily. "If you're selling something, I don't want to know. Just go away and leave me alone!"

This querulous, tired looking woman could not possibly be Bridie, Catherine thought wildly, and yet, she could see that it was her, she had just aged somehow – rather shockingly.

She said quietly, compassionately, "Bridie, it's Cathy. Nick's wife, remember?"

"*Cathy*? What are you doing here?" A pregnant pause, then, "Go away and leave me alone, I have nothing to say to you. Why now, after all this time?"

"I'm sorry, but I really must talk to you."

With an effort of will, Bridie said, "Very well, you'd better come in then."

*   *   *

87

Bridie's long and lovely summertime had faded, and she had grown careless with her appearance over the past fifteen years. Catherine could not believe the change in her.

Her long, ash-blonde hair was grey now, and wispy, dragged back from her wrinkled face into a kind of bun, secured by hairpins and an elasticated net to keep it in place.

Gone was the enchanting creature who had once worn the flimsiest of lace-trimmed underwear to keep her warm. Now, clad in layers of jumpers, she moved forward to the drawing room, no longer a gypsy figure in a low-necked blouse, shining hair, with a clear, high voice, no longer the woman who had looked forty when she was fifty, but an older woman, clearly shaken by this intrusion into her privacy, who looked every bit of her sixty or so years.

"How can I be sure you are who you say you are? You don't look like the young, plump girl who came with Nick all those years ago."

Catherine said, "People change, Bridie. But I notice your Chinese bowls have gone."

"My bowls?"

"They used to stand on the windowsills."

The tired eyes peered, a leaf-like hand fluttered briefly.

"You remember that?" she asked.

"I have remembered everything about this room."

The older woman seemed moved.

"You must forgive me, my dear. I've been discourteous. Come, sit down. Tell me what you want of me."

Catherine could not get over the shabbiness of the room. Memory had painted it in glowing colours, and she trusted her memory. Now it seemed that some richness had gone from the cottage, as though Bridie herself had become impoverished, not merely in spirit but in material possessions also.

The Chinese bowls were just a part of the missing treasures. The lovely inlaid satinwood cabinets and their contents – silverware, Dresden and Meissen figures – were gone, and so were the oil paintings and the exquisitely-fashioned Georgian side-tables, and there was a nervousness about Bridie which she could not clearly define or come to terms with.

As they faced each other across the hearth, she wondered what had become of the independent personality she had so admired. This woman had become impoverished in every way. But why? The greying hair, wrinkled skin, were to be expected over these years, but ageing alone could not account for the woman's apathy. People like Bridie did not diminish with age, usually they became more forceful and eccentric to compensate for their lost youth, channelling their vitality in other directions.

Not so with Bridie. Her frail hands fluttered restlessly, picking at nonexistent cotton threads, plucking at imaginary beads.

She had not expected to find herself the stronger personality of the two, but she knew that she was. And this seemed all wrong, somehow. Unnerving, faintly shocking.

And there were those curious, apologetic phrases – 'I'm sorry, my dear'. 'You must forgive me'. 'Please excuse me'. 'I'm afraid that I . . .' so out of character with the forceful Bridie she remembered so well.

So far, Bridie had apologized for the dustiness of the room, its lack of warmth, the weakness of the tea she had made.

The heavy silver tray had gone from the dining room, so had the Regency sideboard and table and the Waterford decanters, Catherine noticed when she followed Bridie to the kitchen to help her with the teatray.

Once the pulsating heart of the house, cluttered but clean, rich with the fragrance of herbs and spices, Catherine noticed, with a pang of regret, that the kitchen now reeked of stale fat, and the loggia beyond, where cyclamens had once blossomed in bright profusion, was thick with cobwebs.

"I'm sorry, I have no biscuits or cake to offer," Bridie said, making the tea in a pot with a chipped spout.

"It doesn't matter," Catherine assured her.

Bridie appeared not to have heard, then Catherine wondered if she was playing for time? Was she deliberately foiling her attempts to talk about Nick?

The younger Bridie would have said in a clear, ringing voice, "Look here, Cathy, I don't wish to discuss my son or his marriage to you. Let's have a cigarette and talk about something else, shall we?"

This she would have understood and accepted, not daring to do otherwise. But now – they had fenced round the issue long enough.

When Bridie had poured the tea, and they were sitting near the drawing room fire, Catherine came to the reason for her visit.

"Please tell me," she said, "where is Nick?"

A strange note of defiance rose in her voice. "My son is in New Zealand," Bridie said brusquely. "Why? What is it to you?"

Her eyes clouded with tears, Catherine looked about the room, remembering all that it had meant to her long ago; firelight gleaming, pools of lamplight, music, laughter, the scent of flowers – a strange new enchanting world, so far removed from her normal environment that she had looked back on it all these years as something quite perfect; the days she had spent beneath this roof as the happiest she had ever known.

Even now, she could see clearly, in her mind's eye, Jimmy, relaxed and smiling, his injured right leg resting on a footstool, a glass of Bridie's home-made wine in his hand, his walking stick propped up near his chair; Nick, his eyes half closed, listening to Debussy's 'Claire de Lune', his arm about her shoulders, getting up now and then to replenish their wine glasses or re-start the record, giving his mother's hair a tweak as he passed her chair, dislodging the hairpins so that the heavy mass had snaked down onto her shoulders.

Bridie had not cared tuppence Cathy had thought at the time. Her glance in Jimmy's direction had said more clearly than words, 'Am I desirable to you, my love, with my hair about my shoulders?' Not that she had fully understood or approved of the relationship between Bridie and Jimmy that early morning when she had bumped into Jimmy on the landing, leaving Bridie's bedroom in his dressing gown and slippers.

Later, she had come to accept that this house, this place, held a special magic all its own, unbounded by convention, as the people who dwelt there were unfettered by hidebound rules, the conventional behaviour of other people, free to live their own lives as they saw fit.

Memories. So many memories . . .

Nick running down the stairs to the garden, pausing to look up at her bedroom window, calling to her to hurry or she'd be late for breakfast.

Jimmy coming down to breakfast; Bridie cooking eggs and bacon in the kitchen; listening to the latest news on the wireless as she did so; drinking piping hot coffee at the dining room table; Jimmy talking of borrowing a couple of horses from the riding stables in the village so that he and Nick could ride before lunch – if she, Cathy, didn't mind. Or perhaps she'd like to come with them?

Bridie calling out in her clear, fluting voice, "Will someone go to the village shop for me? I need a loaf of bread!"

Nick glancing at her over his shoulder, saying light-heartedly, "Well, come on, Cathy, let's get going!"

The overwhelming happiness she had experienced then, an uncertain, unsophisticated girl in a blue cotton dress and a hand-knitted cardigan, following in Nick's wake to buy a loaf of bread at the village store . . .

And now, facing Bridie across the dusty hearth she said, "Please don't think that I'm being idly curious about Nick. It's just rather terrible not knowing what became of him after – the divorce. I – that is – I still care for him, you see?"

Bridie said slowly, "The past is over and done with, best forgotten. I did warn you, remember, that Nick was not an easy person to come to terms with. But I was never his confidante, only his mother."

"I remember; you warned me that he was selfish. I also remember that you asked me if I knew Frank and Estelle Winter. I wondered why, at the time. Now I think you knew about Nick and Estelle even then. I'm right, aren't I?"

"I can't remember. In any case, you have no right to question me. I didn't invite you here. What happened between you and my son was none of my doing, if that's what you think."

"I know. I'm sorry. I'm not here to accuse you, simply to find out what happened to him after the divorce. Please, I really need to know."

"I've told you, he went abroad to live."

"With – Estelle?"

"Of course. Who else?"

"But before he went abroad? Did he – did they – come here?"

"No, they did not! At least, not to stay. A week or two. I can't remember. Then they went away." Bridie wrinkled her forehead, fluttered her hands. "Now I want *you* to go away and leave me in peace."

"Yes, of course, I understand." Catherine stood up. Collecting her gloves and handbag, "I'm sorry," she apologised, "I didn't mean to distress you in any way. Please forgive me."

Turning at the front door, "Just one thing more before I go," Catherine said quietly, "have you any idea where Nick and Estelle went to when they left here?"

She thought, at first, that her reluctant hostess had not heard the question, or had decided not to answer. Then, "They went to a place called Lessing, near Oxford," Bridie said wearily. "Nick had taken a pub there, the name of which escapes me. But that was a long time ago. Now he's in New Zealand."

Catherine knew that to probe further would be fruitless – and unkind. There was nothing more to be said, except goodbye.

And yet, hearing the closing of the front door behind her, she retained a strong feeling of having been got rid of by a woman not nearly as vague and confused as she had pretended to be.

But – why?

Chapter Nine

In her hotel room, stirring restlessly, sleep would not come. The pillow had bunched into a hard lump beneath her aching head.

At one o'clock in the morning, Catherine got out of bed, put on her dressing gown, and lit the gas fire.

The hotel was deathly quiet. There was no sound of traffic in the street below. Gripped with a terrifying feeling of solitude – as though she was the last person alive on earth, she sank into the chair near the fire to relive her meeting with Bridie Willard.

What a curious interlude it had been; nightmarish in retrospect; unreal – seeing the cottage as it now was, stripped of its treasures. Even worse had been coming face to face with the living ghost of a woman she had once deeply admired for her charmingly bright and unorthodox outlook on life.

What in God's name had happened to change Bridie into a shadow of her former self? If only she *knew*!

Pondering the problem, staring into the past, she wondered what had happened during that brief time Nick and Estelle had spent at the cottage? Had there been a quarrel? Had Bridie begged Nick not to go to Lessing to start another venture that might well end in disaster?

And while all this was going on, Catherine thought, she had been trying to get her own life into some kind of order, knowing that to survive, she must learn to stand on her own two feet.

It had been a rough passage. Instinct had opposed reason. Reason had clashed, head on, with instinct. In the long run, there had emerged a strong determination not to be beaten, to work hard, to make a success of her salon, to pay off her bank loan.

Work had been her salvation during the dreadful time following Nick's departure. At first she had clung to the belief that he would return to talk things over. *There is nothing further to discuss . . .'* he'd written in the note he'd left propped on the mantelpiece. But there *was*. Marriage meant far more than two people living together under the same roof, sharing the same bed, at least it did to her. It meant shouldering certain responsibilities, the honouring of vows solemnly declared on the wedding day, striving towards a better understanding when things went wrong.

She blamed herself more than Nick for the accusations he had levelled against her, that night, regarding her appearance. Nick admired well-groomed women like Estelle Winter, slender, sophisticated women, poised and self-contained. How ashamed and embarrassed he must have felt escorting her into that Italian restaurant – wearing a creased blouse and a baggy skirt, plus the added humiliation of having to ask her for money.

If only she'd possessed the *savoir-faire* to hand over the five pounds without comment, instead of going on about the weekend groceries and the rent money. No wonder he'd accused her of possessing the mentality of a ten-year-old child.

Given the chance, she'd have told him that she was sorry for the humiliation she had caused him. But she had not been given that chance.

Returning to the flat one evening after work, she found another note on the mantelpiece, stating briefly that he had been to collect his belongings, that he was joining Frank and Estelle in London to manage the 'old boy's club' Frank had mentioned. The message ended with the words: *'I suggest that you get on with your own life from now on, and leave me alone to get on with mine.'*

Soon, the flat she had shared with Nick, the setting of so much pain and grief, had begun to get on her nerves to the extent that she had made up her mind to leave it, and the unhappy memories contained within those four cramped rooms.

Nick had made it abundantly clear that, so far as he was concerned, their marriage was over and done with.

Flat hunting had become a spare time occupation. Her mother had told her she was daft seeking another flat when there was room to spare in the Sussex Street house. "Why fork out more money for rent?" she'd said matter-of-factly.

"I'm not thinking of renting," Cathy confessed. "Mrs Gallard – you know the one who comes to me for henna-packs? – says there's a top floor flat for sale where she lives, suitable for one person."

"What? Lumber yourself with a mortgage as well as a bank loan?" Annie Mitchell looked shocked. "Well, I doubt you'd get it."

"As a matter of fact, Mum, I've already seen the bank manager, and he'll be more than happy to extend my loan. He thought it would be a wise move to invest in a place of my own."

"I see. So where is this flat?"

"On the South Cliff, quite near the Esplanade and the road to Oliver's Mount and, oh Mum, it's lovely. Just what I want."

"So it's all cut and dried, is it? Well, you're a dark horse and no mistake! You might have told me what was in your mind. Mavis would've done. But then, you've always been secretive, our Cathy – getting wed the way you did in such a hurry; never letting on to me or Mavis till afterwards. And look where *that* landed you!"

"I'm sorry about that, Mum. There just wasn't time to tell anyone. I thought I'd explained. Nick was posted abroad so quickly, I . . ." Tears sprang to her eyes.

"All right, all right, the least said about it the better. I'm just thankful he's gone, and if a place of your own is what you want, I'll say no more about it. Just as long as it makes you happy." Mrs Mitchell paused. "So when are you going to take me to look at it?"

"We could go tonight, if you like," Cathy sighed with relief, and smiled like a sunburst. "Thanks, Mum."

*   *   *

"It's a good depth up," Mrs Mitchell complained, puffing from the three flights of stairs, "but it's a nice solid house, and you've got your own entrance. Hmmm, a nice little hall too, with a good useful cupboard."

"And this is the drawing room," Cathy stood back proudly to let her mother enter.

"My God, what a size!" Annie looked round the room in amazement, deeply impressed by its dimensions, deep skirting boards, nooks and crannies, and the wide window at the far end. "And have you thought what it'll cost you to carpet a room this size, let alone furnish it?"

"I'll make do with lino for the time being," Cathy said, "and saleroom furniture. Besides, I have a few bits and pieces already." Refusing to be put off or defeated. "I'll creep first, then walk. Come and look at the rest of it."

Mrs Mitchell particularly admired the bathroom and the kitchen. The latter appealed to her because of the number of shelves and cupboards, the bathroom because of the coloured suite and the glass shelf above the washbasin.

"Hmm, well it's all very nice, I must say," she admitted, "as long as you haven't bitten off more than you can chew."

"I don't think so. In fact I know I haven't." She was young, strong, not afraid of hard work. Her business was flourishing, and now she had a new goal in life – the creation of the kind of home she had always dreamed of – filled with lovely things, chosen with care, as and when she could afford them.

In time, the hurt she had suffered when Nick left her, would gently heal, she thought. Not that she would ever forget their happier moments together, or cease to regret that their marriage had ended the way it did. She had thought about it a great deal during the year that followed, turning things over and over in her mind, reaching certain conclusions, realizing that the future could not be built on bitterness or despair.

Nick's final message had been clear and succinct – '. . . *get on with your own life from now on, and leave me alone to get on with mine.*'

In one sense, she had Nick to thank for making her take a good long look at herself in the bedroom mirror. What she had seen there had appalled her. Until that night, she'd had no idea how fat and frumpish she had become, how undesirable.

Later, pride had come to her aid. She'd started eating salads instead of sausages; steamed instead of fried fish coated in batter; roast meat and vegetables on Sundays, leaving out the roast potatoes, Yorkshire puddings and gravy.

Then, when she had started to lose weight, she had bundled the contents of her wardrobe into carrier bags, and carted her old clothes to the Salvation Army, Westborough, glad to see the back of them.

Unable to afford an entirely new wardrobe, she had settled for a couple of smart skirts, jumpers, and a double-breasted blazer from Marks and Spencer; a few items of lingerie from the haberdasher's in Falsgrave, and two pairs of shoes from Dolcis' autumn sale.

Occasionally, busy about the creation of her new home, painting skirting boards preparatory to the laying of the moss green carpet she had chosen for the drawing room, or hand-sewing the matching curtains, she would pause to wonder what Nick would think if he could see her now – getting on with own life as he had decreed.

Then, invaded by a momentary sadness that they would, in all probability, never meet again, she would shrug aside her sadness in positive action, accepting the fact that their marriage was over and done with forever, that Nick would never come back to her.

She had been wrong. Painfully wrong . . .

He had come back into her life just when she was beginning to enjoy her new-found feeling of independence; subtly imposing his will on hers; tearing down her barriers of self-defence so carefully erected against the heartbreak of the past.

One afternoon at the salon, when the phone rang she had answered, thinking it would be a client wanting to make an appointment.

"Hello, Cathy."

She would have known his voice anywhere, that deep, slow, confident voice. She was surprised to hear from him. It had been nearly eighteen months since he had gone.

"Nick? Where are you?" Her hand had trembled on the receiver.

"Look out of the window."

Lifting the nylon curtain, she saw him standing in the phone-box across the road. He was wearing an open neck shirt, his hair was damp, as if he had been swimming.

She said faintly, "Why have you come? What do you want?"

"We'll talk about that later. I'll be waiting."

He had hung up, leaving her bemused, unable to cope adequately with her afternoon's work.

"Are you feeling all right, Mrs Willard? You've gone ever so pale," Vera, her assistant had said anxiously.

"Yes, I'm fine." But she wasn't fine. She had felt churned up inside, anxious and uneasy, dreading the thought of meeting Nick face to face again after all this time; wondering what she would say to him, what he would say to her.

Closing the salon, she had said good-night to her assistant and glanced nervously about her. Then she saw him standing beneath a street lamp. Slowly, she walked towards him.

"Cathy, my love," he said, taking her hand, speaking gently, "you look stunning, really beautiful."

"Please, don't," she said wearily.

"Then you haven't forgiven me?"

"For what? Those notes you left me? Walking out of my life without a backward glance? The fact is, I don't give a damn any more what you think of me or my appearance, I've been too busy getting on with my own life to care tuppence about your approval – or otherwise. So why the pretence? What are you after? What do you want?"

"Look, darling, we can't talk here in the street. Please, say you'll have a drink with me for old times' sake. I haven't come to pester or bother you in any way, simply

98

to say I'm sorry for the way I've treated you. To beg your forgiveness."

Slowly, reluctantly, inevitably her defences had crumbled beneath the weight of his far stronger personality.

Sipping a glass of wine, seeing his well-remembered face across a table for two in a quiet corner of a hotel bar, she had felt a stirring of an old magic as potent now as it had been the night they met, when they had danced together to 'Begin the Beguine'.

She had known then, noticing the way his dark hair sprang back from his forehead, the way he smiled with his eyes as well as his lips, the boyish, vulnerable look about him, despite his innate selfishness, that she was still in love with him. That his many faults and failings were part and parcel of the man she had married; that her life had been the poorer without him.

He said contritely, "I can understand your bitterness towards me, my love. I've treated you shamefully, and I'm sorry. What more can I say? That's why I came, to tell you that I still care for you. To say goodbye the way I should have done that night I walked out on you — decently and honourably, if such a thing were possible.

"The truth is, I was a bloody fool to leave you alone the way I did; so wrong, so arrogant, so conceited, so mixed up, that I couldn't see straight at the time. I blamed you, my love, when I should have blamed myself for all the trouble I caused you; using you as a kind of 'whipping boy'! Oh, Christ, Cathy, I really am sorry!"

"Goodbye? But where are you going? What are you going to do?"

"That needn't concern you, darling." Getting up from the table. "I'll find somewhere to lay my head."

"Of course it concerns me. Nick, where are you staying?"

"Oh, that? Tonight, you mean? Somewhere near the station, I expect. I'll fix that up later, when I collect my luggage." He smiled. "In any case, I'll be leaving sometime tomorrow, by the early train, I imagine. I daresay Bridie will put up with me until I've decided what to do next."

"I don't understand. What about your job?"

"Oh, the employment agency? It flopped rather dismally, I'm afraid. Poor old Binky Charlton lost every ha'penny he put into it, so did Frank. All I lost was my job."

Making up her mind in an instant she said, "Let's go to the station and pick up your luggage. Then you're coming home with me. Please, Nick, I – I want you to stay, for a little while at least."

"You mean this place is yours? Your own property?"

Cathy laughed. "Not quite yet. In about twenty years from now, when I've paid off the mortgage. It's still a bit bare, I'm afraid."

"For the time being, maybe, but I can see the potential. It's a charming flat. You've done wonders, darling. I see now what you meant about getting on with your own life." He added regretfully, "The reason why I can't stay here, as much as I'd like to, is that it just isn't possible." Holding her hands, speaking softly and gently. "You do see that, don't you?"

"No, Nick. Quite frankly, I don't! Unless, that is, you don't want to stay with me?"

"Of course I do. More than anything else in the world, but it goes deeper than that, my love. How do you think I'd feel, a man without a job, reliant on his wife for his existence? A case of history repeating itself, I'd say. No, I'm sorry, Cathy. I have my pride, for what it's worth."

She said hoarsely, close to tears, "But you'll find another job. You're sure to, sooner or later!" Resting her head against his shoulder, "Oh, Nick darling, forget about your pride. Can't you see, don't you know how much I love you? How much I need you?"

"Have you taken leave of your senses?" Annie Mitchell turned on her daughter in a fury. "You mean to stand there and tell me you've taken him back? That rotten little sponger? My God, our Cathy, you must want your brain testing!" Eyes blazing she said, "Have you no pride?"

100

"Pride? Who cares about pride? It was my fault he left in the first place."

"So he's talked you into believing that, has he? Well, all I can say, if you bring him here, I'll show him the door!"

"Please, Mum, you don't understand. He's a changed person."

"Huh, leopards don't change their spots! Doesn't it strike you as a bit of a coincidence that he should come back to you now your business is doing well and you've found yourself a nice place to live?"

"That's not fair, Mum! He didn't want to stay for those very reasons, because I'm doing well and he hasn't a job. He was pretty cut up about it. I had to beg him to stay."

"Ay, I can well imagine. And how long did he hold out? Five minutes? Ten? A quarter of an hour?" Then, less aggressively she said, "I don't want to see you hurt again, that's all."

"I know, but Nick is still my husband. You seem to forget that."

"He's the one who did the forgetting, if you want my opinion – and I can see that you don't. You have that mulish look about you, so I might as well stop wasting my breath." Annie sat down abruptly, her face the colour of clay.

"What is it, Mum? What's wrong?" Cathy cried out in alarm.

"I don't rightly know. I've got a queer pain in my chest."

Easing a cushion behind her mother's back Cathy said, "I'll send for the doctor," picking up the phone.

"You'll do no such thing! It's indigestion, that's all! Just fetch me a bismuth tablet from the bathroom cabinet, and make me a cup of tea. Just do as I say. I've had it before. It'll soon pass off."

Cathy did as she was told. This is my fault, she thought bleakly, but she'd had to break the news about Nick's return, to her mother, even though she had known how upset she'd be.

101

Riddled with guilt, she made the tea, and sat with her mother until the colour had returned to her cheeks.

Then, with a touch of her usual asperity, "Well, you'd best be off now, hadn't you?" Annie Mitchell said. "Knowing that husband of yours, he'll be sitting, knife and fork at the ready, wanting his evening meal!"

"Mother! How could you? What a cruel thing to say!"

Annie's attitude softened suddenly. "I'm sorry, love," she admitted, "I shouldn't have said what I did. But you are my daughter, my own flesh and blood, and I can't bear to see you put upon by a – well, never mind. Just you be careful, that's all, our Cath, and remember what I said – leopards don't change their spots!"

It seemed her destiny to be torn two ways, she thought on her way home, to be constantly at war with herself and her circumstances.

Entering the flat, seeking the solace of Nick's arms, she had burst into tears.

"Darling," he said quietly, smoothing her hair, "this is all my fault. I told you I shouldn't have stayed."

"Don't say that! You are making things worse, not better!"

"All right, darling, sit down, try to relax. Tell me, is there anything to drink? Brandy? Whisky? No? But you need something to calm you. Look, love, I'm going down to the off-licence to buy a bottle of brandy!" He paused briefly. "Oh, blast, I haven't enough money!"

"Look in my purse."

"Thanks, darling! Just stay where you are. Don't move, I'll be back in a few minutes!" Turning at the door, he blew her a kiss.

At four o'clock in the morning, Catherine returned to the bed she had left three hours ago. Utterly exhausted from remembering the past, she sank into oblivion as soon as her head touched the pillow.

Chapter Ten

"Good-morning, Mrs Willard. Did you sleep well?"

The landlady of the Station Hotel glanced at the clock as she spoke. Half-past nine, and the list of rules and regulations pinned up near the reception desk stated quite clearly that breakfast would be unavailable after nine-thirty. But Mrs Willard was a nice lady, and business was slow at this time of year. Besides which, the poor woman didn't look very well, as if she had the weight of the world on her shoulders.

"I'm sorry I'm late," Catherine apologized, "but all I want is a cup of coffee."

"That's not much of a start to the day, if you don't mind my saying so," the landlady said briskly, poking the dining room fire. "It's bitterly cold out. At least have a boiled egg and a slice or two of toast."

"Oh, very well then, if you're sure I'm not being a nuisance."

"Not at all, my dear. And there's a nice fire in the lounge, so no need to dash out if you don't feel like it. I could lend you a book to read, if you like. An Agatha Christie thriller I borrowed from the library. I do so admire her Miss Marple, don't you?"

"Yes, indeed, and thank you."

Breakfast, when it arrived, consisted of a pot of slightly bitter coffee, two boiled eggs capped with hand-embroidered cosies, a rackful of toast, several pats of butter in foil wrapping, a pot of marmalade and a jar of honey, none of which Catherine really wanted.

Later, going through to the lounge, sitting beside the roaring coal fire, picking up the Agatha Christie thriller the landlady had left on the table near her chair, turning the pages, briefly scanning the lines of print, Catherine wondered what she was doing here, reading a book, or trying to, when all she really cared about was solving her own problems.

So Nick had gone to New Zealand after all? He had gone away from her forever, and there was nothing she could do about it. His departure, the distance between them, meant that they were destined never to meet again, that her quest must end here, in this backwater hotel.

Nick, the love of her life, had finally and forever eluded her.

Giving up all pretence at reading, she looked out of the window to see that the first flakes of a fresh snowfall were beginning to descend.

She wondered where Nick was at that moment. On some warm beach with Estelle beside him? Had the sun browned that white skin of hers? How many children had he given her? She imagined sons, dark-haired sons the image of their father, perhaps a daughter. She might have asked Bridie about that, despite the pain of knowing – and the jealousy. Of course she was jealous of Estelle. How could she be otherwise? Estelle who had taken Nick away from her as easily as a child might pick a flower and idly tear off the petals, for the wanton pleasure of watching them fall. Or perhaps now that Nick had got what he had wanted all along, he had grown tired of Estelle, just as he had grown tired of her? Strange to think he would be in his late thirties now.

She could see the station from where she was standing; more of a halt really – 'Lower Minter' – twenty-odd miles west of the industrial town of Swindon with its bustling main line station. Watching, she saw a main line train, presumably from Swindon, on its way north, approaching the platform, stopping briefly to pick up 'daddy', his wife and their offspring, who must have breakfasted earlier, packed their belongings, paid their bill, and departed while she was in the dining room.

The thought occurred that, catching a later train, she could be back in Scarborough, safely at home by six, perhaps seven o'clock that evening. The landlady was sure to have a railway timetable to hand. All she had to do was find out the time of the next train north, pack her suitcase, pay her bill, and head for home; give up the hopeless quest of finding out what had happened to Nick after their final confrontation. And yet . . .

"They went to a place called Lessing, near Oxford," Bridie had told her. "Nick had taken a pub there, the name of which escapes me."

Her mind made up, Catherine went down to the reception desk.

"Yes, Mrs Willard, what can I do for you?" The landlady appeared from the parlour, holding a duster.

Catherine smiled. The woman had been kind to her, and she was grateful. "I'd like my bill, please," she said. "And, I wonder, have you a railway timetable?"

"It's here somewhere. Oh yes, I always keep one handy. Going home, are you? Scarborough, isn't it? Can't say I blame you. The weather's dreadful. You've just missed the 10.35 am to York. The Daytons caught that one a few minutes ago. You know, the couple with the three children? The next train's not due till, let me see, 1.35 pm. So will you be wanting lunch first? We serve bar meals, soup and sandwiches, that kind of thing."

"Thanks, but I'm not going home just yet. I'm going to a place near Oxford. A place called – Lessing."

The slow moving branch-line train from Oxford threaded its way through snow-covered scenery pinpricked with the lights of outlying farms and villages.

The train was due to arrive in Lessing at four-thirty. There had been a lengthy wait at Oxford, coffee and sandwiches in the refreshment room, the inevitable doubts following in the wake of a quickly reached decision. Was she really doing the right thing, or laying herself wide open to more hurt?

She thought, he went to Lessing, near Oxford. When he and Estelle left Cloud Merridon, they bought two tickets to Lessing because Nick had taken a pub there. Why Lessing? What was the name of the pub? Bridie said she couldn't remember. Or had she her reasons for not wanting to tell her the name of the pub?

A pub! Why not? Nick would be in his element close to the source of forgetfulness, the bottle-filled shelves, the beer-pumps, the subdued lighting, the fugginess of the bar, the camaraderie of the customers, the small talk. But what about the hard work? The effort involved in running a business, however small, required far more than a charming manner, and Nick was, by nature, a drone, not a worker.

Hunched in a window seat, staring out at the dark void beyond the creaking, lumbering train, her optimism dispelled by the lack of heating, the seemingly endless journey to a strange place on the map, she wished that she was on her way to Scarborough, not Lessing.

What, after all, had she hoped to achieve by an uncomfortable journey to the middle of nowhere? And even if she chanced upon the name of the pub of which Nick had once been the landlord, what then?

It was just this gut feeling she had of wanting to continue her search to the bitter end, to the point, if necessary, of finding out the name of the vessel in which he and Estelle had sailed to New Zealand.

Obsessive, Adam had called her, and perhaps he was right. Poor Adam, how worried he must be about her. Or had she forfeited her right to his concern? Small wonder if she had. He'd be far better off without her. Adam deserved a nice, uncomplicated wife who would enjoy living in a modern, detached house on the outskirts of York; a wife who believed that the sun rose and set in him. Why settle for less?

As the train rocked on towards Lessing, closing her eyes, memory drew her back to the night of her final confrontation with Nick. Hearing the slam of the front door behind him, shaking uncontrollably, she had sunk down in a chair near the fireplace, scarcely able to believe that it was she who had told him to go, to get out of her life once and for all. But what choice had she, other than to go on suffering the humiliation of his affair with Estelle Winter?

106

How could she have borne to go on living with a man who no longer loved her? But then, had Nick ever really loved her? Even in their intimate moments, when he had made passionate love to her, had he been thinking of someone else at the time? And yes, she thought bitterly, of course he had been thinking of someone else – Estelle, Estelle, Estelle . . . Always of Estelle, never herself.

Later, when she was calmer, when she had stopped shaking, in need of solace, she had switched on the radio near her chair. Not bothering to switch on the lamp, she had listened intently to Beethoven's 'Moonlight Sonata'.

She had been thinking about death at the time, about dying – possibly a far simpler solution than to go on living in a world devoid of love, of hope for the future.

Then suddenly, looking up, she had seen, on the opposite wall, the outline of the window thrown into sharp relief by the headlights of car coming down the road from Oliver's Mount. And there was her window, complete in shape and outline, the panes clear and distinct, etched momentarily on a wall without a window.

A momentary illusion. Nothing more, and yet she had known, in that moment, that the switching off of one light, or the failure to switch on that light, did not necessarily mean oblivion, that death held no dominion over living – all the seeking, striving, yearning, the continuance of hope as long as one retained the willpower to battle on, no matter how dark the days ahead might be.

As the train rocked monotonously towards Lessing, Catherine held onto the memory of the window, the hope that, somehow, someday, she would see Nick once more; tell him, face-to-face, that she still loved him.

In the plummy atmosphere of a lounge bar in Lessing, Catherine sipped a brandy and dry ginger. Acting a part for a nonexistent audience, she kept on looking at her watch, pretending that she was waiting for someone.

People came in, locals, obviously well known to the landlord.

107

"Evening Harry, Maude, Bob! What's it doing outside?" he asked, flattening his hands on the bar, his face wreathed in smiles.

"Bloody freezing! We slid here, if you must know!"

The landlord laughed. "The usual?" he enquired. "Two halves of Guinness, and a rum and Crabbie's for the lady?"

"Eeyah, just you be careful, my lad," the one called Harry riposted drily, "Maude's no lady, she's my wife!"

The landlord reminded Catherine of someone. Yes, of course, Frank Winter. Poor, dear Frank . . . Memory drew her back to that night in Scarborough when, thrown together by the disappearance of Nick and Estelle, they had faced, however obliquely, the knowledge that they were expendable. "Where have your husband and my wife got to, by the way?" he'd asked, turning a blind eye to the obvious, as she herself had done.

"Give the fire a poke, Bob, will you?" the landlord asked the second male. "Thaw yourselves out a bit."

"With pleasure." Bob strode across to invoke more flames.

A piece of coal shot out of the fire and landed on the carpet close to where Catherine was sitting. "Whoops!" Bob cried out in mock alarm, seizing the fire-tongs. "Sorry, Miss, didn't mean to scare you."

"That's all right. No harm done."

"You're sure, now?"

"Quite sure." She smiled at the man – sixtyish, wearing badly, with a set of happy-looking false teeth.

"Even so, you must allow me to buy you a drink to calm your nerves. What'll it be?"

"No, really. Thanks all the same."

"Nonsense! I won't take no for an answer!" Hailing the landlord he said, "Mac, a brandy and dry ginger for the lady, and a half of bitter for yourself."

She laughed. Acting her part, needing to communicate, to ask questions, feeling a bit like Agatha Christie's Miss Marple. "That's very kind of you."

"My pleasure entirely."

108

A good-looking woman, he thought, handing her the drink, and not many attractive women smiled at him nowadays. Flattered, he kept on including her in the conversation.

Harry, Bob's brother, was taller and thinner, with a less spectacular smile and a reputation for being the dry, humorous type – a bit of a wag, droll – after the fashion of Stanley Holloway.

Maude, his wife, was the large, unworried type whose shape, hidden beneath layers of clothing, was immaterial anyway – one of those blessedly extrovert women who couldn't give a damn that her side of the bed sagged to the floor when she got into it.

Large fur-lined boots were clamped solidly onto her feet, the zips at half-mast to accommodate her calves. She wore lots of rings squeezed onto sausage-like fingers, and long earrings which swung and rattled as she laughed uproariously at the landlord's jokes. Her handbag, the size of a portmanteau, was crammed with letters, bills, purses, cigarette packets, football coupons, and sweet-breath cachous, because she had a 'thing' about halitosis, and did not wish to cause offence.

Catherine liked her enormously. She was merry, uncomplicated, and real.

"Excuse me for asking," Bob said, speaking to Catherine, "but you're new here, aren't you?" Gallantly he continued, "I'd have remembered if I'd seen you before, that's for sure."

"Actually, I'm on holiday."

Maude threw back her head and laughed. "On holiday? What? In a godforsaken hole like this – in the middle of winter? Blimey! Now I've heard everything!"

Playing her Miss Marple role for all it was worth Catherine laughed and said, "Yes, I know it sounds daft, but there's a lot to be said for winter holidays when the hotels are nice and quiet, and people are not too busy to talk."

Bob's teeth seemed even happier. "Where are you staying?" he asked, fancying her like mad.

"At The Mason's Arms. Do you know it?"

Maude broke in, with a peal of laughter, "Cor, I've always wanted to spend a night in The Mason's Arms!"

Bob grinned. "Know The Mason's Arms? I'll say I do. I know every hotel in Lessing. Mind you, there aren't all that many. How many, Mac?" Consulting the landlord he asked, "Six? Or is it seven?"

"Six," Mac advised him, turning his attention to a new influx of customers.

Intrigued, Bob asked curiously, "But why Lessing?" then, slid onto a stool at Catherine's table. "There's nothing much to see here. Not like Oxford. Now that's what I call a place – plenty of shops and cinemas, cafés and 'resterongs'." He paused hopefully. "Fond of the cinema, are you?"

"Yes, but – well – as a matter of fact, I knew some people who lived here once. Wartime friends of mine. We lost touch. You know how it is? I'd like to contact them again, if possible . . . They kept a pub."

"Oh?" Edging his stool a bit nearer, Bob asked, "Which pub?"

"That's just it. I've forgotten the name. But the people – my friends – are called Willard. Nick and Estelle Willard."

"Willard?" Bob rubbed his chin thoughtfully. "No, the name doesn't ring a bell, and I'm pretty good at names, as a rule, aren't I Harry?"

"About the only thing you are good at nowadays," Harry said drily, pulling triumphantly at his glass of Guinness.

"Oh, take no notice of him," Bob said easily. "Mr Clever Dick! I'll ask Mac. He'll know. Hey, Mac! Remember a party called Willard? The lady tells me he once kept a pub here."

Mac frowned. "No, but I haven't been here all that long myself." Holding up a glass to the light to make sure it was clean, he said, "You'd best ask Dave Fellowes at The Rose and Crown. He was born here, the poor devil!"

Smiling happily, "There you are then," Bob told Catherine. "Problem solved. Now, how about another drink, Miss – er?"

"No, I'm sorry. Another time perhaps?" She rose to her feet.

Bob said urgently, "I'm not married, if that's what you're thinking, and I really do like you. We could go to the pictures tomorrow night, if you like, or for a quiet drink."

"Thanks, but I may not be here tomorrow night."

He said desolately, "At least let me walk you back to The Mason's Arms."

"Very well, then." She hadn't the heart to be cruel to him. Everyone deserved a taste of happiness once in a while.

Stepping into the street with him, his hand tucked firmly in the crook of her elbow, she thought suddenly of wartime meetings and partings; love affairs begun and ended within the space of hours – or what one had thought of as love affairs at the time – often nothing more than a fleeting kiss or two beneath the stars; a certain look, a certain smile . . .

Walking beside him, she knew that, in Bob's eyes, she epitomized all the women he had loved and lost during his lifetime, that this nice human being, guiding her along the ice-filmed pavements towards her hotel, would not even expect the accolade of a good-night kiss. This was the reason why, at the last moment, in memory of the wartime years, on the doorstep of The Mason's Arms, she had leaned forward to kiss his cheek, with a breathlessly whispered, "Good-night, my friend, and thank you."

"Mr Fellowes?"

"Yes, that's me. What can I do for you?" Peering across the bar counter at his first customer of the day, he asked, "Do I know you? Have we met before?"

The landlord of The Rose and Crown, a thin, wiry individual, resembled a ferret, albeit a successful ferret wearing a green cashmere sweater, heavy gold watch, and a particularly pungent brand of aftershave.

Catherine smiled charmingly and replied, "No, we've never met." Not wanting to appear in too much of a hurry she continued, "I'm a stranger here, actually, staying at The Mason's Arms Hotel for a day or two."

"Oh, I see." Mr Fellowes nodded sagely. "I've a good memory for faces as a rule, the reason why I asked if I knew you, if we'd met before. I'm sure I'd have remembered if we had."

He looked at her expectantly, wondering what was on her mind, awaiting an explanation.

She said, "May I have a drink, please? Medium sherry – and one for yourself."

"That's very civil of you. Thanks. I'll have half of bitter."

How strange, she thought, that she was fast becoming an *habituée* of pubs; ordering drinks she did not want, assuming a bright, false persona – as alien to her as the expression 'actually'.

She had talked to Dave Fellowes, attempting a light-hearted approach, wanting him to see her as a bit of a scatterbrain – a woman whose natural milieu was a pub at opening time. On the other hand, medium sherry was a dead giveaway, she realized. The kind of woman she wished to portray would have ordered something more potent.

She said apologetically, "Sorry, landlord, forget the sherry. I'll have my usual – brandy and dry ginger."

Smiling shamefacedly, hitching herself onto a bar stool, she explained, "It's just that one prefers not to begin on the hard stuff too early in the day. But, well, I am on holiday, so – what the hell!"

"As you so rightly say, Miss," Dave replied good-naturedly. "In other words, a drop of what you fancy does you good."

"It's just that I had a bit of a – heavy session, last night, with some friends of mine – Maude, Harry, and Bob, and they told me that you would be the best person to contact . . ."

"You mean Maude, Harry and Bob Carpenter?"

"Yes. You see, I'm trying to trace a couple I met during the war. Thought I'd look them up since I'm in the neighbourhood. Trouble is, I've lost their address. To cut a long story short, Bob said you might have heard of them – Estelle and Nicholas Willard. I believe they kept a pub."

The landlord sucked in his lips and blew them out again, a habit of his when thinking. "How far back are we going?"

"Well, a good few years," Catherine said, hopefully.

"Naw," Dave shook his head, "I'd have remembered. Pubs aren't all that thick on the ground in a small place like Lessing. The last one to change hands was Mac's, about five years ago, and yet the name rings a bell. Willard? Willard?"

"Tilly," he called out. "Come in here a sec, will you?"

Tilly, a tall thin woman with blonde hair, presumably Mrs Fellowes, emerged from a door marked 'Private'. "Yers," she enquired tersely, "what is it?"

One sensed her fragility, the thundering headache beneath her straw-coloured thatch, the remnants of an almighty hangover from the night before.

"Does the name Willard mean anything to you, love?"

Tilly treated her husband to a look of extreme displeasure. "I'll say it does, if you mean that damned interior decorator chap who conned us into parting with a couple of hundred quid for a job I could have done better myself for a quarter of the price!"

Catherine's heart lurched suddenly. Mrs Fellowes continued aggressively, "At least I had the pleasure of telling him what I thought of him, the jumped-up young devil! In fact, I told him straight, I did, that if he showed his face in here again, I'd send for the Police!"

With that, Tilly marched into the room marked 'Private', and slammed the door behind her.

"Er," Dave said nervously, wetting his lips with the tip of his tongue, "sorry about that, Miss. My wife's a bit off-colour this morning."

Abandoning pretence, Catherine said quietly, "Please, Mr Fellowes, I'd like to hear the whole story, if you don't mind. It *is* rather important to me."

Dave said unhappily, "It's true what my wife said. That

113

Willard chap did take us for a bit of a ride one way and another. But the last thing I want is to cause trouble. After all, it happened a long time ago – the reason why the name didn't ring a bell at first – and with you saying he owned a pub . . ."

"I understand, Mr Fellowes. Even so, I'd like to know the truth."

"Very well then." Dave stared into the past. Wrinkling his forehead, he said, "Mind you, I felt a bit sorry for the chap. He struck me as a well-educated bloke down on his luck.

"You know how it was after the war? A lot of young fellers came out of the Forces with big ideas, and damn-all else. I think Willard was one of them, wanting to get rich quick. And he was on to a good thing, if only he'd buckled down to a bit of hard work.

"People were crying out to have their places done up a bit. I know, I was one of them. Things had got kind of run down during the war. When I saw his advert in the evening paper, I asked him to come round and give us an estimate for decorating our flat upstairs." Dave paused uncomfortably.

"Please, go on," Catherine urged him quietly.

"Well, no way was I prepared to fork out that amount of money, and I told him so. No messing! Then his wife came to see me."

"His – wife?" Catherine's heart missed a beat.

"Yeah," Dave reflected, leaning his elbows on the bar, "a nice looking woman, as I recall, but nervy. You know what I mean? Kind of strung up, and as thin as a rail.

"Well, to cut a long story short, she said there'd been a mistake in the estimate. Apparently her husband had got his sums wrong to the tune of a couple of hundred quid. She begged me to reconsider, to accept the new estimate, and so I agreed. But the job was a mess from start to finish. He hadn't the men, you see, to carry out the work, and he had no intention of soiling his own hands. All he did was prance about giving estimates."

Dave sighed deeply. "Of course he came unstuck in the end, on account of Bill Stone. Now Bill was a decent

114

decorator, a married man with a couple of kids. And what happened? Soon, Willard stopped paying Bill a regular wage. 'Here's eight quid,' he would say, 'I'll give you the rest on Monday.' Well, that was no use to Bill. He had a family to support, so he asked Willard for his cards. Trouble was, Willard couldn't give them to him for the simple reason they hadn't been stamped for the past six months.

"So Bill was in a real fix. He couldn't live on what Willard was paying him, and he couldn't get hold of his cards to find himself another job."

"So then what happened?" Catherine asked wearily, sick at heart.

"Bill went to the Employment Exchange. There was nothing else he could have done, was there? But Willard was one step ahead of him. Talk about the devil's own luck. When he knew the employment inspector was on his trail, the wily bastard shoved up a 'Closed' sign on his shop window. A Friday night, that was. Somehow, during that weekend, Willard had managed to raise the couple of hundred quid he needed to stamp Bill's cards. And there he was, by all accounts, licking the last stamp when the inspector called again on the Monday morning."

Dave chuckled gently. "I couldn't help but admire the man's nerve, though I could have gladly punched him on the nose when he had the gall to demand immediate payment of a bill for two hundred quid for the mess he'd made of the upstairs premises. That's when my wife got in on the act – and what she said to him was nobody's business."

"Where did they, the Willards, live?" Catherine interjected.

Dave frowned. "Over their shop in Cook Street, as I recall. Mrs Corrigan, who used to clean up for them once in a while, said it was a queer place, and no mistake. They had no carpets on the floors, only mats, and very little furniture. But like I said before, I couldn't help feeling sorry for the bloke. It must have been a bit of a comedown for a former RAF Wing Commander trying to earn a living

115

doing something he knew sod all about – if you'll excuse my 'French'.

"Talking of French, he knew it like the back of his hand. I'll never forget the night he got into conversation with a French tutor from Oxford. Marvellous, it was, to hear them yattering on together, in French. It struck me, at the time, that Willard should have found himself a job as a translator, not a decorator. But some people can't see the wood for the trees, in my opinion."

"Dave!" Mrs Fellowes poked her head through the door at that moment. "The draymen are here!"

"Not before time! I'm coming, love."

"Please, before you go, where I can I find this Mrs Corrigan you mentioned?" Catherine asked him.

"Oh. Let me think. She lives further along the street. Number 10. Top flat. You'll have to shout, she's a bit deaf. Now, if you'll excuse me."

Mrs Fellowes took her husband's place behind the bar.

Leaving her glass of brandy and ginger on the counter, untasted, Catherine walked out of The Rose and Crown into the whirling whiteness of a fresh snowfall.

Unseeingly, her mind in a turmoil, Catherine walked the streets of Lessing until, at last, she came full circle to The Rose and Crown. At least walking had released a little of her inner tension. She hadn't realized how deeply affected she would be at Dave Fellowes' reference to Estelle. "Then his wife came to see me," he'd said, "a nice looking woman . . ."

'His wife'. Nick's wife. Estelle, not herself. Jealousy had bitten into her. How could it be otherwise? The past had suddenly come too close for comfort, and she had no one to blame but herself. Bridie had warned her to leave the past alone, but no, she'd gone on blindly, pig-headedly, digging and delving, too stupid to heed Bridie's warning.

Of course Bridie must have known about all this, Catherine thought bitterly. Then why, in God's name

116

hadn't she said so? Why some vague reference to a nonexistent pub?

These and other thoughts had jumbled together in Catherine's mind during her hour long walk in the snow – not knowing where she was going, not really caring, just walking and walking until, close to exhaustion, she had come to terms with her bitterness, jealousy and anger.

After all, she thought wearily, mounting the front steps of Number 10, what right had she to feel bitter, jealous or angry about events which had taken place a long time ago? All she had wanted, from the outset, was to find out what had happened to Nick after the divorce, to come to terms with the past, not to rail against it. And no matter what she did, nothing could change it. A case of 'The Moving Finger writes, and having writ, moves on. Nor all thy piety nor wit shall turn it back to cancel half a line, nor all thy tears wash out a word of it.'

An untidy grey head appeared round the edge of the door.

"Mrs Corrigan?"

"Yes."

"Mr Fellowes told me where to find you."

"Who? You'll have to speak up. Who did you say?"

"Mr Fellowes."

"Oh, Dave at The Rose and Crown!"

"Yes."

"You'd best come in then. It's too cold to stand jawing on the doorstep."

Catherine followed Mrs Corrigan up three flights of stairs to her abode on the top floor of the house.

"Now then," the woman said, bunching an ancient dressing gown more closely about her, "what can I do for you? Want some cleaning done?"

"No, not that, and I'm sorry to trouble you. I just wanted to ask you about the Willards."

"*Who?*"

"It's going back a bit," Catherine explained. "They had a decorators' business here in Lessing. You worked for them at one time, I believe."

117

Mrs Corrigan scratched her head perplexedly. "You'd best come through to the kitchen," she said. "There's some tea in the pot, if you want a cup. I don't get up very early these days. Sit down, dearie. Now, tell me again. I didn't quite catch what you said the first time. I have a hearing-aid somewhere, not that it makes much difference one way or t'other. The doctor says it's me age, but I know it's wax."

There were no fewer than six cups on the table, all containing dregs of tea or coffee, a three-quarters full milk bottle, and the congealed remains of a fried egg on a plate.

"Now, who was you asking about?" Mrs Corrigan enquired, resting her forearms on the table.

"A Mr and Mrs Willard," Catherine said patiently. "Dave Fellowes told me you cleaned up for them at one time – a matter of eight, possibly nine years ago. Please try to remember. It's very important."

Light dawned. "Oh, you mean that poor woman whose husband went bust? Of course I remember. Shall I ever forget? What a blooming carry on that was to be sure." Mrs Corrigan sighed deeply.

"Truth to tell, I felt real sorry for the lass. Not that she invited sympathy. A bit stuck up she was. Not that she had owt to be stuck up about, living in a place like that, with no furniture to speak of 'cept second-hand stuff – bits and bobs from the saleroom – chests of drawers and the like, stripped down to the bare essentials, with all the knots showing, if you take my meaning – her liking what she called 'modernistic' furniture.

"It looked plain ugly to me. So did those Mexican blankets she was so fond of, and those earthenware jugs and bowls she kept filled with dried flowers and summat she called pot-purry or somesuch fancy name.

"Mind you, I could tell she was bad that day I went in to clean up and found her in the bathroom spewing her heart up, so to speak. Well, it weren't none of my business, strictly speaking, but I've had five myself, and I fancied I knew what was wrong with her.

118

"So I asked her, point blank, if she was expecting, and she said yes. In a dreadful state, she was, sobbing her heart out, so I put her to bed and made her a nice cup of tea.

"Then she told me that her hubby was in serious trouble. Financial trouble, that is. No wonder the poor thing was so upset. Anyway, when I went round on the Friday morning, 'I shan't be wanting you today, Mrs Corrigan,' she said, and I could see why. The place was stripped bare ready for the removal van. Then suddenly the door barged open and in *he* came. Her hubby.

"Ever so cheerful he was, as if he hadn't a care in the world. And, 'You needn't look so miserable, darling,' he said, 'I told you it would be all right. Perry and Wynne have turned up trumps, God bless 'em. So Reading, here we come!'"

"You're quite sure about this?" Catherine asked quietly.

"Sure? Course I'm sure!" Mrs Corrigan bridled slightly, "I may be deaf, but I ain't daft!"

"I'm sorry, Mrs Corrigan, I didn't mean to upset you in any way."

"Here, just who are you anyway?" Mrs Corrigan asked suspiciously, "The Police? A private detective?"

"No, Mrs Corrigan." Catherine rose to her feet. "Just someone who knew the Willards a long time ago." She placed a five pound note on the table. "Thank you for your help. You have been most kind. No, please don't move. I'll see myself out."

Even so, the old woman rose from the table to accompany her visitor to the door of the flat, her eyes bright with curiosity when she asked, "They were friends of yours, then?"

Catherine smiled. "I suppose that's one way of describing them," she replied, her hand on the banister.

Mrs Corrigan called after her, "What's *your* name, by the way? You didn't say."

Pausing on the stairs, "My name's Willard," Catherine called up to the face on the landing.

"Eh? What did you say?"

"It doesn't matter. Goodbye, Mrs Corrigan, and thanks again for your help."

She returned to The Mason's Arms, deep in thought.

Chapter Eleven

The hotel was quiet, not surprising considering the time of year, the weather, and Lessing's close proximity to the City of Dreaming Spires.

One felt that The Mason's Arms seasonal trade would stem from its availability as an overspill area when the Oxford hotels and boarding houses were bursting at the seams with overseas visitors.

Certainly, Catherine thought, having afternoon tea in the deserted lounge, no one would stay in Lessing for reasons other than necessity and convenience.

Why Nick had chosen to come here remained a mystery. Oxford was more his milieu, and he had gone to endless trouble during the early days of their relationship to impress her with his knowledge of the place, particularly Queen's College which he referred to as the Alma Mater.

It had come as a shock when Bridie had said that first night at the cottage: "Nick might have gone to university had I taken the trouble to . . . Well, I won't go into that."

So many lies. Dave Fellowes had said, "It must have been a bit of a comedown for a former RAF Wing Commander trying to earn a living doing something he knew sod all about." But Nick had been a Flying Officer, not a Wing Commander.

She hadn't tackled him about the university lie. Even had she done so, he would have laughed and told her she'd got hold of the wrong end of the stick, had gained the wrong impression, and she'd have ended up feeling small, begging his forgiveness for having misunderstood his reference to Queens as his Alma Mater. He'd have said, with exaggerated patience, "My dear girl, what is this, the Spanish Inquisition? I referred to Queens as *'the* Alma Mater' not *my* Alma Mater. There *is* a subtle difference."

How curious, she thought, drinking tea in the hotel lounge, that even Estelle – the love of his life – had come up against the destructive element in Nick's character; and had been dragged to the brink of financial disaster as she herself had been.

Looking into the past, she remembered the summer of Nick's return to Scarborough. She had really believed that what she had told her mother so confidently, was true – that he *had* changed.

He had spent the first two months idling on the beach, swimming and sunbathing. At first she hadn't cared. It was so wonderful to have him home again, and his attitude towards her had been much gentler, much kinder. She hadn't even minded, at first, that he had begun borrowing small amounts of money from her purse without asking, until the small amounts had become larger, and she had known without a shadow of doubt, that he had started drinking again.

The wheel had turned full circle. Nick was spending her housekeeping money as fast as she earned it; contributing nothing towards his upkeep. She was on a tight budget at the time, deeply aware that the bulk of what she earned must be set aside towards the repayment of her bank loan, the upkeep of her salon, her assistants' wages, and so on. Soon, the housekeeping money she kept in her purse, a carefully worked out monthly amount from which she paid the milkman, the newsagent, the butcher, the baker, the grocer, the greengrocer, had begun to dwindle so rapidly that she had no choice other than to marginally increase her overdraft, which had seemed to her the road to nowhere.

And so, as a matter of survival, she had tackled him about his 'la dolce vita' lifestyle, albeit apologetically, because loving him so much, she couldn't bear the thought of losing him again.

"Oh, I see," he said light-heartedly, "so you want me

122

to buckle down to work, is that it? Well, fear not, Cathy my love, the message has come across loud and clear! Funny, isn't it?" he laughed, "I've always seen you as a generous-hearted, warm, sympathetic human being, but you're not, are you? Deep down, you're as hard as the Rock of Gibraltar – a kind of female Shylock wanting your pound of flesh!"

A few days later, he had come in, thrown down on the settee an expensive Rolex camera and a couple of rolls of film.

"What's that?" she'd asked, staring at the camera.

"What does it look like?"

"Obviously I know what it is, but who does it belong to?"

"Technically speaking, to Dick Ralston, my future employer, but I'm the one who'll be using it from now on."

"Your future employer? Oh, Nick! You've found yourself a job?"

"No need to go into raptures. Hadn't much choice, had I, after your reading of the Riot Act the other day?"

"Never mind that. Tell me, what does this job of yours entail?"

"Nothing too mind-boggling, I assure you! I'm simply going to take photographs of all the charming visitors treading the Spa walks during the daytime. At night, I'll be on duty in the Ballroom, snapping happy couples on the dance-floor, doing a nifty Samba, or whatever. A piece of cake really!"

"Oh, Nick darling, I'm so pleased," she'd said warmly, entering his arms.

"Why? Because I'll be doing a job that any moron could do at the drop of a hat? Or are you thinking in terms of your bank loan?"

"I just think it will be better for both of us if you have something definite to do. You said before that you didn't want to be dependent on me, remember? You told me you had your pride, and I respected that." She spoke soothingly. "In any case, this job isn't the be all and end all. Something better will turn up, you'll see."

*   *   *

123

So far her mother had refused to see Nick, although she seemed eager enough to hear about him. A difficult situation as far as Cathy was concerned, listening to Annie's carping criticism of her son-in-law.

"Hmm, so he's still idling his time away, is he? He should be as brown as a berry after all the sun and fresh air he's been getting lately. When I think how your poor father worked, and him so poorly. Worked till he dropped, he did. I wonder what he'd have had to say about a young healthy chap who'd rather laze about all day than bring in a penny-piece."

"Please don't, Mother."

"Oh, I suppose you'd like me to sit here and say nowt? Well perhaps it's time I did see that husband of yours, tell him what I think of him."

There was no pleasing Mrs Mitchell apparently. When Cathy told her that Nick had found a job, and explained what it entailed, "Huh, that's a queer kind of way to earn a living, isn't it!" Annie exclaimed scornfully. "A fine comedown for a chap with a university education, if you ask me, taking photographs folk don't want taking likely as not. And how did he come by this job, may I ask? More to the point, will he be earning a decent wage?"

Realizing the futility of pulling the wool over her mother's eyes, Cathy replied, "Nick told me he'd met this man – Dick Ralston – on the beach one day—"

"In a pub, more like," Annie interjected.

"Oh well, if you don't want to listen—"

"All right, no need to get on your high horse! Go on! So he met this man on the beach. Then what happened?"

"They got into conversation. Mr Ralston said that one of his photographers had let him down, and—"

"Oh yes, I get the picture," Mrs Mitchell smiled grimly at her own joke, "so Master Nicholas begged this Dick Ralston for the job, did he?"

"No, quite the opposite as a matter of fact. Mr Ralston asked Nick . . . Oh, what's the use? You keep asking me questions and then answer them yourself! No wonder I can't talk to you. You never even listen to what I'm saying!"

"I'm sorry, love, it's just my way. It's not you I'm getting at – it's *him*!"

"And that's supposed to make me feel better? Well, it doesn't! I know you hate Nick, but he's my husband, and I love him! If that doesn't suit you, I'm sorry!"

Collecting her belongings – handbag and a couple of bags containing food – "I'm going now, Mother! I'll see you again – whenever."

Walking home, once more had come that deep-seated feeling of guilt. But how could she possibly have told her mother that Nick would be working on a commission basis only, that he had never been to university?

Nick had brought home fifteen pounds the first week.

There was nothing to it, he said blithely, all he had to do was raise the Rolex to eye-level, say 'Smile', and hey presto!

Snapping happy holidaymakers strolling along the Spa eating ice-cream cornets was a doddle; as easy as pie handing them a ticket reminding them that the photos would be available from Ralston's 'Happy Snaps' kiosk on the seafront, at four o'clock.

Even more of a doddle was taking photographs in the Spa Ballroom when the dance-floor and the bar were packed with couples dancing cheek-to-cheek, or raising high their glasses of beer or gin and orange.

How she had laughed, at first, listening to Nick's tongue-in-cheek anecdotes of his evenings in the Spa Ballroom and bar – the honeymoon couple, for instance, who had insisted on being photographed in the middle of a fond embrace which left little doubt about what would happen later in the privacy of their hotel room. "The band were laying bets whether or not they'd be able to wait that long," Nick joked, "which reminds me."

He had proved to be an ardent lover since his return, and she had responded warmly to his passion, had felt more self-confident of her attractiveness in view of her weight-loss and something more besides – an intangible feeling that her luck was beginning to turn at last, that the teething troubles of their marriage were a thing of the past.

She might have known . . .

For no apparent reason, Nick had suddenly grown tired of his job, and decided to pack it in.

"But *why*?" she'd asked despairingly. "I thought you liked it."

"It bores me stiff, if you must know."

"That's not what you said last week."

Dick Ralston came round that evening, she recalled. He and Nick had gone into the kitchen to talk, closing the door behind them. Even so, she had caught quite clearly the drift of the quarrel. They were shouting, not talking.

"Look here, Nick, you knew damn well you weren't supposed to handle any money."

"Frankly, I can't see what all the fuss is about."

"Rules are made to be kept, and you've broken the strictest rule of all! Your job was to take the photographs and hand out the tickets. Nothing more than that. The financial side of the business is handled at the kiosk when the customers come along to collect the photos."

"I was merely doing you a favour, old boy, making damn sure that they paid in advance."

"Look here, Willard, this is *my* business and *I* make the rules, not you. There was bloody chaos at the kiosk with folk turning up saying they'd already paid for the photos, and with nothing to prove that they had!"

"Then perhaps the rules need changing?"

"According to yours, Willard? I don't think so! The fact is, fifty quid has gone missing, and I want to know what happened to it. Hazarding a guess, I'd like to bet that it ended up in your pocket. Perhaps I'd better notify the Police – 'old boy'!"

"Do as you bloody well please, I couldn't give a monkey's about you, your rules, or your job! As a matter of fact, I've a damned good mind to wrap your Rolex camera round your miserable neck and kick you down three flights of stairs!"

In a state of panic when the shouting match was over, searching in her handbag for her chequebook and pen, quickly Cathy wrote out a cheque for fifty pounds which she handed to Dick Ralston on his way from the kitchen.

"I couldn't help overhearing," she said apologetically. "About the fifty pounds, that was my fault, I'm afraid. Nick gave me the money to take care of and, well, somehow, it just got mixed up with my housekeeping money. You know how it is?"

"Yes, Mrs Willard," Dick Ralston said gallantly, "I know *exactly* how it is!"

The day was drawing on. Darkness had fallen when Catherine went up to her room in The Mason's Arms, after tea. Dinner was served at seven. There were no other guests in the hotel as far as she knew. The silence nagged at her. Looking out at Lessing's town centre square, she saw lighted shop and office windows, a few desultory shoppers, a scattering of lamp standards shining orange coloured lights on patchy wet pavements and the piles of shovelled snow lying thick and white in the gutters.

Lessing reminded her of one of those hick, Mid-Western towns seen in old Hollywood movies, where nothing much happened apart from high school kids drinking chocolate malts in the corner drugstore, and the editor of the local newspaper, smelling corruption in high places, deciding what to do about it. Then would come the obligatory rough stuff, the smashing up of his printing press by hired henchmen, the posing of a moral dilemma; the newspaper editor ending up the hero of the piece.

Moral dilemmas were something she knew about from first-hand experience. That night, for instance, when she had handed Dick Ralston the cheque for fifty pounds and lied to him to save Nick's skin. She had done something that was morally wrong without thinking twice, and precious little thanks she had got for it.

Coldly furious, Nick had turned on her savagely. "You realize what this means, I suppose? Any fool could have seen through it! And Dick Ralston's no fool! You might just as well have handed him a signed confession!"

"I did it for your sake, Nick, to save further trouble. What if he'd carried out his threat? Brought in the Police?"

"So what if he had? He couldn't have proved a damn thing! As for you, my own wife, you thought what he said was true, didn't you? You really thought I'd pocketed that fifty quid?"

Facing him squarely she'd said, "No, Nick, I didn't *think* you'd taken it. I *knew* you had!"

He had calmed down then. Later, "Look, darling, I'm sorry," he said, cradling his head in his hands, "I don't know what came over me. Cathy, sweetheart, can you ever forgive me?

"The thing is, I'm just so tired of struggling on the way I am. I need a real job of work, something to call my own. Know what I'd really like to do?" He'd looked up at her then, bright-eyed and eager. "I'd like to start a travel agency. Believe me, I know what I'm talking about. I've had lots of experience. All I need is the capital."

"How much – capital?"

"A thousand. Fifteen hundred! You could swing it for me, darling, and you'd never regret it, I promise."

"*I*? Are you out of your mind? I couldn't lay my hands on that amount of money, and you know it!"

"You could if you put your mind to it. Boring Mr Grogan, the assistant bank manager, thinks the sun shines out of you."

"Because he trusts me to repay my loan on the agreed terms, which, thank heaven, I've been able to do so far. But I've only one pair of hands, and there are only so many working days in a week. No, Nick, it's out of the question!"

"All right, Cathy, if you don't want to help me, I know someone who will. Bridie! The old girl's loaded. My sire was a rich man. He didn't give a damn about me, of course, or her either, come to think of it, but he did right by her financially, and that's all that matters in the long run, isn't it?" He laughed bitterly. "God, if you could have seen your face when you handed Ralston that cheque! I felt like tearing it into a thousand pieces!"

"Then why didn't you?" Drawing in a sobbing breath she continued, "I wish you had! That way I'd have known for certain that you hadn't taken his money!"

"Oh, I get it! So I'm in the doghouse again? My puritanical wife doesn't approve of me any more?"

"You've never really understood, have you?" she said quietly, "How much I love you?"

The venture had been launched. For the first few months he had worked like a demon. With money to burn, he had rented a shop in the town centre of Scarborough, the windows of which he had stuck over with brightly-coloured posters advertising steamer trips on the Rhine; weekends in Paris; coach trips to Austria and Switzerland.

It had all seemed so bright, so promising at first, until gradually had begun a series of complaints from irate customers threatening legal action in respect of lost tickets, inferior accommodation in second-rate hotels for which they had paid first-rate prices; misinformation regarding plane and train departures which had left them stranded in the middle of nowhere.

Turning away from the view of Lessing's main square seen from her hotel window, Catherine recalled the agony of mind she'd endured when Nick's business venture had finally hit rock bottom, when, against her better judgement, she had asked the young assistant bank manager, Mr Grogan, for an extension of her loan to repay her husband's debts.

Explaining the situation to him, she thought she saw a glimmer of disapproval in his face. Then he burst forth, "I know I shouldn't say this Mrs Willard, but you deserve better than this. Forgive me for saying it, but there is no cure for dry rot other than to get rid of it once and for all. You take my meaning?"

She had replied, "But it isn't that simple." Then had burst into tears.

He gave her a handkerchief. "Catherine, I hope you

don't mind me calling you that, but I know nothing is ever that simple. However, from what I know of you, I have decided to grant you a personal loan of one thousand pounds to cover your immediate needs. But that is the absolute limit, I assure you, bearing in mind your health and well-being."

Catherine replied, "Thank you, Mr Grogan—"

"Please call me Tim," he interrupted.

"Tim, thank you so much," she continued, close to tears again, "you'll never know how much I appreciate all that you have done for me these past few months."

Leaving Tim Grogan's office, she had thanked God, in her heart, that Nick was safe at last, that she would soon have the wherewithal to pay off his debts, to refund the money he owed to his irate customers . . .

Then something had happened which she remembered as clearly now, and with the same feeling of shock she had experienced at the time.

The telephone in the flat had rung suddenly late one night, and she had known instinctively, when Nick answered the call, that something dreadful had occurred.

She had been sitting in the armchair near the fireplace at the time, worrying about money – the thought uppermost in her mind most of the time – until the phone rang, and she had thought immediately that it must be bad news – her mother perhaps, or her sister had been taken ill. People didn't ring up at eleven o'clock at night for a cosy chat.

Nick was speaking hoarsely, asking questions. "Why? For Christ's sake, *why*? When did it happen?"

Standing up, she had gripped the mantelshelf, trying to make sense of the conversation, piecing together that the subject of the call was Frank Winter, that something terrible had happened to him.

Then Nick said, "Look, I'm coming. I'll catch the early train tomorrow morning . . . I can't give you an exact time, but I'll be there as quickly as possible, my love."

She had waited there, by the fireplace, filled with a numbing sense of despair, realizing the identity of the caller – Estelle Winter, whom Nick had called 'my love', knowing with a deep, inner certainty, that Frank was dead.

Hanging up the receiver, Nick slumped on to the settee, head bent forward, his shoulders heaving with sobs.

Kneeling down in front of him, she'd longed to cradle him in her arms, to comfort him, and yet she knew instinctively that she must not attempt to touch him, that anything she said or did would prove futile at the moment, in his present state of shock and overwhelming grief.

He muttered into his hands, "Why the hell did he do it? *Why?*"

"What has happened? Please tell me."

"Frank has killed himself!"

"Killed himself!" This was the last thing she had expected to hear. Death by natural causes was one thing, suicide another.

"But why?"

"Why? Sick of the whole bloody shooting match, I suppose. Sick of this incredibly stupid circus we call life. Sick of trying and getting nowhere. Why the hell ask me? Anyway, what does it matter? He's gone and that's that."

Tears rolled down her cheeks.

"Don't do that," Nick said sharply. "Why are you crying anyway? You never liked Frank."

"That's not true."

"Isn't it? Come on, Cathy, be honest, didn't his drunkenness appal you? Didn't you feel embarrassed in his company?" He laughed bitterly. "The trouble with you, you're not capable of understanding anyone who doesn't conform to your pattern. You disapproved of Frank, at rock bottom, just as you disapprove of me. Why be hypocritical about it?"

"You're wrong, Nick. Terribly wrong."

He said harshly, "You have no great concept of life, have you? You don't see it as a glorious gamble, the way I do, the way Frank did. Blame the war, if you like. Would you believe it, we used to lay bets on which one of us would survive the longer – him or me! Bloody funny really, don't you think? Well, this time Frank gambled on

131

a bottle of sleeping pills to put paid to his life, and he won! I glory in that! He's better off dead than going through the motions of living. And I don't believe for one moment that suicide is the cowards' way out. It takes a brave man, in my opinion, to go out alone into the darkness . . ."

Now it was almost dinnertime at The Mason's Arms Hotel.

Washing her face, running a comb through her hair, applying a touch of lipstick, Catherine walked down to the dining room – empty apart from herself.

The waitress brought her Brown Windsor soup, roast saddle of lamb, mashed potatoes, and sprouts, steamed ginger pudding and custard. When the meal was over, "Would madam prefer coffee here or in the lounge?" the girl asked her.

"In the lounge," Catherine told her, wishing she dare tell the lass to make the most of her life, to treasure her youth and beauty as a gift from God, not to fall head over heels in love with the first man she met, however handsome and desirable he may seem.

But what would be the use? No one, in her experience, ever learned from other people's mistakes. The point and purpose of life, she imagined, if there was any point and purpose to it at all, lay in the working out of one's own mistakes along the way. Hopefully to find the peace of mind necessary to carry on with the rest of one's life with no regrets.

Drinking her coffee in the lounge, bemused by the leaping flames of the coal fire near her chair, she recalled a summer Saturday afternoon long ago, when, tired beyond belief by her busy week at the salon, haunted by the tragedy of Frank's suicide, tormented by thoughts of the autopsy, the inquest, the funeral, above all by Nick's silence, the lack of a telephone message from him to set her mind at ease, she had fallen fast asleep on the settee in front of the fireplace, restfully lulled by the sound of the sea in the distance, the high-pitched laughter of children at play near the water's edge, the hooting of a pleasure-steamer emerging from the harbour mouth, the strange, almost human cry of the seagulls swooping down from the Castle Hill in search of food.

Awakening much later, the first thing she had noticed was a change in the degree of light shining through the drawing room window, a turquoise light betokening eventide, the appearance of the first stars in a sky washed over with the fading colours of a long, hot summer day.

Lying flat on her back, she imagined the summer visitors flocking down to the seafront to revel in the glory of a perfect summer night. Hazily relaxed after her long sleep, it had occurred to her that what she needed most, right then, was a leisurely bath followed by a light meal, an early night, the joy of listening to classical music on her bedside radio.

Instead of which, hearing the turning of a key in the front door lock, sitting bolt upright, hair awry, she had seen Nick standing on the threshold.

With a cry of delight, getting up, she had run to him, needing the safety of his arms after the long lonely days without him, the touch of his lips on hers.

And then, "Oh," she'd said, halting in mid-flight when she had realized that he was not alone, that Estelle was standing in the shadowy hallway behind him.

She hadn't thrown herself into his arms as she wanted to, she'd simply stood there, staring at Estelle, not knowing what to say to her.

"What on earth's the matter?" Nick said roughly. "You look as if you'd seen a ghost. Estelle's going to stay for a while. Can you fix up the spare room and organize something to eat? We're starving."

"I'll put the kettle on. I've been asleep," she added lamely.

"Come on, Stella, I expect you're feeling sticky, I know I am. I'll show you the bathroom. Perhaps when Cathy wakes up properly she'll start making noises like a hostess."

"Be fair, Nick. She didn't know you were coming, let alone me."

He shrugged. "I'll take your bag into the spare room."

Was the bathroom basin clean? Cathy wondered. Was

133

there a fresh towel? Had she cleared her sewing things off the spare room bed? Oh God, why couldn't Nick have phoned to say he was coming and bringing Estelle with him? She could have spent the afternoon cleaning up, shopping, baking scones, arranging fresh flowers, making herself look more presentable.

While Estelle was in the bathroom, she cleared her sewing things from the spare bed, smoothed the cover and dusted the dressing table. Then she went through to the kitchen to make a start on the meal, uncertain what to give them. The fridge was comparatively bare. All she had was eggs, lettuce, tomatoes, potatoes, cheese, bread, a few tins of soup, a tin of corned beef. If only she'd known, she would have bought steak or chops, mushrooms, paté, fresh fruit and vegetables.

Nick came into the kitchen. "Is this all you've got to offer? Bloody corned beef salad?"

"I'm sorry, I wasn't prepared."

"Cathy, my love, you never are."

"That's a rotten thing to say. You might have phoned—"

"Oh, I get it! All this is my fault, I suppose? I'm in the doghouse as usual, am I? Because I brought Estelle with me, is that it?"

"Keep your voice down, Nick, she might hear you!"

"I hope she does hear me! That girl's been through hell these past few days, and she's been magnificent. No self-pity, no tears. She didn't want to come with me, I made her! What the hell did you expect – that I'd leave her on her own after the funeral?

"God, it was terrible, sick making. Frank hadn't played by the rules, you see. He'd committed the unpardonable sin of going to meet his Maker before time, and the clean living, high-minded young snot who conducted the service wanted it over and done with as quickly as possible.

"What did he know about Frank, that clean living, high-minded so-called Christian who had the misfortune to bury him? I knew his kind the minute I saw him. Never had a drink in his life except communion wine; never had a cigarette or a woman; never been up in an aircraft."

Nick laughed bitterly. "There was a man who had never needed to drown his sorrows in drink, to drink himself stupid because that was the only way he could face living. Worse still, he didn't want to know! To him, poor old Frank was an embarrassment, some poor old stiff in a wooden overcoat who didn't merit a kind word at the end of things.

"Oh, what's the use of talking? You wouldn't begin to understand what I'm getting at in a million years, any more than you understand why I brought Stella home with me.

"Was it really too much to expect a decent welcome, a show of hospitality, a good meal, a bottle of wine? You didn't even speak to Stella; didn't say you were sorry about what happened to Frank. But you're not, are you? All you care about is yourself and money."

"That's not true." He could not have hurt her more if he had struck her. "I hate money; the trouble it's caused between us."

"I thought you'd changed, Cathy, I really did, when I came home. You seemed more mature, more organized. I was wrong. Look at you. You've never understood, have you? That I need someone calm and wise and full of pith. Someone for the bad days when life's too much to take."

"Someone like Estelle, you mean? But I'm not Estelle. I can't look like her or be like her. I'm myself. Why do you want me to be something I'm not? Why did you marry me in the first place if I was so unlike the person you wanted me to be?"

She burst into tears and ran into the bedroom.

A little while later, she heard voices.

Estelle was saying, "It was a stupid thing for me to do. Coming here. I shouldn't have listened to you."

"You're not leaving. I won't let you!"

"Don't be a fool! You can't stop me."

"But where will you go? It's getting late."

"Don't worry about me. I'll find somewhere to stay overnight, catch the first train tomorrow morning."

Cathy entered the drawing room. Nick and Estelle were

135

standing close together. His hands were on her shoulders. She said dully, "You're welcome to stay if you want to. And I really am sorry about Frank."

"Thanks, but my mind's made up." Estelle picked up her suitcase.

"I'm coming with you," Nick said, "to make certain you find somewhere to stay, to buy you a decent meal."

He turned at the door. "You'd best go to bed, Cathy," he said coldly, sarcastically, "get more sleep; you look as if you need it. Don't worry, I shan't disturb your slumbers. I'll sleep in the spare room!"

That had been the thin edge of the wedge, Catherine thought, finishing her coffee in the deserted lounge of The Mason's Arms Hotel.

From that night onward, Nick had continued to sleep in the spare room. From that night, an insurmountable barrier had sprung up between them.

Later, she had understood why.

Estelle had not left town after all. She had found herself a job as a hotel receptionist; had established herself as Nick's mistress in a rented flat in Albemarle Crescent.

How had she found out the truth? Because Nick himself had told her so; had bragged about it.

Why?

That also had become apparent in the fullness of time. Because, in the event of divorce proceedings, she must shoulder the blame for the break-up of their marriage. She must be the one to give him his marching orders from the marital home. As long as he remained beneath her roof, as her husband, he could prove co-habitation up to the hilt, and no court in the land could prove otherwise.

On the other hand, if she told him to leave, the failure of the marriage would be her fault entirely.

All these facts she had known and clearly understood on the night of their final confrontation when, coming home late, reeking of whisky and Estelle's favourite perfume – Estee Lauder's 'Youth Dew' – uncaring of the consequences, she had told him to pack his things and get out.

Smiling foolishly he asked, "Are you sure you mean

136

that, Cathy darling? I am still your husband, remember?"

Standing her ground, she had begun at the beginning, speaking slowly, weighing her words.

She said, "I didn't believe Heather Harper at first, when she told me you'd danced with me to make her jealous. She was wrong, of course, it was Estelle Winter. And Estelle married Frank to make you jealous. That's right, isn't it? Then you married me to get even with Estelle for having married Frank.

"Bridie did her best to warn me that I was barking up the wrong tree, but I wouldn't listen. I really thought that you loved me, you see? And I loved you enough not to question you about your 'university' education. I was so afraid of losing you. Why, God alone knows!

"You never loved me, I know that now. But I loved *you*. I thought the sun rose and set in you, and no matter how badly you treated me, I kept on loving you.

"I'm still in love with you, heaven help me, but I know when I'm beaten. As for Estelle, the woman *sans* self-pity or tears at her husband's funeral; Estelle the magnificent! How noble of her not to weep for a man who meant less to her than the dust beneath her feet!

"Well, Nick, now that you've got what you wanted all along – a relationship with a woman as incapable of loving, as self-centred and calculating as yourself, who am I to stand in the way of your future life together? From where I'm standing, you richly deserve one another. Now, pack your things and get out!"

And that's the way it was one spring evening long ago when she had finally plucked up the courage to get rid of the dry rot that Tim Grogan had warned her about.

"Boring Mr Grogan," Nick had called him unheedingly. But Tim Grogan wasn't at all boring, despite his neatly combed hair and horn-rimmed glasses, Catherine thought, just a very nice man, in his late twenties who had done his best to help her through a minefield of financial traumas to do with the purchase of her business premises, her home, and the failure of Nick's travel agency venture. A

137

man who had given her comfort and help when she had needed it. She would always be grateful to him for that.

But all she clearly remembered now, going upstairs to her room, was the final closing of the front door when Nick, carrying a couple of hastily packed suitcases, had left her, without a word of regret, to hurry back to his mistress.

She had never seen Nick again from that day to this, and yet his influence had continued to overshadow her life to the exclusion of all else.

So where should she go from here? Reading, of course. It had to be Reading.

Chapter Twelve

She left The Mason's Arms after breakfast the next morning, and took a taxi to the station, where she bought a ticket to Reading, first stop Oxford.

On an impulse, because she had always wanted to see Oxford and this opportunity seemed too good to miss, leaving her belongings in the Left Luggage department, she set out to discover the City of Dreaming Spires.

Enchanting was the only word to describe it. A pale sun had emerged briefly to gild and warm the façades of the ancient buildings, to light up mullioned windows and glisten on the undisturbed snow lying thick on the college lawns and gardens glimpsed beyond the iron gates and railings.

It seemed miraculous to see winter-flowering jasmine blooming in a grey world, showering golden sparks against sombre stonework, and there were snowdrops pushing up through the moist earth where the sun had melted the snow a little.

Soon there would be hosts of yellow and purple crocuses, Catherine thought, a valiant tide of crocuses awash beneath the trees. Then would come the daffodils, betokening springtime, a renewal of hope for the future after the long dark days of winter.

At long last she dared think about an aspect of her conversation with the cleaning lady, Mrs Corrigan, which she had pushed to the back of her mind.

She recalled the woman's words exactly: "I fancied I knew what was wrong with her, so I asked her point blank, if she was expecting, and she said yes."

So Estelle had had at least one child by Nicholas, she thought bleakly, retracing her steps, fighting hard to overcome her deep-seated jealousy of the woman who had not merely taken her husband away from her but had borne his child.

It still hurt, after all this time, that Nick had given to Estelle the one thing she had longed for above all else, which he had laughingly denied to herself; the one vital element – motherhood – the bearing of a child which might have made all the difference to their marriage as a stablizing influence. Too late now. But the passage of time had not softened or altered her deep-seated hatred and jealousy of Estelle, the woman who had taken not only her husband, but his name; but the whole of him – his love, his body, his seed . . .

Wending her way towards the city centre, standing on a corner near the Martyrs' Monument, feeling hungry, glimpsing a restaurant on the opposite pavement, she crossed the road in quick bursts to avoid the oncoming traffic.

January sales' notices were plastered across shop windows, and there were women pushing through swing doors, women wearing the eager, expectant look of inveterate sales' goers, laden with shopping bags and parcels.

From the restaurant she had spied, came the inevitable smell of roast and two veg, accompanied by the rattle of knives, forks and spoons. Confronted by a sea of faces, she glanced round for a spare table.

The manageress bustled up to her. "One, madam?" she asked. "Would you mind sharing with this lady?"

The woman already seated at the table indicated by the manageress, smiled at Catherine. "I don't mind if you don't," she said, moving her shopping bags from the vacant seat opposite.

The moment she was seated, a teenage waitress appeared at her side, order pad in hand. "What'll it be?" she asked snappily.

"I don't know. I haven't seen the menu yet."

"It's on the table," the girl said reprovingly.

"Roughly speaking, it's a toss up between steak pie,

roast lamb or fish and chips," the woman at the table murmured, *sotto voce*, "preceded by something grandly termed 'Potage St Jules' – more commonly known as Brown Windsor. I'd give that a miss, if I were you."

"Oh, very well then. Steak pie, please," Catherine told the waitress.

"What about the Potage St Jules?" the girl asked coldly.

"No, thank you, just the pie."

"Any veg?"

"Potatoes and peas?" Catherine ventured hopefully.

"No peas. Carrots or brussels?"

"Brussels, please."

The waitress flounced off to place the order.

"Tell me," the woman opposite asked, "do girls of that age make you feel old all of a sudden? They do me!"

"Like something from Noah's Ark," Catherine admitted, warming to her table companion; her bright intelligent face lit with blue-grey eyes.

Her hair, Catherine noticed, was cut short, streaked with grey, naturally curly, that her hands were thin, capable hands. She wore no jewellery apart from a thick gold band on her wedding finger.

"I realize, of course," she said, tongue-in-cheek, "that I am flouting the rules of civilized British behaviour in talking to a complete stranger in a crowded restaurant. The fact is, I feel terribly embarrassed looking at someone and not speaking.

"My name is Rose Jarvis, by the way. I came to Oxford to buy a couple of sweaters in the sales. My daughter's starting a new school and needs navy blue instead of green which she had at the last one. The trouble is I get sidetracked into buying things I don't need. Take this for example."

She dug into her shopping bag and brought out a blouse with a foaming lace jabot and frilled cuffs.

"It's very pretty," Catherine said.

"Yes, isn't it? I love it, but what am I going to do with it? I never go anywhere much nowadays, not to

141

concerts or parties or cocktail dos. In any case, I'm not the frilly-blouse type as you can see."

"But does that really matter? I mean, you could just hang it in your wardrobe and get a thrill from seeing it there when you open the door."

"Funny you should say that." Rose Jarvis held her head a little on one side. Her eyes were very soft, very tender.

"Why?"

"That's just what my husband would have said, and I've never met anyone, since he died, who doesn't think in terms of usefulness, or common sense. Even my daughter will say, 'Mum, you waste your money on such silly things.' Of course she wouldn't say that if I'd bought the blouse for her."

The waitress brought Catherine's steak pie. When the girl had gone, Catherine said, "I waste money too. My weakness is flowers. I remember one Christmas, ages ago, buying a bunch of carnations because I knew they'd look just right on a little rosewood table I have. Mother thought I was mad, but ah, the pleasure they gave me. I think my father would have understood, but he died when I was little."

"As long as there is one person who understands, life is possible. When that person no longer exists – well, at times the emptiness seems unbearable." Rose smiled. "Sorry, I was thinking aloud. You must think me a little strange. In a table sharing situation, one is meant to talk about the weather, not ponder the mysteries of life. I hope I haven't embarrassed you."

Catherine said, "When I came into this restaurant, I didn't want to talk to anyone." She hesitated. "I didn't want to share a table. But meeting you has done me good. A bit like, 'Of all the gin joints in all the world, she walks into mine'."

"Oh, you mean *Casablanca*? A lovely film. Bogart and Bergman. 'As Time Goes By'. I wept buckets."

"My name is Catherine Willard."

"I'm very happy to know you, Catherine."

This sort of thing doesn't happen in real life, Catherine

142

thought. One doesn't make a friend in ten minutes. But she was wrong. One could fall in love in ten seconds, as she had done with Nick. Time had nothing to do with the emotional response towards another person; liking, loving or loathing. She knew that Rose Jarvis was someone she liked and trusted. Blade straight, steel true.

They ate for a while in companionable silence. The waitress came to clear the plates. Rose chose apple pie and cream for dessert, Catherine ordered cheese and biscuits.

Over coffee, Rose said, "Tom – my husband, and I used to come to Oxford occasionally to see a show. We loved the theatre. Or sometimes we'd just walk arm-in-arm looking at houses, choosing the ones we liked best, planning what we'd do when the children grew up and left home. We said we'd sell our Victorian monstrosity and buy a cottage with a garden backing on to the river; have a studio where we could paint or write or put people up for the weekend.

"It all sounded so romantic, and yet it seemed entirely possible. Something to look forward to when Tom retired. Then Tom died suddenly three years ago. Still, I'm glad we shared a belief in there being a future for us; a cottage with roses round the door and petunia-filled window-boxes." She quoted softly, "'With a knocker of pearl, a silver dream for a latch, and a carpet of little blue feathers to lay on your floor'."

"I'm so sorry about your husband," Catherine said quietly.

"Thank you." Rose sighed, then smiled. "Now I'm stuck with the monstrosity, and how I've blessed it since Tom died. I mean it. That house has been my salvation. It has given me a means of livelihood. I take in paying guests, you see, and I grow most of my own vegetables, so I'm quite independent."

"Where is your – monstrosity?" Catherine asked, finishing her coffee.

"Not far from Reading," Rose said, "in a village near the Thames, which gives me plenty of summer trade. American tourists in particular."

143

"Reading? You did say near Reading?"

"Yes. Why?"

"Because that's where I'm going later this afternoon."

"How extraordinary," Rose said delightedly. "You will stay with me, won't you, unless you have made other arrangements, that is?"

"This is your room." Rose opened the door. "I've given you this smaller one because it's above the kitchen and you'll feel the warmth of the Aga. The big front rooms are cold at this time of year. I hope you approve?"

Rose had made matching curtains and bedcover from sprigged cotton material. The chest of drawers and the wardrobe were painted white, the walls emulsioned in a delicate shade of green. The carpet was a warm shade of pink which matched the lampshades exactly and picked up the pink in the curtains.

"It's a lovely room," Catherine said gratefully, realizing the amount of care and attention to detail which had gone into its creation.

"The bathroom's just across the landing. I'll go and put the kettle on while you're unpacking." Rose paused at the door and said shyly, "I'm glad you're here."

Later, Rose brought in the tea-trolley which she placed near the sitting room fire. "I baked a few scones before I set off this morning," she said, pouring the tea. "Julie, my daughter will be in any moment now, I imagine – starving hungry, as usual."

Handing Catherine her tea and offering her a plate of delicately-cut sandwiches, she continued, "She'll have gone to the library to change her books. She's a serious-minded child, my Julie. I suppose she takes after her father, except that Tom was serene rather than serious, with a great sense of humour."

"You said 'children' when you talked about the cottage you wished for," Catherine said. "Have you another child?"

"Indeed I have. David. He's spending a few days in Wales with a university chum of his whose family own a rather swish house on the Gower Peninsula. He's

144

nineteen, studying – or should I say reading – modern languages, at Cambridge."

She smiled wistfully. "David's very much like me to look at. As skinny as a yardstick. We see eye-to-eye about everything – well, most things anyway."

"You must be very proud of him."

"Yes, I am, though he'd kill me for saying so."

Here was a woman who had turned possible defeat into positive victory, Catherine thought, understanding the struggle Rose must have had to come to terms with the death of a beloved husband, the education of her children, the maintenance of a very large house and garden.

As if reading her thoughts, Rose said, "I have help with the cleaning. I couldn't possibly manage without my marvellous cleaning-lady, Mrs Wickett, and her married daughter Sally, who comes in as a stand-by during the summer months. But I do all the cooking myself, and see to the garden. It isn't all that difficult. I offer breakfast of the full English variety; bacon, eggs, sausages, tomatoes, fried bread, toast and marmalade – and a three-course dinner. You know the kind of thing? Soup, roast and Yorkshire puddings, three veg, and a hefty pudding to follow. The Americans in particular would feel they'd been cheated if they didn't have what they call 'traditional English cooking'. Lots of fat, starch and gravy!" She burst out laughing.

"What made you and Tom buy such a big house?" Catherine asked, joining in the laughter.

"Mainly because nobody else wanted it, and it was going for a song. The estate agent was tearing out his hair in despair of ever getting rid of it. Prospective buyers turned pale and headed for the gate when they saw the state it was in and the size of the garden. The poor man, he almost fell on his knees and thanked the Lord for his deliverance when Tom and I came on the scene and actually wanted the place.

"He, the estate agent, must have thought he was dreaming when Tom went into raptures about the skirting boards. 'Just look at the depth of them,' he said, oblivious to the fact that they had been painted with something that

145

looked suspiciously like treacle, then went on to enthuse about the stained glass landing window and the ceiling rosettes. At which point I said something feeble about how much it would cost to furnish and redecorate a house this size. But I knew Tom wanted it, and to be honest, so did I.

"We'd spent the first few months of our marriage in furnished rooms, you see, and we were knocked sideways by the sight of so much space. In any case, we were young, full of health and optimism, so we set to work with a will; painting, papering, and gardening. In due course, I had my babies, the children we'd both wanted so much.

"Thankfully the house was paid for long before Tom died, and so, when I was left on my own I decided to stay. I think that's what Tom would have wanted. In any case, there was really no choice. My roots are here, you see, buried deep in this home we created together."

"What was his job?" Catherine asked intently, deeply moved.

"He was a draughtsman, but he hated office routine. He did what was necessary to earn a living, but his real happiness lay here, in this house, or working in the garden at weekends. I suppose some people thought him dull. Dull because he had no hobbies beyond his home and family. But he wasn't dull to me. He was the most exciting person I've ever known! We shared a kind of secret life together, Tom and I. The most marvellous thing of all, he was always so utterly *there* for me. In his eyes, I could do nothing wrong. I knew that no matter how tough the going might seem at times, when the children were young and money was tight, that I could depend on him to see us through. I miss him so terribly."

Catherine said softly, "And yet you seem so self-sufficient and happy."

Rose smiled wistfully. "I try to be. As the saying goes, 'Laugh and the world laughs with you. Weep, and you weep alone.' Besides, I have the most tremendous faith in our being together again one day. I regard my life as a kind of journey, a road leading to a bright light at the end of a tunnel.

"But no, it's far simpler than that, not half so dramatic. I'm sorry, I sound like the soppy heroine of a wartime film, don't I? I just happen to believe that love remains the strongest force of all; a source of joy linked to happiness and hope for the future."

She broke off suddenly. "Why, what is it Catherine, what's wrong?" she asked concernedly. "You're crying!"

"It's nothing. I'm just a bit tired, that's all."

The front door opened and closed at that moment, and Julie, carrying a satchel of library books, entered the room.

"Oh," she said abruptly, "I didn't realize you had company, Mummy. Shall I make myself scarce?"

A hiatus occurred. Catherine said quickly, "No need. I'm just leaving. If you'll excuse me, I'm going up to my room for a little while."

She hadn't meant to be rude, to allow her feelings to run away with her, to cry in front of Rose Jarvis, to brush past her daughter so abruptly. She had, quite literally, come to the end of her tether. She was emotionally and physically drained.

Rose's words had brought home to her the paucity of her own marriage. She had never known what it felt like to have someone entirely on her side. Hers had been a one-sided love affair from the beginning. So why not go home and forget about Nick?

Rose knocked at the door. "Catherine," she called softly, "are you all right? May I come in?"

"Of course." When Rose entered, she said, "I'm sorry, I made a fool of myself I'm afraid, rushing off the way I did. Please forgive me."

"Was it something I said?" Rose perched on the bed end.

Useless to lie. Catherine knew she owed Rose an explanation. She said, "What you told me about your-self and Tom – it's hard to explain – it's just that you had the kind of marriage I hoped for and never had.

"I thought, mistakenly, that the strength of my love for the man I married would be strong enough to see us

147

through. It didn't work out that way. He loved someone else, you see."

"Oh, my dear, how dreadful for you." Rose paused. "You – divorced?"

"Yes, but I had the feeling that it was my fault, if I'd tried a bit harder or done certain things differently, the marriage might have come right in the end."

"Do you want to talk about it? If so, I'm listening."

"Not now. Later, if that's all right. You have things to do, Julie to see to."

Rose nodded understandingly. "Try to rest now, my dear. I'll call you when dinner's ready. We'll talk afterwards, when Julie goes upstairs to watch television in her room."

Rose had cooked lamb chops with rosemary, and made a lemon meringue pie, which they ate in the dining area of the big, Aga-warmed kitchen. Julie had seemed restrained at first in the presence of a guest, whom she eyed suspiciously, as if fearing a second outburst of tears. Really, grown-ups acted very strangely at times, she thought – even her own mother, buying silly things in the winter sales.

She perked up a little when Rose said, "That blouse I bought today, you can have it if you like, love. It's far too young for me." Catching Catherine's eye, she smiled conspiratorially.

Later, relaxing in an armchair near the sitting room fire, after Julie had kissed her mother good-night and gone upstairs to her room, Catherine knew how much she had needed this caravanserai, this oasis of peace after the traumatic events of the past few days.

This was a lovely room, she thought, warm and welcoming, with its leaping log fire and red-shaded lamps, the heavy red velvet curtains drawn against the night, its solid Victorian furniture set against a background of magnolia emulsioned walls, so that the furniture was in no way overpowering or intrusive.

In a way, it reminded her of home, her own flat. Home . . .

148

Speaking slowly to Rose, hesitantly at first, she began piecing together snippets of her life in the manner of stitching, from memory, a multi-coloured patchwork quilt; many of the facets out of sequence, some seemingly irrelevant; inconsequential, just little things which had stayed in her mind for no apparent reason. Her mother's brass fender, for instance, and the china dogs on the mantelpiece; the way she had felt when her father died, not understanding why he had left her without a word of goodbye. Always thinking that he would come back to her, one day, to share with her his boiled egg at breakfast.

She spoke of the war years, the way she had felt when she had learned of the death of the handsome High School boy she had so admired as a tongue-tied 15-year-old, whose ship had been lost at sea, whose boyish frame now lay fathoms deep in the cold waters of the Atlantic Ocean.

"His mother never recovered from the shock of her son's death," Catherine said slowly. "Now I know why. Incompleteness is worse than death." It was then she told Rose about Nick, her need to find him again.

Rose sat quietly, listening, her eyes upon a log which, catching the flames, sent the sweet, smokey scent of last summer's apple boughs flooding into the room.

I have known fulfilment, Rose thought. Tom is dead, but in no way did his dying diminish the happiness of our lives together. We had explored together every avenue of delight; had children, tended our garden; planted trees to survive a thousand storms. This woman has no history of contentment.

Under similar circumstances, she wondered, would she feel motivated to pursue lost happiness? Impossible to say. So much depended on the individual concerned, the depth of the suffering involved.

What Catherine most needed, Rose thought compassionately, was absolution — not the kind of absolution administered by priest or parson at a Sunday morning service — but something far deeper — a kind of self-administered absolution — a healing of one's own soul.

And now Catherine was speaking of a new man in her life, someone called Adam who had been good to her, who had asked her to marry him.

"This – Adam, are you in love with him?" Rose asked gently.

"No, but he's a kind man, deserving of happiness."

"And could you make him happy?" Rose persisted kindly, "Or are you clutching at straws? Be honest with yourself, my dear. Could you give him the happiness he deserves?"

"I don't know. I honestly don't know." Catherine shook her head. "Not as things stand at present, perhaps when I've come to terms with the past."

"Then you are going on with the quest?"

"I think I must. You see, Rose, I have a strange feeling that something is wrong. I think Nick's mother is hiding something from me. Call it intuition, but I don't think he went to New Zealand at all. I believe that he is still here in England – quite close at hand, if only I knew where to look."

150

Chapter Thirteen

One felt that Perry and Wynne had ferried the British Raj to India when Brunel was building his iron ship. There was an air of solid respectability about the building far removed from the modern, up-market travel agencies with their garish posters advertising cut-rate coach trips to the continent of Europe: to Italy, France, Spain and Austria.

Catherine had caught an early bus into Reading. Understanding her need for action, Rose had provided an early breakfast of toast, marmalade and piping hot coffee.

Their conversation of the night before had proved an eye-opener to Rose Jarvis, who had realized, compassionately, the depth of Catherine's love for a man unfit to tie her shoelaces, in her opinion. Not that she had given the slightest indication of her feelings on the subject, believing, as she did, that it was up to Catherine to work out her own salvation in her own way, without the benefit of well meant, possibly spurious advice to cloud the issue.

In her book, friendship meant accepting people as they were, being there for them when needed, providing the creature comforts of warmth, food and drink; a shoulder to cry on, if necessary, at the end of the day.

All she really had to go on, Catherine thought, was the cleaning lady, Mrs Corrigan's word that Nick had mentioned the name Perry and Wynne, and Reading, the day he had walked into the stripped-bare flat in Lessing, saying, "You needn't look so miserable, darling. Perry and Wynne have turned up trumps, God bless 'em. So Reading, here we come."

Now here she came, marching in where angels might

fear to tread, standing on the pavement outside Perry and Wynne's, her breath whirling away like smoke in the bitterly cold air, marshalling her thoughts, mentally rehearsing what she would say when she had plucked up enough courage to cross the threshold.

Eventually, squaring her shoulders, she opened the door and walked up to the counter behind which stood a fresh-faced young man sorting through a pile of travel brochures, who looked up and smiled at her approach.

"May I help you?" he enquired brightly.

"I hope so. That is, I'd like to see the person in charge here."

"You mean – Mr Garrard?" The clerk swallowed nervously, his face clouded. Had something gone wrong, he wondered, dreading a possible complaint. "Er – have you an appointment?"

"No, not at all. I thought there might be a Mr Wynne or a Mr Perry I could speak to. It *is* rather important."

"Oh no," the clerk said quickly, "Mr Perry died some time ago, and Mr Wynne seldom comes in nowadays, but Mr Garrard is related to Mr Wynne by marriage. More specifically, Mr Garrard is Mr Wynne's son-in-law."

The clerk, who hadn't been with the firm very long, felt as if he was giving away state secrets.

"I see. Well, may I see Mr Garrard?"

"He's in his office. Just a moment, I'll find out if he's free."

Ducking from behind the counter, the clerk knocked on a door marked 'Private', brushing, in his nervous haste, against a low table containing a vase of tulips, spilling some of the water, adding to Catherine's own nervous tension.

Opening the door a crack, "There's a lady to see you, sir," the clerk muttered unhappily. "All right if I show her in?"

Hugh Garrard, a tall man, thin, with a receding hairline, clicked his teeth in annoyance. Irritated by the clerk's intrusion, his manner of speaking – 'All right if I show her in?' indeed! – he wondered what the younger generation was coming to these days. He might at least have found out the woman's name beforehand, and the nature of her visit prior to knocking on his door. He'd have something to say to young Compton later . . .

Stifling his irritation, switching on the charm as Catherine entered the office, Garrard rose from his chair behind an imposing mahogany desk, extended his hand in greeting, smiled, and invited her to sit down in the chair opposite. "Now, madam, how may I help you?" he asked smoothly.

It was like being ushered into the presence of a solicitor. "I'm sorry to trouble you," she said. "I imagine you're a busy man so I'll come straight to the point. I'm trying to trace someone who worked for you some time ago. At least I think he did. I may be wrong, and in any case you may not remember him."

"I see." Garrard took stock of the woman. She reminded him of someone. Of course, his sister-in-law Grace Wynne. They were roughly of the same height and build, with similar features and fair hair, the same air of having been treated badly somewhere along the line.

He smiled to put his visitor more at ease. "Well, that shouldn't prove too difficult," he said urbanely. "We do keep a record of our employees. Now, if you would care to tell me the name of the person you are looking for."

"His name is Willard – Nicholas Willard. I have reason to—"

She stopped speaking abruptly. Hugh Garrard had risen to his feet, his face the colour of clay.

"No need to continue," he said hoarsely. "The name you mentioned is well known to me, I assure you. One that I, and members of my family are unlikely to forget."

Fighting to control his emotion, "You must excuse me," he murmured, "a slight heart condition. Over there, the corner cupboard. A spot of brandy."

"Sit down, Mr Garrard. Shall I call the clerk?"

"No, no. Just give me a small brandy. I'll be all right in a minute."

"I'm terribly sorry, I didn't mean to distress you," she said when he had finished the drink. "Are you feeling better now?"

153

"Yes, I'm fine. It was just the shock of hearing that name again. One tries to forget such painful incidents. In this case, an impossibility I'm afraid. We have all suffered the consequences."

"Are you feeling up to this? Mr Garrard. I could come back later if you like."

"No, I'd rather get it over with. But first may I ask why you wish to find Willard? Are you here in an – official capacity?"

"Official?" She wondered what he meant. "No, not at all. He – Nicholas, was my husband. My reasons are purely personal."

Garrard looked bemused. "You mean that he married again after . . .? I'm sorry, I appear to have lost the thread. I recall Willard's wife as a tall, pale-skinned woman, strangely remote, somewhat haughty."

"You are referring to his present wife, Mr Garrard. Nicholas and I were divorced some time ago. I am Catherine, not Estelle Willard."

"Ah yes, I see." Taking a pristine handkerchief from his breast pocket, he mopped his forehead. "Frankly, this has come as a shock. When you walked into my office, you reminded me of someone – my wife's sister, Grace. Grace as she used to look before Willard came into her life.

"She was quite beautiful then, bright, intelligent, with everything to live for." He paused. "If you could see her now, Mrs Willard, you would realize why I have reason to remember and to regret the day he came to work here.

"Need I say that this firm enjoys a unique reputation for fair dealing. Indeed, since it was founded in the year 1860 by my wife's great-grandfather, Sebastian Wynne – one of the Old School of English gentlemen. Never, in all that time, had there been a breath of scandal to tarnish that reputation, until . . ." He paused unhappily. "May I speak freely?"

"Please do, Mr Garrard."

"Very well then, though I should warn you that what I have to say may cause you distress."

"I understand, and thank you. Even so, I'd rather hear the whole story, the absolute truth."

154

Garrard continued. "It all began with Bridie Willard whom I had met in my younger days as a friend of my sister. To cut a long story short, my sister and she remained on friendly terms after Bridie's marriage to Willard's father had ended in divorce.

"We knew of the circumstances, that her husband had left her for another woman, and I must say that we felt extremely sorry for her. Not that she elicited sympathy, far from. Indeed, we greatly admired her self-sufficiency and courage in making a new life for herself and her son.

"We knew her to be a proud woman, unwilling to ask favours of anyone as a rule, the reason why when she came to see me one day to ask if I could find a place here, for her son, I was only too pleased to assist her in any way possible. To that end, I arranged an interview with him the following week.

"My father-in-law, Basil Wynne, was active in the business at that time. We met Nicholas and thought him a charming young fellow, which he was – at least on the surface. Moreover, he appeared to have all the right qualifications – prior experience as a courier, and a quite remarkable command of the French language. And so we offered him a job. Quite a responsible job as it happens.

"At first he worked hard – he was far too clever to do otherwise, I imagine. Soon he inveigled himself into our family circle – my father-in-law's influence, I'm afraid. He had taken a strong liking to the man. At any rate, my wife and I invited Willard and his wife to our home quite frequently in those early days, to dinner and cocktail parties, which my wife's sister Grace also attended as a matter of course, as a member of the family.

"I have to say that neither my wife or I cared much for Willard's wife, but we made allowances for her because of her – condition. In all honesty, we found her a difficult person to come to terms with. I can't explain, she seemed frozen somehow, incapable of laughter."

Catherine knew exactly what he meant. The cool, elegant withdrawn Estelle with her cropped hair and colourless skin, her unhappy, unsmiling mouth, a woman capable of destroying the lives of others without compunction – Frank's first, then hers . . .

Garrard went on, "Our friendship with Willard's mother went a long way towards winning our confidence, of course. My father-in-law who thought the sun shone out of Willard, sent him abroad to the continent to discover how the land lay so far as tourism was concerned, to find suitable hotels and report back to us the result of his findings. To be entirely fair, his judgement was sound. The trouble started when, on his return to this office, my father-in-law entrusted him with the key to the safe."

Garrard groaned wearily. "The bloody young fool robbed this firm of several thousand pounds. Worst of all, when the theft was discovered, he laughed in our faces; threatened to tell the world and its wife that he had taken the money to keep his mistress in the style to which she had grown accustomed. He meant my wife's sister Grace!

"We didn't believe a word of it at first. How could we? Not until Grace confessed that everything he had told us was true, that they had been abroad together, that she was carrying his child. Can you begin to imagine the horror of it all?

"My father-in-law suffered a stroke from which he has never fully recovered. Even so, he would not budge an inch from his intention to make Willard pay back every penny he had stolen, either that or face a stiff prison sentence for the embezzlement of funds from the company's safe of which he was a key-holder.

"In the meanwhile, he had my wife's sister taken abroad, to Italy, to await the birth of her baby, which died two days later. Six months afterwards, Grace returned home a shadow of her former self, broken in mind and body. She had been in and out of mental hospitals ever since. What became of Willard's wife I have no idea.

"Of course Bridie Willard had to be told what had happened. To her everlasting credit, she immediately offered to repay every ha'penny of the money her son had stolen. At first I refused to hear of her doing any such thing, but she wouldn't listen. She said,'I'll repay

156

my son's debt if it means selling everything I own.' And I knew I could trust her to keep that promise."

The interview was over.

Rising to her feet, "Goodbye, Mr Garrard," Catherine said quietly, "and thank you for taking the trouble to talk to me."

They shook hands solemnly.

On her way out, she noticed that the tulips on the little table the clerk had brushed against, had begun to bend and contort in the way that some flowers do when picked. Like lupins – like some human beings, she thought, incapable of standing straight without bending.

She had no other choice now than to go back to Cloud Merridon, to the cottage, to face Bridie once again. Bridie who held the key to the past, who knew Nick better than anyone, as no other human being ever could.

Chapter Fourteen

Catherine face Bridie across the littered hearth.

"Why have you come back?" Bridie asked heavily.

"Because things did not ring true at our last meeting."

Bridie's face, once so lovely and appealing, now seemed so lifeless, so wrinkled. Now Catherine knew why; sensed the suffering which had produced those lines, and the dispirited droop of her shoulders.

Bridie sank down on the settee.

"I prayed you wouldn't come again. I kept on telling myself that you were the same naïve girl you used to be, that you wouldn't trouble me any more. Apparently I was wrong."

The room was a mess, dirty, littered with old newspapers and dog-eared magazines. At least Catherine knew now what had happened to those missing Chinese bowls, the silver, the porcelain, the elegant antique furniture, the oil paintings in their thick gilt frames.

Bridie had sacrificed a great deal for her son. But then, everyone who had come into contact with Nick had made sacrifices, had become impoverished in some way or other.

The room was bitterly cold.

"I think we need a log on the fire," Catherine said, taking command of the situation. Picking up the hearth brush, she swept up the litter of ash lying there, thinking of Estelle, Hugh Garrard's sister-in-law, Grace Wynne, Bridie, herself, all of whom had been touched in some way by Nick's presence in their lives, all of whom had been hurt by him.

Kneeling by the hearth, turning to face Bridie, "I don't want to trouble you," Catherine said gently, "only to talk to you. You see, I met Hugh Garrard yesterday, and he told me about Nick's affair with Grace Wynne."

Bridie's hands trembled in her lap. "Hand me a cigarette," she said hoarsely. "That packet on the table, and the lighter." Inhaling deeply, she burst forth, "Did you indeed? And what business was that of yours?"

"None whatever." Catherine sighed deeply. "You know, Bridie, I was always a bit afraid of you. You were so efficient, so self-contained, all the things that I was not and never could be."

Bridie said scornfully, "Obviously you are not afraid of me now, otherwise you would not have had the effrontery to come here again."

"I came because I had to. Nick was my husband. Do you think I have gone through life not caring what became of him? And then I discovered that you hadn't been quite straightforward about Lessing. You told me that Nick had owned a pub there, but that wasn't true."

"You went there? You actually went there to check up on me? How utterly despicable!"

"Not to check up on *you*, Bridie, to find out what had become of Nick. Then, when I found out you'd lied, I asked myself why. Why didn't you simply tell me the truth, that Nick had started a decorating business, that he had gone bankrupt? It didn't make sense that you had tried so hard to cover his tracks. Why did you, Bridie? Do you hate me so much?"

"Hate you? Why should I hate you? You overestimate yourself if that's what you think. Let me put it this way, I knew when Nick first brought you here that you were not my kind of person. You seemed so weak, so soft, such a starry-eyed little ninny! Not at all the kind of girl my son should have married. He needed someone strong and reliable to lean on." She laughed bitterly. "Not a silly young girl who thought the sun shone out of him."

"Perhaps you were right in that respect." Catherine rose to her feet. "But that still doesn't explain why you lied to me. I want the truth this time." Looking down at the older woman on the settee she asked "Why are

159

you so reluctant to talk to me? What are you trying to hide?"

Bridie flung her cigarette into the hearth. "Talk to you? Why should I?" she cried out, close to tears. "What more can I tell you? Why rake up a past best forgotten? Why can't you leave us in peace?"

"*Us?*"

Bridie stared up at her, aware that she had said too much.

"Us?" Catherine repeated. "You mean that you are not alone here? Who is with you?"

There came a well-remembered voice from the past.

"It seems that Cathy has found some spirit at last."

She turned to face the door. A gaunt figure stood there, a drab facsimile of the glamorous woman who had haunted her life.

"*Estelle!*"

The woman moved slowly into the room. There still remained a vestige of proud arrogance in her bearing, but the white skin had started to wrinkle, and the once burnished brown hair was streaked with grey, unattractively cut. The slender figure which she had so envied and Nick had so desired, was now too painfully thin, and the column of her throat, once so smooth and taut had become sinewy, like whipcord.

The cool dark eyes flicked over Catherine with that familiar expression of dislike.

For a moment she was conscious of the old feeling of inferiority, until she remembered the courage of Rose Jarvis, and knew that she had a friend in all this, someone completely on her side.

Watching, as Estelle walked slowly to the fireplace, she knew that to allow herself to be intimidated would mean the loss of her pride and self-respect, that all she had suffered and endured, her struggle for survival and sanity, would count for nothing, that the future would not be worth living.

How could these two women hurt her now? She looked at Estelle and thought how much she had changed, not just physically but in some other, less tangible ways. The

160

drooping, unhappy line of her mouth was all too apparent now without its armour of bright red lipstick, but there was something more besides.

Estelle was not as self-controlled as she appeared to be. Aware of the tension about her, Catherine scented fear. Estelle was afraid. Bridie was afraid. Why?

Attempting a nonchalance which sat oddly with her nervous tension, Estelle lit a cigarette and drew the smoke deeply into her lungs, and then she coughed, as Frank used to cough.

She looked tired and strained. Catherine imagined her waking up each morning to reach for the cigarettes which had become her consolation in life. A drug – an anodyne.

The silence was spinning out, becoming unendurable. A long time ago Catherine would have broken it nervously, saying something trite and stupid, giving Estelle the advantage. Now she stood watching and waiting, filled with a new and exhilarating sense of courage.

It was Bridie who broke the silence, irritably, nervously.

"Oh, for God's sake! It's no use, Stella. She knows something is wrong. I can't stand much more of this."

"Be quiet," Estelle snapped.

"It will come as a relief in some ways. A relief," Bridie whimpered. "I'm so tired. Sick of the strain. I tried to put her off, Stella, you know that I did. You heard me the last time she came here. You told me not to worry. 'She won't come back,' you said. But she has come back, and I don't understand why."

"I told you why," Catherine said quietly. "All I want is to talk to Nick, to ask him questions that only he can answer."

Estelle laughed bitterly. "Why he married you, you mean? I can answer that. He married you to get at me, because he could fool you into thinking he loved you."

She sat down in one of the shabby chairs near the fire and crossed her legs, revealing the tears in her stockings. "You haven't changed much after all. You were blinkered then, and you still are. I can tell you this much, Nick never loved you, he merely used you to get under my skin.

"I knew what he was up to, of course I did. He used you as a lever, a weapon, to get back at me because of Frank. But I never dreamt he'd go as far as marrying you."

Catherine noticed the trembling of Estelle's hands, the nervous flicking of cigarette ash into the hearth.

"I don't think he really intended going that far himself. The night he announced that you were going to be married – well, you were just as surprised as the rest of us, weren't you? I knew he'd made the announcement to gauge my reaction – to punish me because I had refused to sleep with him." She smiled cruelly. "Because, you see, he still wanted me."

"*Still* wanted you? I don't understand."

"How could you? I don't imagine Nick told you that we had known each other long before the war, that I had had a child by him. If you don't believe me, ask Bridie.

"It was all a dark and deadly secret, of course. In those unenlightened days, nicely brought up girls, especially in my family, were not expected to produce illegitimate offspring. If they did, they were whisked away, as I was, to a quiet place in the country – the offending infant quietly adopted."

Inhaling deeply, she continued, "Bridie told you there were reasons why Nick never made it to university. Or did she? I daresay she didn't tell you that Nick was expelled from his grammar school because of the scandal?"

"I did try to warn you," Bridie broke in piteously. "Do you remember? That time you came here with Nick, engaged to be married, I warned you, at least I tried to, not to take too much for granted."

"You knew about Estelle all along?"

"Of course I did. And I was fond of her. If I'd had my way, that child would never have been adopted by strangers. My grandson!"

Sick at heart, Catherine asked, "Did Frank know?"

The log broke in two, sending up a shower of sparks.

Estelle continued, "No, Frank never knew. I never intended that he should. Meeting Nick again during

162

the war was a coincidence pure and simple. The old attraction was still there. I knew that Nick still wanted me physically, as much as I wanted him."

She laughed bitterly. "Can you imagine? Nick even tried a little blackmail. Said he'd tell Frank about the child, if I refused to sleep with him."

"Then why didn't he?"

Estelle shrugged. "Nick was fond of Frank, and Frank thought the world of Nick. Besides, it amused Nick to play games with other people's lives. And that's what it amounted to all along – a bloody silly game played against a wartime background."

She threw her cigarette end into the hearth, where it lay smouldering.

"I wouldn't sleep with Frank most of the time. I made all kinds of excuses not to have sex with him – tiredness, not wanting to start a baby during wartime. The fact is, I couldn't bear him to touch me. He was weak and foolish, but he'd been decent to me.

"Of course I wanted Nick, what woman in her right senses wouldn't have wanted him? But I wished to punish him a little for what he had put me through in the past; leaving me alone to face the birth of his child, with never a word from him, not even a letter, a card, or a bunch of flowers . . .

"And then you came on the scene." She glanced contemptuously at Catherine. "You with your innocent little girl face, your shining eyes and hair, thinking the sun shone out of him.

"Ha! Well, Nick had it all figured out. He knew how to turn the knife in the wound, right enough. 'Think of me making love to my child-bride tonight,' he would say, and laugh when I called him a cruel, unfeeling bastard!"

Tears stung Catherine's eyelids. Would there never come an end to the saga of Nicholas Willard? All the suffering and humiliation he had caused herself and others?

"You shouldn't have told Cathy all those things," Bridie said hoarsely, close to tears. "Why did you, Stella? What was the point?"

Staring into the past, Bridie continued, "I used to think that Nick and I were alike, but I was wrong. He was ruthless, I was just selfish and careless.

"When you came here all those years ago, Cathy, I was so much in love with Jimmy that I didn't give a damn for anyone else, especially not you. If you were about to be hurt, so be it! It was Jimmy I cared about – the only person in the world that I have ever really loved."

Suddenly Bridie began to cry, a terrible abandoned weeping that was somehow shocking.

Estelle got up quickly from her chair to sit beside her. "Stop it, Bridie," she said harshly. "Crying can't change a thing! The past is over and done with!"

But Bridie was not listening. "Why did Jimmy have to die?" she murmured brokenly. "If only he hadn't come indoors when he did! Oh, God, Stella, why did it have to happen? I can't get it out of my mind!"

"Come upstairs and lie down, " Estelle said, "I'll give you something to make you sleep."

"I'm so cold," Bridie complained.

"It's snowing again, that's why," Estelle said, leading Bridie from the room.

Catherine watched, filled with a strange foreboding, as if something terrible was about to happen.

She shuddered. Glancing out of the window she saw that the view of the village green had been blotted out by the thickly falling snow. The chill of the room struck at the core of her. Soon daylight would be swallowed up by the encroaching darkness of a winter afternoon. Then night would fall over the clustered houses of Cloud Merridon, and the wind would whisper down the lamplit streets, like ghostly voices from the past.

And yet it seemed to her that the past was here now, in this very room. She looked about her nervously, imagining that someone, some unknown presence, was lurking in the shadows.

She recalled Bridie's words: "Why did Jimmy have to die? If only he hadn't come indoors when he did . . . I can't get it out of my mind."

So why had Jimmy died, and how?

164

Noticing a few pieces of wood in the log basket, she threw them recklessly on the dying fire, and switched on a table-lamp, then she crossed to the kitchen and began collecting and stacking dirty plates, cups and saucers; creating order from chaos, scraping bits of bacon-rind into the rubbish bin. Squeezing suds into the sink, she began washing-up, and switched on the electric kettle for some tea, forgetful of the fact that she was a guest of sorts in someone else's house.

There was obviously a shortage of money, worse still, a lack of interest or concern in keeping the place clean, as if the whole house had become affected by the lethargy of its occupants, as if past events had cast a shadow over the cottage, and no laughter or joy existed there any more.

Washing and rinsing the plates, cups and saucers, Catherine thought about her mother – Annie's implicit belief in housework as an antidote to despair.

Mother, Catherine thought, whom she had never really valued since the shadow of Nicholas had fallen between them, towards whom she had often been impatient or coolly dismissive because Annie had dared to speak her mind about the state of her marriage – "Tell the truth and shame the Devil," as she had once said during a particularly heated confrontation between the pair of them.

But things would be different from now on, Catherine decided, between herself and her down-to-earth mother. Returning home when all this – her apparently futile quest to make sense of the past – was over, she would tell her mother how much she loved her, how much she had always loved her.

Estelle's voice cut across her reverie.

"Oh, you're playing the role of a char-lady now, I see," she said caustically. "Come to 'muck us out', have you? In more ways than one!"

"Not at all. I just needed to do something positive. The kettle has boiled, by the way. I thought that Bridie would appreciate a cup of tea. I know I would. She seemed so – upset."

"How kind of you to feel concerned about her," Estelle said mockingly, "since you are the cause of her upset."

Refusing to be intimidated, "But that's not strictly true, is it?" Catherine said coolly, facing Estelle. "Talking about Jimmy upset her. How could I have had anything to do with that? I didn't even know that he was dead!"

"I'll make some coffee." Estelle measured powder into the cups Catherine had just dried. "I hate tea. Coffee and cigarettes are my staple diet. No use taking Bridie any, she'll be no use to herself or anyone else until this crying spell's over. She'll calm down in a while, she usually does."

She walked through to the drawing room, cup in hand, not bothering about a saucer. "Huh," she snapped, seeing the fire, "you've used up all the wood, now I'll have to fill the damned basket again."

Ignoring the remark, Catherine asked, "How did Jimmy die?"

Estelle hesitated momentarily, then replied, "If you must know, he fell downstairs and broke his neck." Her voice was tired, flat, unemotional.

Deeply shocked, Catherine said, "How did it happen?"

"He fell because Nick hit him. It doesn't take a very hard blow to knock a lame man off-balance."

"You're telling me that Nick – killed Jimmy?"

"As surely as if he'd stuck a knife in him." Estelle drew a packet of cigarettes from her skirt pocket, lit one, and gulped in the smoke.

"But why? Surely it must have been an accident? Nick couldn't have meant to kill him? He and Jimmy were friends."

"Not any longer, they'd quarrelled about . . . It happened because of the money Nick had stolen – or 'borrowed' as he put it – from Perry, and Wynne.

"Nick came home to sponge on Bridie, despite her having promised to pay back every ha'penny. She'd already put up her important items of furniture, china and pictures, for auction. To make matters worse, Nick's father had died, putting an end to her allowance, and he hadn't left her a penny piece in his will.

"Jimmy was angry. He came into the kitchen one day to hear Nick badgering Bridie for more money, and he lost his temper completely; told Nick to get out and leave her alone."

Estelle was speaking in a flat monotone devoid of anger or sarcasm. "Nick laughed at him, 'You're telling me to get out of my own home?' he said. 'Why don't you get out? Who the hell do you think you are to tell me what to do? I'm Bridie's son – what are you? Just a lame dog she happens to fancy in bed.'

"The 'lame dog' jibe must have hurt Jimmy pretty deeply. He'd been damn near killed in the Battle of Britain. Nick turned to go upstairs. Jimmy went after him, God knows why. Perhaps he wanted to make Nick apologize. Who knows why? Nick turned on the landing. I can't remember what he said exactly, but it concerned Jimmy's relationship with Bridie.

"Jimmy lost control. Dropping his walking stick, he hit out at Nick. Nick hit back, and Jimmy fell. Bridie screamed and ran to him, but there was nothing to be done. Jimmy was dead. Nick was still on the landing, looking down at us.

"I'll never forget it for as long as I live. It all happened so suddenly." Estelle's face looked as if it had been carved out of ivory. "I had scarcely got over losing the baby I was carrying when Nick and I left Lessing. We'd had a terrible time there. Little or no money coming in, so many bills to be paid. We were up to our ears in debt. Little wonder I miscarried, I was living on a knife's edge all the time, as sick as a dog, not knowing where the next meal was coming from."

"I really am sorry," Catherine said compassionately, her dislike of Estelle melting away like snow.

Not that she appeared to have heard as she went on, deep in thought, "Do you wonder that Bridie and I enjoy a reputation for being 'strange' in these parts? I believe the villagers think we're witches – or worse – a couple of freaks. Two unhappy women clinging together for support, careless of our appearance." She laughed bitterly. "But why bother? Why care about anything? There's really no point, is there?"

167

Catherine said slowly, "Was there an inquest on Jimmy?"

"Oh, that!" Estelle lit a fresh cigarette. "A verdict of accidental death was recorded."

"Then Nick wasn't blamed?"

"Oh no, Nick wasn't blamed. Because we shielded him, Bridie and I. We swore, on oath, that Jimmy had tripped and fallen over his walking stick. There was no suggestion of foul play. Jimmy was known to be crippled, and he'd become much worse in recent years. Nick and he were known to be friends of long standing, with an RAF background."

As shadows stole deeper into the room, Estelle's face was thrown into sharp relief by the firelight. A sense of numbness, born of shock, had invaded Catherine's mind. In a low voice she asked the vital, all important question. "And Nick? What became of him? Where is he now?"

A long pause, then Estelle said bleakly, "Nick is here in Cloud Merridon, in the cemetery on the hill. He died last February. Well, now you have it. End of story!"

She rose stiffly to her feet, brushing the cigarette ash from her skirt. "And now, it's time for you to leave. You've far outstayed your welcome. You've achieved your objective in coming here. Raked up the past. I hope you're satisfied."

"*Satisfied*?" Close to tears, yet standing her ground, facing Estelle she asked, "You really think that I intend leaving here without knowing how Nick died? He was comparatively young, not even forty, for God's sake, full of life! So what happened to end his life? I warn you, Estelle, I shall not leave this house until I know the whole truth!"

The door opened at that moment and Bridie came into the room.

"Sit down, Cathy," she said dully. "You have asked for the truth, now you shall have it in full measure.

"When Nick died, the coroner recorded a verdict of Death by Misadventure. I was so grateful for that. It was, you see, the verdict I had prayed for. Nick would

168

have hated a verdict of Suicide whilst of unsound mind, or words to that effect."

"For God's sake, Bridie, think what you're doing!" Estelle exclaimed.

"I have thought, Estelle, and my mind's made up. I've come to the end of my tether. I'm going to tell Cathy everything that happened."

Chapter Fifteen

"Jimmy's death marked the beginning of the end for all of us," Bridie said, staring into the fire. "Nick bitterly regretted the quarrel, and lashing out at Jimmy the way he did. Had I believed otherwise, I would not have shielded him.

"After the inquest and the funeral, Nick went away. We didn't know where to at first. He didn't write. I nearly went out of my mind with worry, waiting for news of him; letters which never came.

"Meanwhile, I had repaid his debt to Perry and Wynne. My possessions had sold well at auction, even better than I had expected. There was some money left over, enough to get by on."

Bridie's mouth twisted into a half smile of pain and regret, her eyes misted with tears. "I would have given everything I had, and more, for news of my son.

"A year went by. One day, Nick returned as abruptly as he had left. All he would say, was that he had been in London. No mention of what he had been doing there. My guess is that he'd been living rough with tramps and down and outs, his appearance, the state he was in, convinced me of that.

"He was gaunt, unshaven. All he had were the clothes he was wearing. He was a changed man whom I scarcely recognized as my son. Gone was that devil-may-care charm of his. He was silent, morose.

"All he craved was whisky. He would sit for hours on end in that chair you are sitting in now, drinking and staring into the fire. He seldom spoke or ate. I doubt if he even slept."

Bridie's mouth worked piteously. "It couldn't have

170

gone on like that for much longer. I knew that, so did Stella. We tried to talk him into seeing a doctor. He wouldn't even listen. Then, one day we found him in a state of collapse, deeply unconscious. Stella rang for the doctor who diagnosed liver damage due to alcoholism, combined with acute malnutrition, and advised his immediate removal to the intensive care unit of the local hospital."

Bridie paused. Estelle gave her a cigarette and a light. The room was now completely dark apart from the halo of light near the hearth. Catherine shivered. Cold air was blowing into the room as if a door somewhere in the house had opened suddenly for no apparent reason.

"For weeks," Bridie continued, "Nick was desperately ill, so ill that we thought he wouldn't make it. And then, thank God, he began to show signs of improvement. My heart rejoiced when the specialist told me that my son was fit enough to come home. Of course there were certain conditions pertaining to his homecoming. On no account must he be allowed alcohol, and his diet must include plenty of nourishing food – fish, eggs, cheese, fresh fruit and lightly-cooked vegetables – what he termed fittening not fattening food.

"At first he was fine, his old self once more, and then . . ." Bridie's lips trembled, her voice faded.

Estelle's voice cut into the silence. "Leave it now, Bridie," she said harshly. "You've said often enough that no good can come of reaping up the past. Why put yourself through the torture all over again?"

Bridie said quietly, with dignity, "Because I must. Because I'm tired of lies, tired of subterfuge, because I no longer care what happens to me. All I care about is the truth."

"This is all Cathy's fault!" Estelle exclaimed bitterly. "What right had she to come here in the first place to dig and delve into our private lives?"

"Because she bears the name Willard," Bridie said softly. "Because, whether we like it or not, we are all bound together by a single common denominator – my son, Nicholas Willard. God rest him."

171

She continued, "As I said, he was fine, his old self once more when he came back to us, and then suddenly he was gone again, without a word. A case of history repeating itself.

"After a while, he wrote to me asking for money, giving the address of a house in Reading, begging me to come to him as quickly as possible. How could I refuse such a request?"

Tears rained down Bridie's cheeks. Struggling for composure, she went on, "I went to the address he'd given me – a cheap lodging house in a seedy area of the town. Entering his room, I found him sitting in a chair. He was cold, shivering, crying out for the drink he needed to make his life bearable.

"All he kept saying, over and over again was, 'For the love of God, Bridie, get me some whisky!'"

In a voice harsh with emotion, she said, "And so I went out in search of an off-licence and bought a bottle of whisky. Beside myself with grief, I could not equate the man I'd found in that filthy bedsit with my handsome, charming son Nicholas.

"The man I'd seen was a human wreck, unshaven and dirty, with the eyes of a wild animal at bay. Was it my fault? I wondered. Or was it the fault of the war? The excitement, the danger of the wartime years; the possibility of there being no tomorrow?"

She bowed her head. Her voice, when she continued, was little more than a whisper. "When I returned with the whisky, I found Nick on the floor, unconscious. He had fallen out of his chair and crawled towards the fireplace to light the gas fire. He was so cold, you see . . . He had a box of matches in his hand, and he'd managed to turn on the tap. The room was filling with fumes.

"My first instinct was to turn off the tap, to call for help. But I didn't. I stood there looking down at him, thinking, 'What will happen to my son? If I turn off that tap, what will become of my son?'

"I knew what would happen. *I knew!* There would be other rooms like that one, more unspeakable agony for him to endure. Nothing left for him to live for – finally his

172

dying somewhere, alone perhaps, with no one knowing or caring who he was or where he had come from. I couldn't bear it! I just couldn't bear it!"

Raising her head, Catherine caught a glimpse of the youthful, indomitable Bridie behind the mask of her age, and her heart went out to her.

"If one owned an animal which one loved, and saw that animal in torment," Bridie said, "would one hesitate for a moment to put it out of its misery? How could I have done less for my son?

"Perhaps I was mad, I don't know. I left Nick in that gas-filled room. I even put more money in the meter to make sure. It seemed the only way out, the only answer for him.

"I remember thinking, he won't feel any more pain. He'll be at peace from now on. No more unhappiness for my beloved son."

Bending forward like a broken doll, racked with the pain of remembrance, she cried aloud, "My son, my son! Oh, dear God, help me! I killed my son, my beloved son!"

There followed a terrible silence, then gradually there returned the small sounds of normal everyday life, the crackle of the fire, the ticking of the clock, and, because this was winter, the keening of the wind, the creak of timbers, the rattling of door and windows.

Estelle said defiantly, "Well, what are you going to do?"

Catherine looked at her. "Do? I don't understand. What is there to be done? Nick is dead. You can't bring the dead back to life. Nobody can do that."

"No, but you could make things unpleasant. More difficult than they already are for Bridie and me."

"In what way?"

"Oh don't be so naïve," Estelle snapped. "You know damn well. You could go to the Police, stir things up, tell them that Nick's death was not accidental. If you brought them here now, Bridie would not have the strength to deny anything."

Getting up, she began nervously pacing the room. Nicotined fingers fumbled for the cigarettes in her pocket. Pausing to light one, she swore when the lighter refused to work, and made a spill which she ignited in the fire.

Watching her, Catherine thought back to the times when her attractiveness had made her painfully aware of her own inadequacies, then she looked at Bridie whose tear-stained face reflected the agony she had suffered, was still suffering.

Catherine said, "You needn't worry, what you have told me will go no further. You have suffered enough, we all have."

Memories flooded back of the Nick she had fallen in love with, vibrant, handsome, charming. Loving him as much as she had, filled with a yearning to see him again, to draw a gentle dividing line between the past and the future, she had come up against a reality too terrible to contemplate. There was nothing more to be done or said. Her mission had ended in failure.

Now there could never be the quiet interlude she had hoped for, the chance to tell him that she had gone ahead with the divorce still loving him. Malice had never entered into it, or a desire for revenge. She had wanted him to know that. Nor would she ever know if their marriage had meant anything at all to him. Somehow she had never believed him capable of that depth of cruelty towards her.

Sick at heart, she heard the clock strike eight. "I must go now," she said dully, thinking of her friendly landlady at the Station Hotel in Lower Minter, knowing the woman would be worried about her if she didn't soon put in an appearance. "May I ring for a taxi?"

"We're not on the phone," Estelle said coldly.

"Then I'll catch a bus," Catherine replied, desperate to get away from the cottage.

"I think not," Bridie said, getting up from her chair. "It has been snowing for several hours. In any case, the last bus leaves Cloud Merridon at seven-thirty in winter. You'll have to stay the night, I'm afraid. We'll do our best to make you comfortable." `

"But there's a hotel in the village," Catherine reminded her. "The Merridon Arms. I know, I've been there before. The first time I came here, remember? Jimmy and Nick took me there for—" She stopped speaking abruptly. "I'm sorry, I . . ."

Estelle regarded her mockingly. "The Merridon Arms is closed for the winter, but there's a phone-box near the village green, if you want to ring for a taxi. I'll fetch your coat."

"Don't be a fool, Stella," Bridie said sharply, "you know as well as I do that no driver in his right mind would risk his vehicle on a night like this. No, Cathy can have Nick's room. There's an electric blanket in the bed, and plenty of spare bedding in the airing cupboard. Please, Stella, go up and see to the room. Meanwhile, I'll make some coffee and sandwiches."

Estelle laughed unpleasantly. "Cathy appears not to welcome the thought of spending a night beneath our roof. Perhaps she thinks she'll be murdered in her bed!"

When Estelle had gone, Bridie moved slowly through to the kitchen, shivering, pulling her cardigan together, with Catherine beside her. "You must make allowances for Estelle," she said quietly, "she has suffered a great deal, and she is bitter. Very bitter. Do you wonder?

"I did warn you, didn't I, that it would be best to leave the past alone? You should have done as I asked. You are still young. You have your life before you, not like me. My life is over. It ended when I allowed my son to die in that gas-filled room. The mistake I made was in leaving that room. I should have stayed there with him to the bitter end. Oh God, how I wish that I had. Cathy, my dear, can you ever forgive me?"

Holding Bridie in her arms, filled with compassion, "Who am I to condemn what you did?" Catherine murmured. "I'm just someone Nick met a long time ago, who meant less than nothing to him, I know that now. I suppose I knew it all along, I just couldn't bring myself to believe it."

"Well, what a touching scene!"

Estelle came into the kitchen. "Wife Number One in

175

mother-in-law's arms, or vice versa. Wife Number Two acting the role of chambermaid, and not a sign of coffee or sandwiches! Oh, what the hell? Leave everything to me, as usual! Go back to the fire, Bridie, I'll make the sandwiches. Cheese and pickle all right with you, Cathy? Or would you prefer smoked salmon or caviare?"

"I'm not hungry! I'll go up to bed, if you don't mind."

"Want me to show you the way? Or can you remember?" Estelle called after her, as she hurried upstairs. "Or does a silly question deserve a silly answer?"

She knew what Estelle was driving at, that she and Nick had slept together before they were married, in his room at the head of the stairs. But she was wrong. She had never crossed the threshold of Nick's room until now.

Inside the room, she felt for the key and turned it. The sense of relief at being alone was overwhelming. Standing with her back to the door, she gave way to tears of despair that Nick was dead.

Standing alone in his room, she heard the wind sighing round the casements. She was sick of winter, when the world and life and time seemed frozen, when the sun is farthest from the equator and the few hours of daylight are bounded by darkness. The time of the Winter Solstice.

There was a single bed, a small table beside it with a lamp which Estelle had left burning when she came to switch on the electric blanket. Too tired to care whether or not the bed had been kept aired, she undressed to her underclothes and lay down, leaving the light on, praying for morning to come; as she prayed for sleep, the blotting out of thoughts too painful to bear – Nick lying alone in a lethal chamber; unconsciousness deepening to a dark and everlasting slumber.

Turning on her side, she pressed her face to the pillow and wept for him, the waste of a life, precious to her, ending in failure and despair.

She fell eventually into an uneasy sleep, awoke in the early hours of the morning shivering with cold. Estelle had not troubled to provide the extra blankets Bridie had mentioned.

Getting out of bed, she put on her jumper, then opened the wardrobe to find something more to put round her. Anything would do.

The first thing she saw was Nick's dressing gown, a shabby woollen robe, green plaid with a tasselled cord and frayed cuffs. Putting it on, fastening the cord, she experienced a strange sensation of comfort, as if Nick was standing close to her, his arms about her, his dark hair falling onto his forehead – the way it had done that first Christmas he had come home to her after the war, and she had looked down at his sleeping face, knowing how much she loved him. But never at any time had he looked deep into her eyes and said simply and truthfully, "I love you, Cathy." The words she had longed to hear. But it was too late now.

The letter she discovered in the dressing gown pocket was addressed to Bridie in Nick's strong, sloping handwriting. The envelope was unsealed, otherwise she would not have taken out the letter and read it. The pages were carelessly folded, as if he had written the letter in a hurry, pushed it into the envelope, and forgotten about it. Or perhaps he had decided not to leave it for Bridie to read after all?

Sitting on the bed, holding the pages in trembling fingers, she saw that the letter was undated. She read:

'Dear Bridie,
I am going away again! Blunt and to the point as usual, except I haven't the guts to tell you to your face that I'm leaving. I've turned coward. But you must have known that when I let you and Estelle cover up for me over Jimmy.

It didn't seem to matter much at the time. I took for granted that you would protect me; save my miserable skin. But I couldn't get Jimmy out of my mind, the fact that he would still be alive if I hadn't lost my temper the way I did. Blame the old enemy! I had been drinking pretty heavily that day.

Poor old Jimmy bore the brunt of my aggression. I really did like him, you know, more than I can say. But you knew that, didn't you, and forgave me? But I have never forgiven myself, nor ever shall.

In London, I hit the bottle harder than ever in a fruitless attempt to blot out the past. I lived among drunks and layabouts, spent my nights in Salvation Army hostels, my days on park benches. You name it, I did it! All I craved was drink, the blotting out of memories too painful to recall.

I was all right during the war – at least I thought I was. Everything laid on for me. Wine, women and song – a smart uniform. Life was exciting, death something we joked about in the Officers' Mess. Now the thought of living appals me, and death seems the easier option.

Forgive me, Bridie. The fact is, I can't stay here any longer. You mustn't blame yourself, it's Estelle I can't stand – the way she looks at me with that disdainful expression of hers. My own fault, I know, but I can't take that silent condemnation of hers any more. Unfair of me, perhaps, but then I've always been unfair, haven't I?

A long time ago, you told me in no uncertain terms that I was being grossly unfair to Cathy, and you were right. I couldn't see it at the time, because I didn't care tuppence about Cathy. She was just a silly, starry-eyed kid I'd decided to marry to spite Estelle.

Funny how things rebound, isn't it? What is that old biblical saying – 'The Mills of God grind slowly but they grind exceedingly small'?

Now I know that the woman I wanted so much was not the right one for me after all. I got what I deserved, God help me, an ice-princess, as brittle as glass.

The one I threw aside, little Cathy, is the one I remember now, and I can't help thinking that, if only I'd given her half a chance, how happy we might have been together.

That funny, star-struck kid I treated so badly had more warmth in her, more guts, more life, more real goodness, than Estelle ever had.

If ever we meet again, I'll tell Cathy how wrong I was, and how rotten; beg her forgiveness; tell her how much I loved her.

I love you too, Bridie. Now, goodbye, and – forgive me.
Nick.'

Holding the letter in her hands, slowly the weight of misery in Catherine's heart began to lift.

Miraculously, the still small voice, the riding light of faith nurtured deep inside her, had not been extinguished; had led her, mysteriously, to this place, this precise moment in time, to the truth, like a pot of gold at the end of the rainbow, awaiting its discovery.

Chapter Sixteen

In time to come, Catherine would recall her stay at the cottage as a dream bordering on a nightmare; an old black and white movie, crackly and out of focus, in which none of the characters or events seemed real.

She had come downstairs from her room to find Estelle in the kitchen, smoking a cigarette and heating a panful of coffee.

"Want some?" she'd asked offhandedly.

"No, thanks."

"Please yourself. I'm going back to bed to drink it." Pouring the coffee into a mug, Estelle shuffled upstairs in her down-at-heel slippers.

Snow or no snow, even in blizzard conditions, Catherine thought desperately, she must get away from the cottage. If the buses weren't running, she would make her way to the phone-box and ring for a taxi.

Opening the front door, she saw that last night's downfall had drifted against the garden gate, which meant she would have to dig her way out. So be it. If necessary, if she couldn't find a spade, she would use the fire shovel.

Then she remembered the loggia where she had noticed a few rusted gardening tools propped up in a cobwebby corner alongside a stack of seedboxes and empty plantpots. Hurrying through the kitchen into the loggia, she found what she sought – a spade, rusty but serviceable.

Putting on her coat and gloves, she set about clearing the snow from the garden path. Panting with exertion, she looked up to see Estelle leaning against the door, watching her, a mocking expression on her face.

"You seem as eager to leave as you were to come," she said caustically. "So what if the buses are still not running?"

"In that case, I'll walk!"

"My, aren't you the energetic one?" Estelle laughed mirthlessly.

"I'm afraid I can't say the same for you." Straightening up, Catherine said, "Or perhaps you enjoy living in squalor, making messes that you can't be bothered to clear up after you? Being too damned idle to fill the log basket! Is it too much to ask that Bridie should come down to a fire in the hearth, a decent cup of coffee, or are you too far gone, too sunk in lethargy to care about anyone except yourself?"

"How dare you speak to me that way? Just who the hell do you think you are?" Estelle's eyes flashed anger. "Do you imagine I give a damn what you think, you stupid ninny! Coming here with your airs and graces, stirring up trouble . . ."

Facing her old enemy, knowing that she had lost the power to hurt her ever again, Catherine said calmly, "Methinks the lady doth protest too much! You know, Estelle, you were quite something in the old days. I hadn't a weapon to use against you, all I could do was stand by and watch as you took away from me everything I had: my marriage, my husband, my happiness. A hollow victory, I'd say. But I still have the one thing that you couldn't take away from me – my self-respect! Now, are you going to fill that log basket, or shall I?"

When Bridie came downstairs, she had been pathetically pleased to see a clean hearth and a blazing fire.

"Are you responsible for this, Cathy?" she asked when Catherine came in with a freshly-made cup of coffee, and toast on a tray.

"No, Estelle brought in the wood and lit the fire," Catherine said, clearing a space on the table beside Bridie's chair.

"Really? You do surprise me. How come?"

"Her conscience got the better of her, I imagine," Catherine said, tongue-in-cheek.

"Conscience? Estelle has no conscience," Bridie remarked wryly. "Where is she, by the way?"

"Oh, she's gone to the village shop for cigarettes."

This was the moment Catherine had been waiting for. Alone with the older woman, she gave her Nick's letter. "I found this in Nick's dressing gown pocket," she said. "Forgive me, but I've read it, that was wrong of me since it was addressed to you. I just couldn't help it."

Putting on her glasses, Bridie read the letter. When she had finished reading she said, "This must mean a great deal to you, Cathy."

"Yes, it does."

"In that case, you must keep it, my dear. It is more yours than mine." Bridie's eyes clouded with tears. "I'm just so happy to know that my son bothered to write to me before he went away the last time. What really matters is that he was still capable of compassion towards those he loved, wanting to make amends for his past sins of omission – particularly so far as you were concerned. But first, I think that Estelle should read it, don't you?"

Catherine shook her head. "No, that's the last thing I want. Let her keep her illusions, such as they are."

Bridie said quietly, "I said that you weren't my kind of person, but I was wrong. It must have taken a great deal of courage to do what you have done. You must have loved my son very much to have followed the trail to the bitter end. And now what will you do?"

"The only thing I can do – go home, get on with my work, try to come to terms with all that has happened. But what about you, Bridie? You and Estelle?"

Bridie smiled wistfully. "No need to worry your head about that. We have come a long way together, Stella and I. We need one another – for obvious reasons. Stella stands in need of my protection, a roof over her head. I stand in need of her discretion, her silence. So there you have it – the strong thread that binds us together – to do with greed, guilt – and fear."

182

"I must be going now," Catherine said. "Goodbye, Bridie. Thank you for the letter, and God bless you."

Impulsively, she gathered Nick's mother into her arms, and kissed her, and knew that she loved her, had always loved her.

Standing beside her at the door, "Goodbye, Cathy," Bridie said softly. "Take my advice, forget about the past. You are still young, still lovely. You have the rest of your life ahead of you. Live it to the full, as I have mine.

"One of these days you'll fall in love again. Oh, I know it won't be the same. That first fine careless rapture of one's first love affair can't happen twice in a lifetime, but it will be every bit as good, even better."

"Well, if you think so – but how will I know?"

"Without the benefit of starlight kisses and all those nostalgic wartime tunes played on old gramophone records, you mean?" Bridie chuckled deeply. "Don't worry, my dear, when love comes your way again, you'll *know*!"

It was late that afternoon when Catherine arrived back at Rose's house near Reading.

First she had caught a bus from Cloud Merridon to Lower Minter where she had picked up her overnight case from the Station Hotel.

The landlady had been vastly relieved to see her in one piece. "I wondered where on earth you'd got to last night," she said concernedly. "My hubby told me not to worry, that you'd be staying the night with those friends of yours, but I had visions of you stuck in a snowdrift. I very nearly called the Police!"

"How very kind of you, but I'm glad you didn't." Catherine laughed.

"Now where are you off to?" the landlady asked when the bill had been settled.

"First I'm going to Reading," Catherine told her, "to stay the night with a friend of mine. Then I'm going home to Scarborough."

"My word," said the landlady, "you do get around, don't you?"

*   *   *

183

Rose said briskly, "Come in and sit by the fire. You look half frozen! I'll just nip through to the kitchen and make some tea. What you need, my girl, is a good strong cuppa, a hot bath and an early night, in that order. I'll bring your supper to bed later!"

Her briskness covered her concern at her friend's appearance, her air of weariness and dejection, the shadows beneath her eyes – as though her mascara had run – except that she wasn't wearing mascara, or powder, or lipstick.

"My dear, what is it? What's wrong?" Forgetting about the tea, Rose knelt at Catherine's feet, within the warm circle of firelight and the glow from a red-shaded lamp near her chair.

Burying her face in her hands. "Oh, Rose," Catherine sobbed, "Nick's dead! I'll never see him again! Never be able to tell him how much I loved him! And I really did love him! He meant all the world to me, and now he's gone!"

Rose, in her wisdom, realized there was nothing she could say to stem the tide of grief. She had been through it herself and knew full well that what really mattered in the depths of distress, was a hand to cling to, a shoulder to cry on.

And so she knelt beside Catherine and held her close in her arms until her grief was spent. And then, quietly, holding her hand, she led her upstairs to her room, helped her to undress, and put her to bed, tucking her in as a mother would tuck in a child, knowing that she would sleep now, until morning, worn out by her weeping.

Night long, Rose kept vigil in her room across the landing, her ears strained to catch the slightest sound of movement from her friend's room. None came.

At five o'clock in the morning, shrugging on her warm woollen dressing gown, she went down to the kitchen to make herself a cup of tea.

The kettle had just boiled when Catherine entered the room. "I'm hungry," she said.

Rose smiled. "Come to think of it, so am I. How about a bacon butty?"

184

Her heart rejoiced, knowing that Catherine had weathered the worst of the storm, that any tears she might shed in the future could never be as soul-shattering as those she had already shed.

Sitting at the kitchen table, Catherine said, "It's time I went home."

"Today, you mean?"

"Yes. Today."

Rose smiled. "Well, you know best. I'll miss you, Catherine."

"Not half as much as I'll miss you."

"But we'll keep in touch? You'll write me long letters telling me all about – what's his name? Adam."

"Adam? Oh yes, of course, Adam . . ."

And now it was almost train time.

Rose had driven Catherine to Reading Station in her ancient car, which had just passed its recent MOT test after a few major repairs to the back axle and the exhaust system.

Standing together on the platform, they said all the meaningless things that people are wont to say at the point of departure, one from the other, when all the meaningful things they really want to say are bottled up inside them.

At the last moment, they simply clung together wordlessly, apart from their whispered goodbyes; two women whose friendship had blossomed as unexpectedly as a Peace rose in winter, and which, both knew, would continue to flourish till the end of time.

The train was due in York at 11.55 am. Thinking about Adam, Catherine decided to break her journey for an hour or two. She had neglected him shamefully, and she must tell him so. How humiliated he must have felt returning home alone, being handed a *fait accompli* the morning she had gone to his room ready for departure. A bitter pill for any man to swallow, especially a man she cared for and had promised to marry.

She had always liked York for its sense of history,

185

ancient houses and narrow streets, romantic city walls and toll-bars, the brooding Minster with its glorious stained glass windows.

Blossom Street brought back memories of a hot summer day during the war, when she had gone there to undergo her Wren medical examination. Looking out from the back seat of a taxi, she saw, in her mind's eye, a plump fair-haired girl of eighteen – the Cathy Mitchell she used to be – nervously approaching the building in which the examinations had taken place.

Now here was the mature Catherine Willard paying the taxi-driver and entering the gleaming car showrooms of Fuller and Jesson. No wonder Adam was proud of the business he and his partner Barry Fuller had built up together from scratch – it was certainly imposing with its plethora of immaculately polished cars for sale, and the troughs of greenery near the glassed-in office to the rear of the showroom, from which a man emerged, smiling pleasantly.

"May I help you?" he asked. "Or are you just browsing?"

"I'm looking for Mr Jesson, as a matter of fact. Is it possible to have a word with him?"

"I'm sorry, you've missed him. He's gone to lunch. I'm his partner, Barry Fuller. May I give him a message?"

"Oh, did he say where he was lunching? It is rather important."

"He mentioned the Royal Station Hotel," Fuller said somewhat uneasily, "but he's with someone. A client, I believe."

"I see. Thank you." Catherine smiled. "Our paths must have crossed. I've just come from the station. My fault, I should have contacted him earlier. Never mind, perhaps I'll pop into the hotel, see if I can find him there. All I want is a word."

"And if you miss him, may I tell him who called?"

"By all means. My name is Catherine Willard. You might tell him that I'm on my way home."

"Yes, of course, Mrs Willard." He swung open one of

186

the heavy glass doors for her. "Mind how you go, it's a bit slippery underfoot."

"Thank you, Mr Fuller. Goodbye."

It had been on the tip of her tongue to ask Fuller how Adam had seemed recently, if he was well and so on, but that would be ridiculous. She would find out for herself soon enough, besides which, she wanted to get back to the station as quickly as possible. With luck, she might catch the 1.15 pm train to Scarborough.

The Royal Station Hotel, adjacent to the railway station, could best be described as a 'pile' – in the context of a massive Victorian edifice erected to accommodate travellers in the early days of the steam-engine. It was, quite simply, enormous – something of an anachronism in the mid-Twentieth century – in which present day travellers, *sans* bustles and bonnets, rattled around like peas in a drum.

No one took the slightest notice of her as she entered the foyer. Encouraged by her seeming invisibility, she walked towards the dining room and looked into the room through the glass-panelled doors.

There, at a window table, almost directly opposite to where she was standing, was Adam, deep in conversation with an attractive, dark-haired woman wearing a lime-green jumper and a tweed skirt.

With an instinct older than time, Catherine realized that this was no business meeting. They were smiling into each other's eyes, touching hands across the table.

Turning away abruptly, she hurried away from the hotel to the station precincts, unable to equate what she had seen with Adam's diffident, somewhat shy personality. She would have staked her life on his faithfulness, his code of honour in view of their engagement.

She simply could not believe that Adam, of all men, was a womanizer. But apparently she was wrong – as she had been wrong about so many things in her life before.

And now she was going home, back to the place she

loved best on earth, the familiar streets of Scarborough, the sound of the sea on the shore, the safe haven of her flat, her refuge from the storms of life.

As the train jogged on amid familiar scenery, past Kirkham Abbey where the River Ouse ran gently between its meandering, tree-clothed banks, she thought of Rose Jarvis whose happiness and strength had derived from a rock-solid marriage to a man who had been there for her unreservedly during his lifetime, so that neither of them had needed to ask the all important question: 'Do you still love me?'

Would she ever know that kind of love? Catherine wondered, so right and true and valid that no questions need ever be asked or answered.

Deep in her heart she knew that what Bridie had said was true. Only once in a lifetime came the thrill of a first ever love affair, with all the trimmings of starlight and nostalgic music played on a wartime gramophone record.

Now, much older and wiser, she also knew that friendship, no matter how meaningful it might seem, could not be dressed up to look like love. Far better to walk through life alone than to settle for second best.

Possibly, she thought wryly, Adam had come to that same conclusion?

So what did the future hold for her? Realistically, work and more work, the rebuilding of bridges between herself and her mother, a coming to terms with the past, a gentle folding away of all save the happy memories she had of Nick.

The letter Bridie had given her was tucked away in a secret pocket of her handbag – as a talisman, a gentle reminder that their marriage had held some meaning for him also, despite its ending.

Suddenly, mysteriously, she experienced a feeling of completeness, as if the first chapters of her life had been encapsulated within the pages of a book, now closed, which she would pick up and read again, from time to time, without heartache or regret.

188

Time? Why worry? She had all the time in the world . . .

And now her journey was nearing its end.

Gathering together her belongings, she stood near a corridor window watching the lights of home springing up against the dusk of a winter twilight. Lights blurred by the tears in her eyes, as the train jogged slowly past the snow-clad slopes of Oliver's Mount and came to a halt near the ticket barrier, beyond which lay the station forecourt with its line of taxis for hire.

Soon, very soon now, she would close her own front door behind her, and savour the full meaning of homecoming: the peace and privacy of her own four walls, her own roof, her own windows, her own bed, with no one to tell her what she must or must not do within the confines of her own space, her own lifetime.

Entering her domain, leaning her back against the door, she saw that the centrepiece of gold and white chrysanthemums on the round dining table, and Adam's roses were dead. Only to be expected, but her tough little ivies had survived the drought.

When she had gathered herself together a little, she made a shopping list and went down to the grocers in Ramshill Road for a few necessities to keep body and soul together for the time being.

Returning home, she telephoned her mother. A matter of priority – although she had sent her a picture postcard of Oxford and a few words of explanation while on her way, with Rose Jarvis, to Oxford station, on the day they had met.

Waiting for Mrs Mitchell to answer, she would not be best pleased, Catherine thought, at being neglected, and she was right. "Hello, Mum. It's me, Cath," she said brightly.

"Oh, so you're back, are you? About time too! I've been worried sick about you, my lass, going off with that feller you told me about. A few days in London indeed! And then I got a bit of a postcard from Oxford. I don't know

189

what's been going on, but I can guess. All this time away from the shop, you'll be lucky if you have a business left when you show your face—"

"Please, Mum, calm down and let me get a word in edgeways. It isn't what you think, but I can't explain on the phone. I'll come and see you tomorrow, after work."

"You *are* going back to work, then?" Mrs Mitchell sniffed audibly. "I thought you'd taken an early retirement, and our Mavis has been trying to get in touch with you. 'And it's no use you looking at me,' I told her, 'I don't know where Cath is any more than you do.'" Another sniff. "For all I knew, you might have gone and got married again, on the sly. I wouldn't have put it past you."

"Well I didn't, and I haven't been with anyone. But I'm not going into details now. I'll tell you all about it tomorrow." She paused. "How are you, by the way?"

"'By the way?', well that's nice, isn't it? I might have been dead and buried for all you cared. I had another one of my funny turns, if you must know. I had to knock on the wall for Mrs Smith next door to come in to me."

"Oh, Mother, I'm sorry. Are you all right now?" Catherine's heart sank. "Perhaps I'd better come down tonight."

"A fat lot of good that would be, like locking the stable door after the horse has bolted! No, there's summat I want to watch on the telly, then I'm off upstairs to bed. I'll see you tomorrow night, make you a bite of supper. Good-night, love."

"Good-night Mum, and God bless."

Hanging up the receiver, she went through to the kitchen, pausing to switch on the immersion heater for a bath. The flat felt chilly, and she felt weary. First she would have something to eat, just a snack, she wasn't really hungry.

After her bath, she would go to bed, listen to music on the radio for a while, then try to get some sleep.

Tomorrow, she must go back to work; pick up the threads of her life once more. For the time being, all she wanted was peace, time to herself to sift and sort through the muddled memories of the past few days. It

190

wasn't going to be easy, but then nothing ever had been easy. Perhaps she was one of those incident-prone people destined to live her life on a knife's edge, never to achieve true peace of mind?

Waiting for the bathwater to heat up, after she had eaten, she switched on her electric blanket, and cleared away the dead flowers, watered the ivy plants, and unpacked her cases. She then undressed, put on her dressing gown, and telephoned Rose.

"Oh, Catherine," came Rose's familiar voice on the line, "I've been praying you would ring. Are you all right, love? You must be exhausted after that long journey."

"I am a bit tired," she confessed.

Intuitively Rose said, "There's something you're not telling me, or would you rather I didn't ask?"

Then Catherine told her about Adam and the woman she'd seen him with. When she had finished speaking, "What are you going to do about it?" Rose asked.

"What can I do? I can scarcely blame him for being fed up with me. I just wish it hadn't happened, that's all. One more problem to be solved."

"I know how you feel, love. But that's life, isn't it? One damn thing after another? The only advice I have to offer, take each day as it comes. As it says in the Good Book, 'Sufficient unto the day is the evil thereof'." She chuckled gently. "Here endeth the First Lesson! You know, Catherine, I often ask myself, since I'm so smart, why I never listen to my own advice? Answers on the back of a stamp!

"Now, do as Mummy tells you, go to bed, get a good night's rest, and I guarantee that things will look a helluva sight better in the morning."

They bade each other a fond good-night.

The time was now nine o'clock. Getting into bed, Catherine switched on her radio. The strains of Elgar's 'Enigma Variations' floated into the room.

The bed was warm, her pillows felt soft and downy, her body relaxed. About to switch off the bedside lamp, suddenly the doorbell rang, and kept on ringing until, at

last, getting up, shrugging into her dressing gown, she
went downstairs to see who it was.

Adam was on the doorstep.

"May I come in, Kate?" he asked quietly. "I need to
talk to you."

Chapter Seventeen

"Couldn't this have waited?" she asked, switching on the fire and the lamps. "Or you might have rung me."

"I'm sorry, I didn't want to talk on the phone. I thought twice about turning up at this hour, knowing you'd be tired after your journey, but there was no alternative. I needed to talk to you face to face."

"That's all right, Adam. It isn't all that late, but I am tired. Sit down, let me make you some coffee."

"You've been away a long time," he said. "Far longer than I expected. Look, Kate, don't bother with any coffee for me. This isn't exactly a social call."

"That sounds ominous." He looked tired too, she thought, and strained.

"What I have to say isn't easy, but first I want to know about you, where you went, what you did, what happened. I thought you'd write or phone."

"I meant to, there really wasn't time. I seem to have been living on trains recently, and in hotel rooms, but it's a long story and I'd rather not go into it. I'm not sure I'd even know where to begin."

"But did you find what you were looking for? That is, the person you were looking for?"

"Yes," she said softly, knowing she couldn't bear to tell him that Nick was dead. Her memories were too fresh, too painful to recount. In any case, what would be the point? Her travels had involved far more than hours spent in cold railway carriages and sleepless nights in hotel bedrooms, they had involved people and emotions, the discovery of a web of deceit involving someone she loved, which she would never divulge to a living soul.

He waited, expecting her to say something more, and

then she continued haltingly, "Yes, I discovered what I was looking for, and it's over now. All is well. Mission accomplished."

"I'm glad," he said. "And now I'd better explain why I'm here. As I said before, this isn't going to be easy for me. The fact is . . ." He paused. "I don't know quite how to tell you. I care for you a great deal, Kate. The last thing I want is to hurt you."

Taking pity on him, realizing his nervousness, not wanting to prolong his agony she said wryly, "You don't need to tell me, I think I already know. There's someone else, isn't there? The woman you had lunch with today? The woman in the lime-green sweater?"

"You saw us together?"

"Yes, accidentally I assure you. Mr Fuller told me that you were lunching at the Royal Station Hotel with a – client. I went there on the off chance of seeing you, not to interrupt your business meeting, simply to tell you that I was on my way home. It seemed the least I could do after my long silence. I looked into the dining room, and – hey presto – there you were."

"Oh, God, Kate," he said abjectly, "I'm sorry. Truly sorry. You see, I never expected to see her again. I thought it was all over between us, then suddenly there she was, and I knew . . ."

Catherine smiled wistfully. "You are talking about Margaret, I assume? The girl you met during the war? Your – first love?"

"Oh, Kate, how did you guess?" Adam's face was a study of relief and guilt intermingled.

"Because I know *you*, Adam. Of course I was angry and hurt at first. Just another womanizer, I thought, but I knew deep down that wasn't true. Then, when you appeared on my doorstep wanting to talk to me face to face, the pieces began to slot together like a jigsaw puzzle. I knew then that you were incapable of underhand behaviour, that the person you were with meant a great deal to you, and the most likely person seemed – Margaret."

"You are absolutely right, of course," he said quietly, looking down at his hands, nervously interlocking his

194

fingers. "I knew, the moment I saw her again, that I had never really stopped loving her. It was as though we'd never been apart, and I knew that she felt the same way too."

"So, what's wrong with that?"

Looking across at her, "You know what's wrong," he said jerkily, "I have you to consider, our engagement, the fact that I still care for you very deeply, that I loved you enough to want to spend the rest of my life with you!"

"Yes, I see," Catherine said gently, "but tell me more about Margaret. I thought she had married during the war."

"She did, but her husband was killed in Italy, at Monte Cassino. When she was demobbed from the ATS after the war, she took up nursing as a career. She was living in Wolverhampton at the time, with her in-laws. Her own parents, who had moved to Hull, had died in an air raid – one of those 'bombers' moon' attacks on the dockland area, so the poor kid had no one of her own left to turn to.

"Before Christmas, apparently, she decided to leave Wolverhampton, return to York, to continue her nursing career. She felt that her roots were there, you see? And then, just after I returned home from London, she got in touch with me, and . . ."

"That, to coin an expression, was that?" Catherine suggested, building up the whole of the jigsaw puzzle in her mind; slotting into place the final pieces. "You fell in love with each other all over again? Am I right?"

"Well, yes, but it's not quite as cut and dried as all that," he said despondently. "I didn't try to mislead her in any way. I told her about us, that we are engaged to be married; how much I admire you, what a wonderful person you are, how good you had been to me after the death of my mother."

Catherine laughed suddenly. "Poor Margaret. I bet she felt like scratching my eyes out. I know I would have, in her place. The truth as I see it, and I'm sure I'm right, is that I wouldn't have made you happy. We just happened to meet at a time when we both

195

needed someone to lean on, and I'm grateful for that, believe me!"

She added more seriously, holding out her hands to him, "But friendship isn't love. We both know that, and engagements were made to be broken. Do you imagine that I would stand in the way of your future happiness with someone that you are really in love with?"

"You mean that?" he said wonderingly, clasping her hands. "Oh Kate, I can't thank you enough."

"It's I who should thank you for putting up with me the way you did, in London. I behaved badly, and I'm sorry."

"You were ill. I took care of you, that's all. I'll never regret having known you."

They stood up. "We will keep in touch?" he asked.

Catherine shook her head. "Better not, for Margaret's sake. It wouldn't be fair."

"But what about you? I can't bear to think of you being ill and unhappy again with no one to turn to."

"You mustn't worry about me, Adam," she said. "What happened in London was a blessing in disguise. Strange how things work out. Had I not been ill, I would never have met Dr Ellerby who gave me the best advice I've had in years. It was he who encouraged me to take stock of my life; reach a firm decision about the future.

"He said I had come to a crossroads and it was up to me to decide where to go next, the reason why I went in search of – Nick. I knew that I stood little chance of future happiness until I had come to terms with the past."

"And have you? Come to terms with the past, I mean?" Adam asked concernedly.

"Not quite yet, that will take a little time. Let me put it this way, all the fret and fever of not knowing what became of him is over now. I discovered that our marriage did mean something to him after all. And that is all I really needed to know."

"I'm glad," Adam said simply. Bending down, he kissed her cheek, and then he was gone, hurrying downstairs to his car, a man in love with a woman who would bring him the kind of happiness he so richly deserved – an undemanding, uncomplicated kind of happiness with no emotional hang-ups.

Going back to bed, Elgar's *'Enigma Variations'* had long since faded. Now, in the silence of her room, she heard the opening chords of Debussy's *'Claire-de-Lune'*, and remembered a springtime evening long ago.

Early next morning, she walked briskly to her salon. Making a mental note to ring the garage, to have something done about her car – she opened the shop door and stood on the threshold breathing in the familiar intermingled smell of shampoo and permanent-wave lotion.

Back to square one, she thought wryly, leafing through the pages of the appointments' book on the reception-desk to find out what had gone on during her absence, what she was in for later on in the day.

As she had imagined they would be, the pages of the book were sparsely dotted with names after the Christmas rush. Even so, she felt guilty that she had left June and Esme to cope on their own for such a long time – almost a fortnight. Really? As long as that? She had lost track of time recently.

Of course Tim Grogan, now the bank manager, knew that business was slack at this time of year, but the takings since Christmas would scarcely cover her assistants' wages, let alone make a dent in her overdraft.

Perhaps she had better pop into the bank later to have a word with him? And yes, she thought, that would be the best thing to do. He was, after all, a very nice man who had done his best to guide her through her many financial storms of the past.

Tim Grogan rose to his feet when Catherine entered his office. He was a tall man, grey-haired now, always impeccably dressed in a well-tailored grey suit, a white shirt and a nondescript tie, with a charming smile and shrewd yet kindly grey-blue eyes behind the horn-rimmed glasses. She felt he was pleased to see her, and knew she could come to him with any financial problem.

After warmly shaking hands with her, he said, "Please sit down, Catherine. Now, how can I help you?"

"I'm worried about my overdraft," she said simply. "The fact is, I've been away from work this past fortnight, not pulling my weight at the salon. I just wanted you to know, that's all."

"Why?" he asked concernedly, "have you been ill?"

"Yes and no. That is, it's hard to explain." Pausing to frame her thoughts, trusting in his discretion – this man who knew about Nick – who had loaned her money to pay off his debts – she continued, "It has to do with my ex-husband . . ." She bowed her head, close to tears.

"You mean he's in more trouble?" Tim Grogan asked gently.

"No, Tim," Catherine said bleakly. "He, Nick, is dead. The fact is, I went away to find out what had happened to him. I lost track of time, I'm afraid. That's it in a nutshell!"

Tim Grogan said slowly, compassionately, "I'm so sorry about your husband. I realize how much he meant to you, how hard you have worked to pay off his debts. That you have managed to do so is entirely to your credit. All I can possibly add is, please stop worrying about your overdraft. I know, as well as you do, that January is a lean month in a seasonal town like Scarborough – and I should know, seeing I was born and bred here."

"Were you really? I had no idea. I thought you might be a Londoner, or whatever, by your lack of a local accent, sent here, against your better judgement, to cope with the likes of me – small fish in a very small pond – owing more than they earn."

Although there had always been a mutual liking and respect between Catherine and Tim from their first meeting, especially after Tim's comfort and support during that awful episode when she had broken down in his office, Catherine had always resisted any inclination to put their conversations on a more personal level, feeling so vulnerable after Nick had left.

Rising to her feet, she said, "Thank you, Tim, for easing my mind about my overdraft."

Turning at the door, she added quietly, sincerely, "You have been a tower of strength to me. I can't thank you enough for all that you have done for me, over the years."

Mrs Mitchell had prepared a steak and dumplings casserole for supper, with mashed potatoes and vegetables.

"There, get that down you," she said, bustling the food on to the table. "You're as thin as a herring, our Cath, after all the chasing about you've been doing lately. What's it all been in aid of, that's what I want to know? And where does this feller you went off with fit into the picture?"

"He doesn't, not any longer. He's engaged to marry someone else. In any case, we were only friends."

"Huh, seems a rum going on to me, rushing off to London with an engaged man. What did his 'fiancée' have to say about it?"

"They weren't engaged at the time." Catherine sighed. "Look, Mum, I promised I'd tell you about it, and I will, but in my own way, in my own time, and I'm warning you beforehand, you're not going to like it."

Catherine gave her mother an edited version of her quest, saying nothing that would add to her dislike of Nick, making no mention of the state of affairs at the cottage, saying simply that she had seen his mother and stayed with her for a while, making it sound almost idyllic, leaving Estelle out of the story.

She told her that the weather had been bad, and they'd been snowed in for a while. Curiously, when Annie learned that Nick had died she murmured, "Poor lad; why, he was no age at all. He was a bonny lad, I'll say that for him."

When Annie asked what was wrong with him, drawing in a deep breath, Catherine said, "He'd been seriously ill with a liver complaint," and left it at that.

"Well, I'm sorry for you, Cath, I know you thought the world of him, and that's to your credit. There's many a lass wouldn't have done for him what you did, so you've nothing to reproach yourself with," Mrs Mitchell said

199

firmly. "But I think there's a lot you're not telling me. Where does Oxford come into it?"

On safer ground, Catherine told Annie about Rose, describing the house in detail, and their meeting in the restaurant. Annie listened intently, nodding and smiling. "She sounds a very nice person," she said. "The change would do you good."

Catherine was about to leave when Mrs Mitchell dropped her bombshell. They were in the hall at the time. "By the way," she said, "Mavis is coming to see you on Sunday – about me going to live with her and Ernie. She wants to settle about putting this house on the market; what's to go to the saleroom and so on."

"You mean it has all been arranged? You really intend giving up your home?"

"No need to look so upset. You knew it was on the cards. Why, our Cath, you're crying! Eh, love, I never thought you'd take it so hard. I mean, it's not the end of the world, is it? I won't be all that far away, and you know you'll be welcome to stay any time you want. Mavis said so. I expect that's one of the things she'll talk over with you on Sunday."

Brushing away her tears, "I'm sorry, Mum," Catherine said. "It came as a bit of a shock, that's all. I – I don't know what I'll do without you!"

"Well I never! I thought you'd be pleased to see the back of me!"

"You thought wrong then. I love you, Mum. Perhaps I haven't always shown it, but I do. I always have and I always will."

Unused to emotional outbursts, slightly embarrassed, secretly pleased yet incapable of expressing her feelings, "Oh, get on with you," Annie said. "I took it for granted you – loved me. I'm your mother!"

Walking home across the Valley Bridge, Catherine thought, first Nick, then Adam, now Mum. She had never felt so lonely in her life before.

Chapter Eighteen

Mavis was shorter than her sister, and plumper. A happy marriage to a successful husband, a nice home, and two serious-minded, clever children, had given her an air of smugness.

She wore 'nice' clothes lacking in style, mainly tweed skirts and bulky woollen jumpers in winter, print dresses and lightweight cardigans in summer, had her hair washed and set once a fortnight, belonged to a Women's Luncheon Club and a flower arranging group, and took a pride in her cooking; played Bridge occasionally, and enjoyed sequence dancing with her stalwart Ernest, who referred to her, irritatingly, as 'Mavie'.

Glancing across at her that Sunday morning, handing her a cup of coffee, Catherine could scarcely equate the matronly woman in the chair opposite with the sister whose hair she had pulled in the old days, and had teased unmercifully about her boyfriend Ernie – 'Ernie the Yernie', she had called him, to Mavis's disgust – who had never had much of a sense of humour, come to think of it.

"The thing is," she was saying, "we, Ernest and I, want Mother to have as many of her own things about her as possible. She'll have her own bedroom and sitting room, of course. But we must be a teeny bit selective. That's where you come into it, Cath. You will make sure, won't you, that she sticks to the essentials?

"What I mean is, no use trying to put a quart into a pint pot. Do try to persuade her to part with the heavy stuff, otherwise she won't have room to move. All she'll really need is a single bed, a small dressing table, and wardrobe, a couple of armchairs, her TV, her gate-legged table, and a few ornaments and pictures to make her feel at home. Well, you know what I'm driving at."

"Oh yes, Mavis, I know exactly what you're driving at! It's as plain as the nose on your face!"

Mavis bridled. "What exactly do you mean by that?" she asked huffily.

"You know damn well what I mean. Mum has slept in the double bed she shared with Dad, all her married life – long before we were born or thought of. It would break her heart to part with it now, and no way would she think of parting with her sideboard and dining chairs.

"With the best intentions in the world, you can't expect an old lady to part with her most treasured possessions simply because, as you so succinctly put it, she won't have room to move. So far as I'm concerned, she'd be far better off staying where she is, under her own roof, with her own four walls about her!"

"Oh, you're a fine one to talk," Mavis burst forth, "sitting pretty in this elegant flat of yours, as selfish as sin! What have you ever done to help mother, I should like to know, apart from popping in to see her occasionally? At least Ernest and I have provided an alternative to her living alone in a house that is far too big for her. I care about our mother! Can you honestly say the same?"

"Yes, I think so," Catherine said quietly. "You see, I visited the estate agents yesterday; asked him to put my flat on the market."

"Oh!" Mavis jerked bolt upright in her chair as if she'd been stung. "Just why, may I ask?"

"Because I'm going home to live with Mum, to take care of her from now on. That way she won't have to part with a thing."

"Huh, all very touching, I'm sure," Mavis said snidely, "but *you* will! All this fine furniture of yours! What will you do with it? Send it to the saleroom?"

Catherine smiled. "I don't see why not. That's where most of it came from in the first place, and human beings are far more important than furniture, wouldn't you say?"

She added kindly, "I'm sorry, Mavis, believe me, the

last thing I want is to belittle your kindness, and you were quite right in saying that I've been as selfish as sin, so please don't think too harshly of me for wanting to make amends. At least, this way, you'll be spared the necessity of trying to put a quart into a pint pot."

"Well, this is all very unexpected and discouraging, I must say," Mavis said haughtily, getting up from her chair near the fire. "A right fool I shall look, having told my friends that Mother was coming to live with me."

"Oh, sit down and drink your coffee. Which comes first, Mum's happiness or what your friends will think?"

"Now you're saying that Mother wouldn't be happy with me!" Mavis remained standing, the picture of injured pride.

"She wouldn't. Look, Mavis, Mum has worked hard all her life, she's had to. How do you think she'd take to being idle all of a sudden?"

"Idle? She wouldn't *be* idle," Mavis retorted, "she'd find plenty of things to do."

"Such as? You mean that you'd give her the run of your kitchen, let her do the cooking and washing-up? And when you have your Bridge friends round for the evening, would you invite her to join you for supper?"

"No, of course not. That's ridiculous! She wouldn't want to. That's the whole purpose of giving her her own space, her own rooms, so she could do as likes – watch television and knit.

"I've thought it all out very carefully. There's a cubbyhole next to the bathroom on the top landing where she could make tea and coffee, and toast. I'll take her lunch up to her on a tray, and she'd have her evening meal downstairs with us. That goes without saying."

"Does it? And what if she wanted to stay downstairs for the evening to join the family circle?" Catherine glanced quizzically at her sister. "You realize we're speaking hypothetically about something that isn't going to happen? Can you really picture Mum making toast and tea in a cubbyhole on the landing? Allowing you to bring up her lunch on a tray? Staying in her room all day? Being treated as a guest in someone else's home?

"You've got it all wrong, if that's what you think. Knowing Mother, she'd want to be down in the kitchen cooking the evening meal, let alone eating it and going back to her room afterwards like a good little girl. In other words, Mum is a strong-minded woman who'd be into everything, making her presence felt, telling you, Ernie and the kids what to do. No, Mavis, it just wouldn't work, and that's why I've decided to go back to Sussex Street to live. It's for the best, believe me."

Mavis sighed deeply, inwardly relieved, trying desperately not to show it. "Hmm," she conceded, "I suppose you're right. But at least give me credit for trying."

Heading for the door, she couldn't help getting in a final dig. "All very well being noble, our Cath, but I can't see you and Mother hitting it off together for long under one roof, especially since you've been on your own so long, and when Mum starts telling *you* what to do!"

Afterwards, it occurred to Catherine that their mother knew nothing of all this. Putting her flat on the market had happened as a result of Friday evening's conversation when Mum had told her she was leaving Scarborough. But suppose Annie didn't want to stay on in Sussex Street? What if she was looking forward to living with Mavis?

Only one way to find out. At two o'clock, she put on her outdoor things and caught the bus into town. Still no car, but it was at least being attended to in the 'sick bay' of a local garage as a result of her Friday morning phone call. "There's summat up with the magneto," the mechanic had told her.

"Well, have you seen Mavis?" Annie asked, without preamble, when they were seated in the back room.

"Yes, that's why I'm here." Catherine felt that she was treading on eggshells.

"Oh, so what did she say?" Never one to beat about the bush. "You haven't fallen out, have you?"

"Not exactly, though we didn't see eye to eye entirely." Now for it. "You see, Mum, I came up with a better idea – at least I hope you'll think it a better idea—"

204

Annie burst forth, "An old people's home! That's it, isn't it? Well I'd sooner die and have done with it! I'm not ending my days in an institution, and that's that!"

Catherine laughed, she couldn't help it. "What's so funny?" Annie demanded.

"You are! Honestly, Mum! Putting you into an old people's home is the last thing on my mind. No, it's far simpler than that. The fact is, I want to come and live with you, if you'll have me. Well, what do you think?"

If she lived to be a hundred, Catherine would never forget the look on her mother's face, the softening of her features, the wondering, tender expression in her eyes as she said huskily, "Do you really mean it, Cath?"

"Of course I mean it."

"What, and give up your flat, your independence?"

Catherine smiled wistfully. "You said yourself, independence is just another word for loneliness. You'll be doing me a favour. I need you, Mum. I don't want to lose you." She paused. "So I take it the answer is yes?"

"There's nowt I'd like better," Mrs Mitchell drew in a deep breath of relief, as if a weight had been lifted from her shoulders, "but only if you're sure. I wouldn't want to be a burden to you."

"You've never been a burden to anyone in your life," Catherine reminded her. "The boot's on the other foot. I've been the burden."

"But I've promised Mavis! What's she going to say when I tell her?"

"She already knows, and she's all for it." A white lie, but a necessary one to set Annie's mind at ease. "Naturally, she was a bit disappointed, but we both want what's best for you."

"Well I never." Annie clasped her hands delightedly. "Now I needn't get rid of my bed and my sideboard. Ah, I don't know what to say. I'm fair flummoxed!"

"I'll make some tea, shall I?" Catherine asked. "You sit still, I'll do it."

When she returned with the tray, Annie said, "I've been thinking. Those rooms on the top floor would make a nice little flat for you if they were cleared out and redecorated.

That way you could keep some of your own things. You'll need privacy, but I could have a nice meal ready for you when you come home from work, then you could please yourself what you do. I wouldn't want to cramp your style. I know you like to go to bed early to read or listen to the wireless."

"That sounds wonderful." Catherine had never felt so close to her mother before.

"I know it'll seem a bit cramped after what you've been used to, and there isn't much of a lookout," Annie said, gazing into the future, painting rosy pictures in her mind's eye, "but it could be made nice and comfortable I daresay." Puckering her forehead she continued, "Happen it'll be a bit on the cold side in winter, being so close to the roof."

"Tell you what, Mum, now that you've decided to stay, let's have central heating installed, shall we, and a coloured bathroom suite?"

"What colour?"

"Any colour you want. You choose."

"Pink, then," Annie said firmly. "I like pink. But won't it cost a lot of money?"

"Not to worry about that. When my flat's sold, we'll be rolling in it! We might even have the kitchen modernized, and new windows to keep out the draughts."

"Cor," Annie said joyfully, "I'll think I'm in Paradise before my time!" Then, pulling a wry face, "But I mustn't start counting my chickens before they're hatched, and there's many a slip twixt cup and lip."

"There won't be this time, not if I can help it," Catherine assured her. "The house will be in a bit of an uproar for a week or so, I expect, but you can come and stay with me until the workmen have finished, unless you'd prefer to stay with Mavis and Ernie for a while. That's entirely up to you."

"No," Annie said quietly, unexpectedly, "I'd rather be with you. You're a good lass, Cathy. I know we haven't always seen eye to eye over – certain things, that I said more than I should have at times, but that was only because I – because I – love you."

A long, gentle silence fell between them, too precious to be broken. It seemed to Catherine, savouring that silence, that all the barriers between them had been washed away on a full tide of love and understanding.

When it was time for her to go, she put her arms about Annie, and kissed her, catching the fragrance of her hair, of Amami Shampoo, and the familiar smell of her mother's favourite coal tar soap which she had used all her life – Annie's maxim being that cleanliness is next to godliness.

"Good-night, Mum," she said tenderly. "God bless, and sleep well."

"You too, love. But I doubt I'll be able to sleep much, I'm too excited."

Walking home in the teeth of the bitter wind blowing in from the sea, Catherine scarcely noticed the weather. All she could think about was the warm feeling she'd experienced when her mother had told her she loved her, the look of joy on her face when she knew she wouldn't have to get rid of her double bed and her wardrobe.

Filled with a sense of purpose, of well-being, Catherine marched home to the drum beat of her happy heart. Her life was about to change drastically, and she was glad. She needed someone to care for apart from herself, something to live for apart from work.

It occurred to her, when she was getting ready for bed, that she would need to tell Tim Grogan what she was planning to do. Poor Tim would think she was haunting his office these days. She would call in to see him tomorrow afternoon around three o'clock, before the bank closed.

"You're looking well this morning, Mrs Willard," June said when Catherine came in to the salon. "I think that holiday did you good even if it was a funny time of year to take a holiday. What was it? One of those winter breaks you read about in the paper?"

"Something like that," Catherine told her, realizing that the girl was dying to know where she'd been and who with. June adored romantic novels with happy endings, and her ears had been flapping the day Adam came to the shop after Christmas.

Catherine said, "Speaking of holidays, you and Esme had better let me know when you want time off. No hurry, just think about it. I expect you'll want to talk it over first, before you decide."

June blushed becomingly. "Well, me an' Pete are thinking of getting married in July. His parents say we can live with them till we've saved up enough money for a place of our own. 'Course, I'll keep on working afterwards, we don't want to start a family till we're settled."

"I see, well that is exciting news," Catherine said, "and what about you, Esme?"

"I dunno, I'll have to ask my parents," the junior murmured shyly.

The poor kid, Catherine thought, her time off would probably be spent looking after her younger siblings, taking them down to the sands for donkey rides and ice-cream cornets, making sure they dried their feet properly after paddling.

Having made noises like a 'boss', Catherine turned her attention to her first client of the day, of all people, Mrs Hobart of the peanut-size engagement ring and ocelot coat, whose main grievance against life, was that there were not enough hours in day to fit in all her social activities.

"I understand you've been on holiday," Mrs Hobart said offhandedly, her mind elsewhere; making conversation, "anywhere nice?"

Catherine said wickedly, tongue in cheek, "Well, London was quite fun, but one really needs to see Paris in the spring, don't you think?"

"Oh?" Mrs Hobart regarded her with awakened interest. "So you've been to Paris?"

"Yes," Catherine replied truthfully, remembering the chocolate stall in the Rue Lafayette, a long time ago, the intermingled smells of dust and petrol fumes – and Nick who had been so angry at the time. All part of

208

the past that she was slowly but gradually coming to terms with.

Later that afternoon, she told June that she was going into town, to the bank to see Tim Grogan, and asked her to lock up the salon at closing time.

"Yes, Mrs Willard," June said cheerfully, "see you in the morning."

Tim Grogan rose to his feet when she entered his office. "A pleasure to see you again, Catherine," he said truthfully, aware of a feeling of warmth, of buoyancy, a kind of protective tenderness towards her, linked to a deep admiration of the way she had struggled to overcome all the odds stacked against her, her innate honesty and charm, her faithfulness towards the man who had brought her to the brink of financial ruin, with never a trace of bitterness or a harsh word to say against him.

"Please, sit down, and tell me what I can do to help you."

She said, "I've decided to sell my flat, in fact it's up for sale now. I rang Ward Price, the estate agents, on Saturday."

"I see, but I thought you were happy there. Has something happened to change that?"

"Not the way I feel about the flat. It's been my refuge, but my mother's getting on in years, and I've decided to live with her. My sister wanted her to move to a place near Darlington – Croft Spa – I don't know if you've heard of it? It's very pretty, I believe, but that would have entailed Mother selling most of her furniture, uprooting herself entirely, and I couldn't bear that to happen."

She went on, "It's quite a big house, so there'll be plenty of room for the pair of us. Mother has suggested my having a little flat made on the top floor, so we won't get in each other's way. It seems the ideal solution. I'll be there if she needs help, and she'll enjoy looking after me." She paused. "What do you think?"

Tim Grogan said quietly, "I was faced with a similar situation five years ago, when my wife died. There I was, alone in a house far too big for just one person, and so

I joined forces with my unmarried sister who was also living alone in a house too big for her, our old family home, as it happens, which she felt reluctant to leave, for obvious reasons. This dragging up of roots can be a painful business for the elderly, I know. My sister was the oldest of four children, and twelve years my senior."

"How has it worked out?" Catherine asked, deeply interested.

"Very well indeed." Grogan smiled reflectively. "At least it did until the death of my sister last October. Now I'm back where I started – living alone in a house far too big for me."

"I'm so sorry," Catherine said sympathetically, thinking that she had never really seen Tim Grogan before as other than her business manager, a friendly but somewhat remote figure seated behind a large desk in a room marked 'Private', certainly not as a vulnerable human being with problems similar to hers.

The phone on his desk rang suddenly. "Excuse me," he said, picking up the receiver. "Yes," he replied tensely, "I see. In that case, you had better put her through."

Looking at Catherine, "This call is for you," he told her.

"For *me*? But who . . .?" She experienced the same feeling she had done the night Estelle rang up to tell Nick that Frank was dead.

"Someone called June," Tim said, handing her the phone, "I have a feeling it's bad news." He spoke gently, wishing desperately that he knew how to spare her, to soften the blow he knew was coming to her. June was ringing to tell her that Mrs Mitchell had suffered a major heart attack and had been rushed into hospital, that she was in the intensive care unit, fighting for life.

Chapter Nineteen

Taking control of the situation, Tim Grogan drove Catherine to the hospital. She was quiet and shaken, but calm. His heart went out to her.

Mrs Mitchell's next door neighbour had gone into the house by the back door, as she often did in the afternoon, for a cup of tea and a chat, to find Annie on the floor of the kitchen, unable to move, scarcely breathing. At once Mrs Smith had dialled 999 for an ambulance.

This she had explained to June tearfully on the telephone, then June had rung the bank, speaking first to Tim's secretary who had relayed the call to his office with a brief summary of the message.

Losing no time, he had taken Catherine through a side entrance of the bank to the staff car park, his arm firmly beneath her elbow. She said, "I must get in touch with my sister."

"Don't worry," he told her, "I'll see to that for you, if you give me her number."

"I feel I'm to blame for what has happened," she said bleakly. "Mum was so excited last night when I left her. Perhaps that's what caused the attack."

"I think that's hardly likely," Tim said, finding a parking space near the main entrance of the hospital, "but you'll know more when you've seen the doctor. I'll check at the reception desk."

He talked briefly to the receptionist. "The doctor's name is Phillips," he told Catherine. "He'll be along in a few minutes to talk to you, then I'll make that phone call to your sister."

"You will come with me when, I mean if . . ."

He knew what she meant. "Of course I will," he

said reassuringly. "I'll stay with you for as long as you need me."

When the doctor, a youngish man with dark hair, appeared on the scene to talk to Catherine, Tim slipped away to the phone-box in the foyer to call Mavis. Scarcely a pleasant duty to perform, but necessary.

At first she had seemed unable to grasp who he was and why he was ringing. "What did you say your name was?" she asked twice. "Grogan? Are you sure it's me you want and not my husband? Oh, a friend of Cath's? Why? Has something happened to her?"

When she had finally stopped talking to listen, and the message had sunk home, she had begun to cry hysterically, then followed a garbled background conversation until a man's voice came on the line, by which time Tim had begun delving in his back pocket for a fresh supply of loose change and worrying about Catherine who had left the reception area with Dr Phillips.

"I'm Ernest Stokes," the man said. "I gather this is about my mother-in-law?"

"Yes, it is," Tim spoke impatiently. "She's in the intensive care unit at Scarborough Hospital. How quickly can you get here?"

"Hard to say. Three hours, maybe four. I have a couple of clients to see first, and Mavie will need to arrange something for the boys – food and so on. It's not just a question of shutting up the house when you've got other people to consider."

"Quite. I leave it up to you, then, Mr Stokes. Goodbye."

Now to find Catherine. He'd had enough of Ernest and Mavis for the time being. Families, he thought wryly, thank God one could choose one's friends.

Dr Phillips had taken Mrs Willard through to the intensive care unit, he discovered from the receptionist. "Through the swing doors," she said, "then along the corridor, turn left, then right. You can't miss it. It's clearly signposted."

He wasn't too sure about that. Following his exhausting conversation with the Stokeses, he felt that he might well miss finding Nelson's Column in Trafalgar Square.

A ward orderly told him that Dr Phillips and a lady had gone into his office a few minutes ago. Tim thanked him and sat down in the corridor to wait; prepared to wait until Doomsday, if necessary.

It was then, perched on a far from comfortable pressed-fibre chair in a clinical hospital corridor, awaiting the opening of the office door, he knew beyond a shadow of doubt that he had fallen deeply in love with Catherine.

This was no sudden rush of blood to the head. He couldn't even say for sure when it had happened. Until this moment, he could not have said with any certainty that it had happened.

He had liked and admired her from the first time she came to the bank to discuss buying Mrs Maitland's salon, all those years ago. There had been an air of straightforwardness about her, of trustworthiness, which had made an immediate and favourable impression on him, quite apart from Mrs Maitland's glowing personal reference to her assistant's capability for hard work and her popularity with the clients.

On these grounds, he had had no hesitation whatever in granting her a purchase loan on the business, or later extending the loan to cover the down payment of the mortgage on her flat.

Over the years, he had watched her progress with a sense of pride in her achievements, had looked forward to her occasional visits to his office with a feeling of pleasure which he had scarcely begun to analyse until now.

Suddenly he remembered a teasing remark of his sisters; one morning as he came downstairs on a day he was scheduled to have a business lunch with Catherine. "My, you look nice today! Are you seeing someone special? Anyone would think you had a lady friend on the QT, with the trouble you are taking with your appearance lately!"

And he had said, "Don't be silly Frances, who'd look twice at a boring old bank manager like me?"

"You're not boring," she'd reminded him. "It's your

job that's stuffy, not you. I always told you you should have been a train driver or a farmer. Given your love of freedom, the great outdoors, you'd have made a splendid farmer. How you ended up a bank manager, I'll never know – putting the fear of God into people. So who is the lady you're so fond of? A rich widow wanting advice on her portfolio?"

"Heaven forbid! What would I want with a rich widow, or any other woman come to that? I have enough trouble with you!"

Things might have been different had she said, "So who is this girl you're so fond of? A young woman with a spendthrift husband who doesn't give a damn about her, sorely in need of your help to save her from financial ruin?"

Then he would have known exactly who she meant. Or perhaps he had known all along; had been too blind or too stupid to admit, even to himself, how much Catherine meant to him.

He knew now.

He rose to his feet instinctively when she and Dr Phillips emerged from his office. One look at her drawn and suffering face and he knew that the worst had happened.

Dr Phillips said quietly, "I'm taking Mrs Willard to see her mother. Will you wait here?" He added, "Mrs Mitchell died an hour ago."

"Yes, of course."

He would never forget the way Catherine turned to him and said, "Would you mind coming in with me?" And he had read in her eyes how much she needed his strength and support.

Holding her arm, he had felt the trembling of her body as they entered the little side ward where her mother lay sleeping her last sleep, as peacefully as a child, all of life's sorrows and hardships washed away, with no sign of struggle, of inner turmoil, the hint of a smile on her lips.

Tim felt that he had no right to be there, in that heart-rending moment when Catherine whispered, "Good-night,

214

Mum, sleep well. Remember, I love you." But he knew he must be there to help her through this ordeal, because she needed someone to lean on. Not himself necessarily, but – someone.

When the doors of the side ward had closed behind them, he said gently, "Come with me, Catherine."

"Where to?"

"Nowhere in particular, just as long as it's away from here for an hour or so. We'll just get into my car and drive somewhere."

"But Mavis and Ernie might arrive at any moment," she reminded him. "I must be here when they come."

"You will be, I promise. Your brother-in-law explained on the phone that there might be some delay in setting off, to do with arrangements for their boys, and so on."

"Yes, I see. How selfish of me to expect them to simply drop everything and run. In any case, even if they had, it's too late now, isn't it?" Her eyes filled with tears.

Seated behind the wheel of his car, Tim drove her away from the hospital, along Scalby Road, then on to the Foreshore, deserted at this time of year.

The Christmas lights outlining the bay had been switched off now, so that the waters of the bay were invisible beyond the darkness of a January night, illuminated merely by the orange glow of the street lamps shining down on snow-filmed pavements, as if the sea had ceased to exist – apart from the pulsating beat of the tide running in on the shore.

"Listen," Catherine said, hearing the music of the sea beyond the darkness, "it reminds me of the poem, 'Dover Beach'. Do you know the one I mean? It's by Matthew Arnold, only I can't quite remember how it goes."

"Yes, I know the one. When he talks about, the sound the pebbles make, when the waves withdraw from the sand."

"Yes," she said quietly, "that's it exactly. The music of my life!"

She sat silently beside him as he drove slowly round the Marine Drive; staring out of the window at the great mass of darkness beyond the curving roadway bordering the bastion rocks of the Castle Hill, and he knew that she was fighting a desperate, silent inward battle to come to terms with the death of her mother, that there was nothing he could possibly say or do to alleviate her distress apart from sitting at the driving wheel of his car, hoping against hope that sooner or later she would give way to the benison of tears.

He longed to say to her, "Let go, my darling, sob out all your hurt and tears against my shoulder," but he dare not. The last thing on earth he wanted was to lose her trust in him as a friend. Falling in love with a woman was one thing, hoping and praying that she would come to love him in return, was a different matter entirely.

If only he could find a way . . .

Turning the car near the Corner Café on the north side of town, he drove back along the Marine Drive and from there to the South Cliff where, signalling right, he turned into the road leading to Oliver's Mount.

"This is one of my favourite walks," Catherine said softly, "I love the view from the top."

"Yes, it is inspiring, isn't it?" He smiled. "Especially by night. Shall we look at the lights?"

Parking the car, he took her hand and led her towards the parapet overlooking the town. Far below lay a fairy-land of twinkling lights shining up through the darkness, as if the crisscrossing streets of home had been strung with diamonds. And beyond the thickly clustered lights, on the clifftops stretching northward to Robin Hood's Bay, as far as the eye could see, glimmered the scattered lights of villages and solitary farmhouses, while out at sea, near the horizon, shone the slow moving lights of a passing ship.

It was a calm, still evening, cold but clear. The scourging wind had dropped. All they could hear was the gentle soughing of the trees in the breeze blowing in from the sea, the muted thunder of the tide coming in on the shore.

"What a lovely night," Tim said. "Look at the stars. I'd

216

almost forgotten there were such things. Strange how one forgets to look up at times. Reminds me of something I read once, 'Two men looked out from prison bars, one saw mud, the other stars'."

Raising her head, gazing up at the sky, Catherine saw that the heavens were littered with scintillating pinpricks of light, rekindling memories of a starlit night long ago.

Suddenly, painfully, she began to cry the pent-up tears of grief she had kept bottled up inside her at the hospital, even when the doctor had broken the news that her mother was dead.

Now she felt the warm, comforting clasp of Tim's arms about her, and heard his voice murmuring sweet, gentle words of encouragement and hope, telling her not to despair, that love remained the brightest star of all, and her mother had died knowing how much she loved her; words that she needed to hear, strong words spoken by a man who had come to mean a great deal to her.

Drying her tears on Tim's proffered handkerchief, she remembered Bridie's parting words to her. "Don't worry, my dear, when love comes your way again, you'll *know*!"

Moving away from him, she said, "I think it's time I went back to the hospital."

"Yes, of course." Taking her hand he led her back to the car.

"You will stay with me?" she asked wistfully.

Scared of saying too much, of losing her, yet wanting her to know how he felt, he said, feeling like a man in love again, no longer just her bank manager, "I'd like nothing more than to stay with you – always."

"Oh, that's all right then," she said, drawing in a deep breath of relief and happiness intermingled, admitting to herself that she felt the same way, and had done for sometime without realizing, "because that's how long I want you to stay with me. Always. Forever."

GW00870930

The XXL Baking Cookbook

Quick and Super-Delicious Recipes for Every Day incl. Bread, Cakes, Pies, Cookies, and More

Amanda Berry

TABLE OF CONTENTS

Introduction

Throughout this book, our intention is to show you some of the secrets involved in great baking. While others maintain that the secret ingredient is love, we know that great baking starts with a great recipe. To give you the best possible chances at creating a culinary masterpiece, we have collected some of the quickest, tastiest, and most cherished baking recipes from throughout the land.

As well as containing recipes that will inject some sparkle into your baked goods, we have collated some top baking tips, straight from the mouths of the chefs themselves. So sit back, relax, and turn your tastebud settings to "tingling." It is time we got down to business... The business of baking.

Baking Vs Cooking: What is the Difference?

Baking is a specific form of cooking. While all baking is cooking, not all cooking is baking. The main difference that separates the two, is the use of the oven.

When we bake goods, we cook them in the oven from start to finish. When we cook, we use a variety of techniques to achieve an edible delight. We can cook everything from sauces to ice cream – but we can only bake if that cooking is performed in the oven.

Baking Vs Roasting: What is the Difference?

Interestingly, and just to confuse you further, not everything baked in an oven from start to finish is thought of as "baked goods." For example, a whole chicken or beef joint cooked in the oven from start to finish would be known as a "roast" dish. This is because we don't refer to meats or vegetables as being baked goods. Why? It is just a colloquialism. We would call meats or vegetables cooked in an oven "roasted" as opposed to "baked."

It is this distinction between being baked or being roasted that conjures two different dishes to mind. If you tell someone you will bring baked goods to the party, they assume you will bring cakes or breads. If you tell someone you will bring a roast to the party, they assume you will bring a roasted meat dish, with or without vegetables.

What Key Elements Make Baking successful?

There are many factors which come together to create a perfect baked dish. The oven temperature, the length of time the dish gets cooked for, and the recipe, are the three most crucial factors. However, other things can make or break a good dish too. Things like beating instead of whisking, folding instead of beating, and sieving your floor to make it extra fine, all come into play.

Let's review some of these factors before we move on.

Oven Temperature

The temperature of your oven drastically affects how your baked goods will turn out. Too high and the food will be undercooked in the centre and charred on the outside. Too low and the food might not be fully cooked.

As a guide: denser foods take longer to cook than foods that are light and airy. A cake might take 20-25 minutes while a bread, whose dough is denser, might take 25-35 minutes, even though they are of comparable size.

A Preheated Oven

An oven which is preheated is cooking your baked goods at exactly the right temperature from the start. When we put food in a cold oven, the food must then pass through all the temperatures up until the correct one. Variations in temperature like this might affect the quality and integrity of the food. If you want perfect, consistent, baked goods, then the same temperature every time is the desired standard.

Length of Time Baked

If you bake your food for too long, it will become tough and carbonated (burned). Bake something in the oven for too little time, on the other hand, and it may still be raw on the inside.

Additionally, you should never open your oven to check on food before the prescribed time has passed. Each second the oven door is open loses 10C//50F of your temperature. As we know, temperature fluctuations affect both cooking times and the quality of our baking. Resist the urge to check.

Recipe

You cannot underestimate the importance of following your recipe. Good baking requires good powers of observation. Following the recipe to the letter means preheating your oven, using the correct amounts of each ingredient, baking at the correct temperature and for the correct timespan, and any other intricacies needed to bake perfect foods.

If you have followed your recipe properly, you will end up with the same appearance, texture, and flavour of food, every time you cook it. The recipe sets the quality standard of your food. How well you follow it will irrevocably impact the quality of baking you end up with.

Top Tips for Baking Success

We can't send you off into the world of bakery without giving you some sound advice on how to be a successful baker. Before you pick up the apron and begin, here are some top tips that professional bakers swear by.

Place cakes in the centre of your oven

Unless the recipe states otherwise, bake everything in the centre of your oven. Be sure there is room for air to move around the food in all directions. This is how a traditional oven heats the food evenly.

Get the weights spot on

Weights and measurements are too important to be given in cups. The size of a cup differs in every household. Stick to g//oz and try to be as precise as possible.

Make adjustments as per the recipe

Where a recipe says "beat" instead of "whisk," follow these instructions. Adjust temperatures too, soft butter, cold butter, or melted butter, can make a significant difference to the recipe. Cooking is chemistry at its heart. Be precise.

Invest in baking parchment and ring moulds

Ring moulds are used for everything from cheesecakes to parmesan crisps. Invest in a set of four if you want to impress your friends and family with baked dessert delights. Parchment paper is your best friend for stopping cakes, breads, biscuits, and cookies from sticking to your baking tins.

Chill cookie dough, warm bread doughs

As a rule of thumb, cookie doughs which are cooled and left to chill for an hour or two, create fluffy, light cookies. When left to heat and go mushy, the cookies are denser and flatter.

Contrarily, a warm bread dough allows the yeast to ferment. You will have a light, fluffy bread. A cold bread dough means the yeast is no longer working. If it gets cooled too soon, the yeast will not ferment and your bread will be flat.

Confectioners' sugar or icing sugar?

Depending on where you live, you may substitute icing sugar for confectioner's sugar and vice versa. To make icing sugar from normal sugar, place caster sugar into a food processor and blend it well. Powdered sugar is just sugar blended into smaller particles than what you would find in caster sugar. Again, caster sugar is simply granulated sugar blended into smaller particles.

Check your substitutions

If you need to substitute an ingredient, be sure to have cooked the recipe at least once beforehand. There are some recipes that can have ingredients switched out easily. For example, if you wanted to make a vegetarian shepherd's pie, switching out the lamb mince for soy mince or Quorn could be a healthy alternative.

Separating eggs

To separate an egg white from an egg yolk, crack the egg open over a bowl. Pour the yolk into one half of the shell, then back into the other half of the shell. Let the white fall out and focus on the yolk. You can use your fingers instead of the yolk, but a professional baker would try not to touch the eggs if they could help it.

Advice on yeast

In general, a recipe for bread will require yeast. The recipe will state which kind of yeast, as it may need dried, active, or fresh yeast. Yeast is activated by adding lukewarm water and sugar (which it eats) and placing in a warm place for 10-15 minutes. Salt deactivates yeast over time. If you are baking bread, try to add the sugar at the beginning and the salt towards the end.

Yeast should always be kept warm, but not hot. Do not pour boiling water straight over your yeast as it may kill it. Instant yeast can be added straight to your recipe without activation. Just keep it away from the salt.

Cooling advice

If you don't have a wire cooling rack, you can cool baked goods using the inside of your grill pan. Be sure your grill is off at the time! Try not to remove cakes and loaves from their tins until the baked goods are properly cooled. To remove them before proper cooling increases the chances that they will break apart. Cutting bread before it is properly cooled is also a bad idea since it will still be cooking for a while after it comes out of the oven. Leave loaves to cool for 15-20 minutes for a warmed, but cooked, loaf.

Checking on baked goods

If you are waiting for a cake to rise and want to check if it is ready or not, inserting a toothpick into the mixture (or a butter knife) in the thickest part will tell you. If the toothpick draws out clean, the food is cooked. If it is still doughy, the mixture needs more time.

Bicarbonate of Soda Vs Baking Powder?

Both ingredients can produce bubbles within your mixture, allowing more air to get inside your baked goods. Bicarbonate of soda requires another acidic ingredient plus liquid to be activated. Baking powder is bicarbonate of soda which has had cream of tartare added into it. This means it does not need an acid to activate, it only needs liquid. Both will produce a light, bubbly texture that keeps baked goods aeriated.

Whether you require baking powder or bicarbonate of soda will depend on the other ingredients. Follow the recipe for best results. As an added aside, many American recipe books stick to baking powder or baking soda, while many British recipes call for bicarbonate of soda. Recipes in Britain from before the 1990s would often call for both bicarbonate of soda and cream of tartare. This can still be found nowadays in old cookbooks.

What Baking Equipment Do I Need?

To start baking at home, you will need some basic pieces of equipment.

Basic Baking Equipment:
- A large bowl, preferably metal
- A whisk
- A wooden spoon
- A spatula
- A fork
- An oven
- A cake tin or baking tray
- Scales, digital or otherwise
- Sieve

As your hobby progresses, you may wish to invest in other baking equipment. We would recommend some of the following.

Optional Baking Equipment:
- An electronic mixer
- An electric whisk
- Parchment paper
- Ring moulds
- A loaf tin
- A muffin tin
- A cooling rack (you can use your grill pan tray)
- Reusable pastry bag and nozzles
- Measuring cups and spoons
- Cookie cutters

- Oven thermometer
- A bench scraper

There are plenty of other optional pieces of baking equipment but if you have all the above, you are well on your way to baking success.

A Glossary of Baking Terms

There are those of us who are complete beginners and we welcome each one of you. However, you need to get up to speed on bakery terms before we go any further. We have outlined the key baking terms below as a reference point for the rest of the book. If you come across a term in a recipe that you do not recognise, you will find it here.

Whisking

When we "whisk" our food we use a specific device to do so, which is known as a whisk. This device can be motorized to make our lives easier. An electric whisk will take egg whites to meringue mix in less than 5 minutes. By hand, whisking egg whites into meringue takes up to three times as long.

As a pro tip: whip cream by whisking it in a metal bowl. Whisking in a metal bowl generates extra friction which will help get the job done faster. This works for anything you need to whisk until stiffened.

Beating

When beating a mixture, you are required to use a metal spoon or fork. Contrarily, beating can mean whisking in some circumstances. The recipe should make this clear. The purpose of beating with a metal spoon or fork is to get air into a mixture that cannot be whisked to stiff peaks.

Folding

We usually "fold" flour into a pre-whisked mixture of other ingredients. Folding is done with a spatula or metal spoon. We run the spatula around the outside of the bowl and fold it on top of itself into the centre. We repeat this until the flour is gone. When we fold, we usually sieve the flour or icing sugar. The purpose of folding is to stop the air from leaving the mixture as we add the heavier flour.

Kneading

We use the term "kneading" to describe the act of working a dough mixture. Typically used in the baking of breads, kneading the dough means to stretch, press, and distort the mixture.

We knead the bread to encourage the formation of gluten strands within a dough mixture. These form when liquid is added to some flour. The more you stretch and work your dough, the stronger these strands will be. This leads to a denser bread, so be careful not to over-knead.

Lining

When we say "lining" in bakery, we mean creating a layer between the baked goods and the tray or tin we are using to cook it. The easiest way to line a tin is with baking parchment, although dessert, cake, and bread tins, are often lined with butter and a dusting of flour. We would "grease" a tin with butter or non-stick spray to help the parchment paper stick.

Proofing

When baking breads, we often leave the dough to rise in a technique called "proofing." Proofing allows the yeast in your dough to do its job of making the mixture rise. It rises because the yeast expels carbon dioxide as it grows. This is a fermentation process which makes a better bread.

Sieving

A Sieve is a piece of kitchen equipment which is used to finely sieve your dry ingredients. It keeps flour particles separated, allowing more air to get into your mixture. We use sieving during baking cakes and desserts which need plenty of air in the mixture so that they are bouncy and light instead of dense.

Creaming

When creaming two baking ingredients together, you are blending them until they form a cream-like consistency. We use this term when referring to blending butter and sugar together, as we do to form a basic blend for many cake recipes.

Rubbing

When we "rub-in" a substance in baking, we use one of two techniques. We use the fingers of our hands and avoid the mixture touching the palms. The aim of rubbing ingredients into one another is to achieve a breadcrumb-like consistency. We usually rub butter into flour to make this texture. It allows as much air into the mixture as possible, while ensuring the two ingredients are well blended. We do not want to melt the butter, which is why we avoid using the palms of our hands.

The two ways to rub-in ingredients are as follows:

a) Pick up a scoop of mixture using only your fingers. This is best done from above, as if your fingers are a crane closing. Hold one hand flat and drop the scoop onto its fingers using the scooped hand. Holding your flat hand facing away from you, flatten your scoop hand and push the material away from your body to the side. This causes friction which rubs the two ingredients together.

b) Using each hand as a scoop, pick up a little material at a time and rub your thumb across your forefingers. Slowly let the material fall through those fingers as you do so.

Remember: if your palms have flour on them, you are not rubbing-in correctly.

Conversion Tables

Where needed, conversions throughout this recipe book will be given in UK//US (ca).

°C	°F	Fan Oven	Gas Mark
170	325	150	3
180	350	160	4
190	375	170	5
200	400	180	6
220	425	200	7
230	450	210	8

Millilitres	Fl Ounces
1ml	0.04
5ml	0.18
10ml	0.35
50ml	1.76
100ml	17.6
1000ml	170.6

Grams	Ounces
1g	0.0353oz
5g	0.1764oz
10g	0.3527oz
50g	1.7637oz
100g	3.5274oz
1000g	35.2740oz

Recipes

Baked Breads

Simple White Loaf

MAKES 10-12 SLICES
PREP TIME: 2 HRS 20 MINS | COOK TIME: 25 MINS | TOTAL TIME: 2 HRS 55 MINS
NET CARBS PER SLICE: 38G//1.3OZ | PROTEIN: 6G//0.2OZ |
FAT: 4G//0.14OZ | FIBER: 2G//0.07OZ | KCAL: 200

INGREDIENTS

- 500g//17.6oz strong white bread flour
- 7g//0.2oz instant yeast
- 300ml//10.1floz of lukewarm water
- 2 tbsp olive oil
- 1.5 tsp salt
- Self-raising flour for dusting

INSTRUCTIONS

1 Mix bread flour and yeast into a large bowl.

2 Make a well in the middle of the mixture, then gradually pour the water and the olive oil into it.

3 Mix with a knife until the mixture becomes a dough. It should be wet enough to remove all material from the sides of the bowl, but stiff enough that you can knead it.

4 Once the dough has come together, sprinkle in the salt to deactivate the yeast.

5 Turn the dough out onto a floured surface and knead for ten minutes.

6 Place your dough back inside the bowl and cover it loosely with clingfilm. Leave to rise somewhere warm (but not hot) for 2 hours or more.

7 When ready to bake your bread, preheat your oven to 220C//428F//gas mark 7.

8 The dough will now be much larger than it was when you left it. Remove it from the bowl and place it on a floured surface. Fold it in on itself twice. Do not fully knead it.

9 Place the dough into a lined loaf tin. If you do not have a bread tin, the dough can be shaped into a ball and placed on a baking tray. Score the surface of the bread with a knife.

10 Place inside the oven and cook for 25 minutes or until the bread has turned golden brown.

11 Do not cut your bread until it has cooled slightly as it will still be cooking in the middle.

Wholesome Wholemeal Bread

MAKES 10-12 SLICES
PREP TIME: 2HRS 20 MINS | COOK TIME: 25 MINS | TOTAL TIME: 2HRS 55 MINS
NET CARBS PER SLICE: 23.64G//0.8OZ | PROTEIN: 3.86G//0.13OZ |
FAT: 2.48G// 0.08OZ | FIBER: 2.8G//0.09OZ | KCAL: 128

INGREDIENTS

- 400g//14.1oz strong wholemeal bread flour
- A pinch of salt
- A pinch of sugar
- 7g//0.24oz instant yeast sachet
- 300ml//10.1floz lukewarm water
- 2 tablespoons olive oil
- Wholemeal flour for dusting

INSTRUCTIONS

1 Mix your wholemeal flour, the sugar, the salt, and the instant yeast together in a bowl.

2 Create a well in the centre, then gradually add the water and the oil to the well.

3 Mix the water into the dough using a knife. Once it is coming away from the sides of the bowl freely you can stop adding water. The mixture should come together into a ball without being sticky.

4 Turn your dough onto a floured surface and knead for 10 minutes.

5 Cover with clingfilm and place somewhere warm (but not hot) for 2 hours or more. The dough will proof and rise.

6 Preheat the oven to 200C//392F//gas mark 6.

7 Remove the dough from the bowl and place it on a floured surface. Turn it over on itself twice.

8 Place the dough into a lined loaf tin or form into a ball and place on a lined baking tray. Score the top of the loaf with a knife.

9 Place inside the oven and cook for 30-35 minutes or until the crust is golden.

10 Allow your bread to cool a little before you cut it as it will still be cooking on the inside.

Sourdough Bread

MAKES 10-12 SLICES
PREP TIME: 8 DAYS 12 HRS 15 MINS | COOK TIME: 30 MINS |
TOTAL TIME: 8 DAYS 12 HRS 55 MINS
NET CARBS PER SLICE: 50G//1.7OZ | PROTEIN: 8G//0.28OZ |
FIBER: 2G//0.07OZ | FAT: 0.9G//0.03OZ | KCAL: 240

INGREDIENTS (STARTER)

- ◯ 700g//24.7oz strong white bread flour
- ◯ Warm water

INGREDIENTS (BREAD)

- ◯ 500g//17.63oz strong white bread flour plus extra for dusting
- ◯ 1 tsp salt
- ◯ 1 tsp sugar
- ◯ 300g//10.58oz sourdough starter
- ◯ 250ml//8.4floz lukewarm water
- ◯ 1 tbsp rapeseed oil

INSTRUCTIONS

1 Place 100g flour and 150 ml of water in a sealable jar and mix well. Leave the jar open for half an hour and then seal it. Place it somewhere warm but not hot.

2 For 6 consecutive days, add an extra 100g flour and 150ml water per day. By day 7 your starter will be usable.

3 You can keep your sourdough starter in the fridge for as long as you need it. You will have to feed more flour and water into the mixture every 4 days to keep the yeast alive.

4 To make your sourdough bread, place all the dry ingredients in a bowl and mix well.

5 Make a well in the middle and pour the sourdough starter and the water into it. Keep the remaining portion of your starter for another loaf and remember to feed it fresh flour over the coming days.

6 Mix the dough together with a knife until it comes freely away from the sides of the bowl into a ball.

7 Turn the ball out onto a floured surface and knead it well for ten minutes. When it is ready, it should have a soft, stretchy texture.

8 Take a clean bowl and line it with oil, then put your dough inside it and cover it with clingfilm. Leave it to proof for 3-4 hrs.

9 Remove it from this bowl and place it into a clean bowl, this time cover it loosely. Leave it to rise overnight. Sourdough takes two-three times longer to rise than any other dough.

10 Top tip: the longer you leave a sourdough to rise for, the better the flavour. When it is ready it will have doubled in size and will have a few air bubbles.

11 Preheat your oven to 230C//446F//gas mark 8 and line a baking tray with parchment paper or prepare a loaf tin.

12 Place an ovenproof dish containing water in the bottom shelf of the oven to create steam.

13 Put the dough onto your tray and score it with a knife. Place the dough in the oven and bake for 30-40 minutes.

14 Remove from the oven and cool for 20 minutes before cutting, as the bread will still be cooking on the inside.

Poppy Seed Rolls

MAKES 8 ROLLS
PREP TIME: 30 MINS PLUS 3 HRS PROVING |
COOK TIME: 20 MINS | TOTAL TIME: 3 HRS 50 MINS
NET CARBS PER ROLL: 48G//1.7OZ | PROTEIN: 9G//0.31OZ |
FIBER: 2.6G//0.09OZ | FAT: 7G//0.03OZ | KCAL: 255

INGREDIENTS

- 500g//17.63oz strong white bread flour
- 1 tsp salt
- 1 tsp granulated sugar
- 7g//0.25oz fast action yeast
- 30g//1oz butter, softened
- 75ml//2.5floz lukewarm milk
- 1 tbsp cold milk
- 2 tbsp roasted poppy seeds

INSTRUCTIONS

1 Mix the flour, salt, sugar, and yeast together in a bowl.

2 Rub in the butter until it has a breadcrumb consistency.

3 Add in the warm milk and combine into a dough.

4 Turn the dough onto a lightly floured surface and knead for ten minutes or until it is smooth.

5 Put the dough back into the bowl, cover it, and allow it to rise in a warm place. Within an hour it should double in size.

6 Remove the dough from the bowl and preheat the oven to 220C//428F// gas mark 6.

7 Knock the air out of the dough by turning it over on itself a few times. Do not overwork it.

8 Separate your dough into 8 portions and place them on a lined baking tray.

9 Brush them with the tbsp of cold milk and sprinkle them with the poppy seeds.

10 Bake for 15-20 minutes or until golden brown.

11 Remove from the oven and leave to cool for at least 15 minutes before serving.

Sweet Breads

Banana Bread Recipe

MAKES 8-10 SLICES
PREP TIME: 15 MINS | COOK TIME: 45 MINS | TOTAL TIME: 1 HR
NET CARBS PER 2 SLICES: 53G//1.86OZ | PROTEIN: 5G//0.17OZ |
FIBER: 2G//0.07OZ | FAT: 11G//0.38OZ | KCAL: 334

INGREDIENTS

- ○ 285g//10oz self raising flour
- ○ A pinch of salt
- ○ 110g//4oz butter, softened
- ○ 225g//8oz caster sugar
- ○ 2 overripe bananas
- ○ 2 drops vanilla essence
- ○ 2 large eggs

INSTRUCTIONS

1 Preheat oven to 180C//356F//gas mark 4.

2 Take a small bowl and sieve your flour into it. Add the salt and mix it well, then set it aside.

3 Place the butter and the sugar in a large bowl and cream them together with a wooden spoon.

4 On a separate plate, mash the bananas until they are gooey and sticky, then add them to the creamed butter and sugar.

5 Next, add the vanilla essence, then take a metal fork and beat the eggs into the wet mixture. The object is to get as much air into the mixture as possible without whisking it.

6 Add a little flour at a time to the mixture and fold it in using a spatula or metal spoon.

7 Line a cake or loaf tin with parchment paper and spoon the mixture into it.

8 Place in the oven and cook for 45 minutes or until the top has turned golden brown.

9 Remove from the oven and leave to cool for at least 20 minutes before serving as it will be extremely hot.

Simple Sweet Baps

MAKES 8 PORTIONS
PREP TIME: 1 HR MINS | COOK TIME: 20 MINS | TOTAL TIME: 1HR 20 MINS
NET CARBS PER 30G BAP: 16G//0.56OZ | PROTEIN: 3G//0.105OZ |
FIBER: 0.9G//0.03OZ | FAT: 2.2G//0.07OZ | KCAL: 96

INGREDIENTS

- ○ 1 7g//0.05oz packet of dried yeast
- ○ 110ml//3.71floz of warm water
- ○ 1 tbsp sugar
- ○ A pinch of salt
- ○ 250g//8.18oz plain flour
- ○ one large egg, beaten
- ○ 25g//0.88oz of softened butter
- ○ 2 tbsp strawberry jam
- ○ 100g//3.5oz mixed fruit

INSTRUCTIONS

1 Mix the yeast and the warm water together with the sugar and stir well. Cover with clingfilm and leave in a warm place for 10 minutes. When it turns frothy it is ready to use.

2 Mix the salt and flour together in a separate large bowl. Make a well in the centre and add in your yeast mix. Add half of the egg and the butter and mix it together into a dough.

3 Knead the dough for ten minutes or until smooth.

4 Return the dough to the bowl, cover it loosely, and set it back in the warm place to rise for 20 minutes.

5 Preheat the oven to 200C//392F//gas mark 6.

6 Remove the dough from the bowl and push the air out of it. Divide it into 8 balls. Roll each of the 8 balls flat on a floured surface.

7 Smear the flattened dough with jam and fill with a little mixed fruit, then pinch the balls closed.

8 Put in the oven for 20 minutes or until golden brown. Leave to cool for 15 minutes or more, the contents will be hot.

Cinnamon Rolls

MAKES 12 ROLLS
PREP TIME: 1HR 45MINS (INCLUDING PROOFING TIME) |
COOK TIME: 30 MINS | TOTAL TIME: 2 HRS 15 MINS
NET CARBS PER 88G ROLL: 47G//1.65OZ | PROTEIN: 3.8G//0.13OZ |
FIBER: 1.2G//0.04OZ | FAT: 9.9G//0.349OZ | KCAL: 290

INGREDIENTS

- ◯ 350g//12.34oz plain flour
- ◯ 7g//0.24oz sachet dried instant yeast
- ◯ 2 tbsp cinnamon
- ◯ 100g//3.52oz granulated sugar
- ◯ A pinch of salt
- ◯ 40g//1.41oz butter
- ◯ 70ml//2.36floz cold water
- ◯ 120ml//4.05floz whole milk
- ◯ 2 drops vanilla essence
- ◯ 1 large egg, beaten
- ◯ 120g//4.23oz icing sugar

INSTRUCTIONS

1 In a large bowl, add the plain flour to the dried instant yeast. Mix in 1 tbsp of cinnamon, half the sugar, and the salt. Set it aside for later.

2 Melt half the butter in a saucepan over a low heat. Add in the water, the milk, the vanilla essence and lastly the egg. The mixture should be no more than warm.

3 Add in the dry ingredients slowly, stirring as you go. Gradually it will come together to make a dough. Remove it from the heat and turn that dough out onto a prepared floured surface.

4 Knead the dough for at least 10 minutes, or until it is stretchable and silken.

5 Return the mixture to the bowl and cover it loosely with either a wet cloth or some clingfilm. Let it rise for approximately 1 hr to 1 hr 30 minutes. The dough will double in size.

6 Preheat the oven to 190C//374F//gas mark 5.

7 Remove the dough from the bowl and knock the air out of it by turning it over on itself a few times but do not knead it.

8 Separate your dough into 12 portions and roll flat. Mix the rest of the butter and sugar together and smear it on the dough.

9 Place rolls on a baking tray and cook for 25-30 minutes.

10 Mix the last of the cinnamon and the icing sugar with water and drizzle over cooled rolls.

English Tea Loaf

MAKES 1 FRUIT LOAF OR 4-5 SERVINGS
PREP TIME: 20 MINS | COOK TIME: 45 MINS | TOTAL TIME: 1 HR 5 MINS
NET CARBS PER 2 SLICES: 47G//1.65OZ | PROTEIN: 5G//0.17OZ |
FIBER: 2G//0.07OZ | FAT: 1G//0.35OZ | KCAL: 279

INGREDIENTS

- ◯ 110g//3.8oz softened butter
- ◯ 110g//3.8oz caster sugar
- ◯ 225g//8oz self-raising flour
- ◯ A pinch of salt
- ◯ 225g//8oz mixed dried fruit*
- ◯ 2 large eggs. beaten
- ◯ 20ml//0.67floz whole milk

*Can be substituted for chocolate

INSTRUCTIONS

1 Preheat the oven to 180C//356F//gas mark 4. Line a loaf tin or baking tray in preparation.

2 Cream the butter and the sugar together in a large bowl until the mixture is smooth.

3 Rub in the flour and the salt until the mixture forms a breadcrumb consistency.

4 Add the fruit into the mixture and stir well.

5 Add in the eggs and mix.

6 Place into the loaf tin or onto the baking tray and brush the dough with the milk.

7 bake for about 45 minutes or until it has turned golden.

8 Place it on a wire rack to cool for 15-20 minutes before cutting.

Light and Airy Brioche Loaf

MAKES 8 PORTIONS OR ONE LOAF
PREP TIME: 45 MINS (PLUS 3.5 HOURS PROOFING) |
COOK TIME: 35 MINS | TOTAL TIME: 4 HRS 50 MINS

NET CARBS PER PORTION: 49G//1.72OZ | PROTEIN: 12G//0.42OZ |
FIBER: 2G//0.07OZ | FAT: 23G//0.81OZ | KCAL: 460

INGREDIENTS

- ⭕ 7g//0.25oz dried active yeast
- ⭕ 50g//1.76oz sugar
- ⭕ 450g//15.8oz strong white bread flour
- ⭕ A pinch of sea salt
- ⭕ 100ml//3.34floz whole milk
- ⭕ 5 room temperature eggs, one beaten to glaze
- ⭕ 200g//7.05oz unsalted butter, softened

INSTRUCTIONS

1 Place the yeast, sugar, and flour in a bowl and mix. Add the salt last and stir well.

2 Heat the milk gently in a saucepan over a low heat.

3 Make a well in the centre of the flour mixture and gradually pour the warmed milk into the hole.

4 Beat your 4 eggs in one bowl and your fifth egg separately. Gradually add the 4 eggs to the mixture, stirring all the while.

5 Gradually feed in the butter while mixing. This recipe is best mixed with a hand mixer or electronic mixing bowl from this point forward. Beating by hand is possible but will take much longer. It should take 10 minutes to feed in the butter and eggs.

6 Line a large bowl with a little butter and place the dough into it. Cover it with cling film loosely and leave it to proof somewhere warm for up to two hours.

7 Place your risen dough in the fridge to chill for 1 hour or more.

8 Preheat your oven to 180C//356F//gas mark 4.

9 Turn the dough onto a floured surface and divide into 8 equal dough balls.

10 Place the dough balls into a lined loaf tin and brush them with the remaining egg.

11 Bake for 30-35 minutes and leave to cool for 15 minutes before serving.

Baked Starters//Appetizers

Baked Camembert

INGREDIENTS

❍ 1 round camembert cheese (250g//8.8 oz) *

❍ 1 sprig rosemary or thyme

❍ (optional) 1 teaspoon chilli flakes

❍ (optional) 1 teaspoon white wine

* Can be substituted with brie

INSTRUCTIONS

1   Preheat the oven to 180 C//356F//gas mark 5.

2   Remove the cheese from its plastic packaging and return it to its wooden container.

3   Slice cheese into 4 quarters, scoring two lines into the surface until you can see the cheese underneath the skin.

4   Place sprig of rosemary or thyme (depending on taste) along the central line.

5   Sprinkle drops of wine and optional chilli flakes over the cheese.

6   Place in the centre of your preheated oven and bake for 20 minutes or until the centre of the cheese has become gooey.

7   Serve with crackers, bread, or garlic bread.

Italian Garlic and Rosemary Focaccia

SERVES 2 PEOPLE
PREP TIME: 1 HR 5 MINS | TOTAL TIME: 1 HR 25 MINS
NET CARBS PER SLICE: 20G//0.70OZ | PROTEIN: 5G//0.17OZ |
FIBER: 1G//0.03OZ | FAT: 4.5G//0.16OZ | KCAL: 142

INGREDIENTS

- ○ 1 sachet dried yeast
- ○ A pinch of sugar
- ○ 300ml//10.1floz lukewarm water
- ○ 400g//14.14oz strong white bread flour
- ○ A pinch of salt
- ○ 20ml//0.7floz olive oil
- ○ 100g//3.50oz semolina flour
- ○ Two sprigs rosemary, finely chopped
- ○ Two garlic cloves, crushed or finely chopped
- ○ A pinch of flaked sea salt

INSTRUCTIONS

1 Place the yeast and sugar in the jug of lukewarm water, stir it, and cover it. Place it somewhere warm, but not hot. Leave it for ten minutes to ferment.

2 Preheat your oven to 220C//428F//gas mark 7.

3 Mix your flour and salt together in a large bowl.

4 Make a well in the centre of your flour mix and add the yeast and water mix a little at a time. It will come together into a dough.

5 Turn the dough onto a lightly floured surface and knead for 10 minutes.

6 Use 10ml of olive oil to line a fresh bowl and transfer your dough into it. Cover it loosely with clingfilm and leave it for 30 minutes.

7 The dough will have risen to double in size. Turn it out onto a floured surface again, this time using the semolina flour. Turn it over on itself to knock the air out of the mixture.

8 Roll the dough out onto until it is about the thickness of a pound coin// dollar coin.

9 Transfer your flat dough onto a baking tray that has been lined with parchment paper.

10 Brush the dough with the remainder of the olive oil, the garlic, and rosemary. Sprinkle with the salt.

11 Cook for 15-20 minutes or until golden brown. Serve immediately.

Goats Cheese and Caramelized Red Onion Tart

MAKES 6 TARTS
PREP TIME: 35 MINS | COOK TIME: 15 MINS | TOTAL TIME: 50 MINS
NET CARBS PER TART: 26G//0.70OZ | PROTEIN: 7.9G//0.17OZ |
FIBER: 1.1G//0.04OZ | FAT: 21.5G//0.16OZ | KCAL: 336

INGREDIENTS

- ○ 500g//17.63oz short crust Pastry
- ○ 1 tbsp butter
- ○ 20ml//0.7floz olive oil
- ○ 3 red onions, finely diced
- ○ 1 tbsp reduced balsamic vinegar
- ○ 1 tsp thyme
- ○ A pinch of salt
- ○ 200g//7oz goat's cheese

INSTRUCTIONS

1   Preheat oven to 200C//392F//gas mark 6 and line your tart cases with butter.

2   Roll out your pastry and insert it into your tart cases.

3   Place parchment paper over the pastry and fill with baking beans or dried lentils to blind bake. Bake in the oven for 10 minutes, until the pastry is starting to brown and holds its shape on its own.

4   Leave the pastry to cool without removing them from the tart cases.

5   Heat the oil in a saucepan over a medium heat.

6   Add the finely chopped onion and the vinegar. Sprinkle in the thyme, add the salt, and lastly break in the goat's cheese.

7   Reduce the heat to a low setting and simmer for five minutes.

8   Once the cheese is beginning to melt, remove from the heat and spoon the mixture evenly into your tart cases.

9   Return tarts to the oven and bake for a further 15 minutes, or until your tarts are golden brown and melting.

10 Serve immediately.

Pull Apart Cheesy Garlic Flatbread

SERVES 4 PEOPLE
PREP TIME: 55 MINS | COOK TIME: 25 MINS | TOTAL TIME: 1 HR 20 MINS
NET CARBS PER 53G//1.86OZ PIECE: 12G//0.42OZ | PROTEIN: 6G//0.21OZ |
FIBER: 0.6G//0.04OZ | FAT: 14G//0.49OZ | KCAL: 199

INGREDIENTS (DOUGH)

- ○ 7g//0.24oz pack of dried yeast
- ○ 200ml//6.76floz lukewarm water
- ○ A pinch of sugar
- ○ 1 egg
- ○ 45g//1.5oz softened unsalted butter
- ○ 300g//10.5oz strong white bread flour
- ○ 2 tsp garlic powder
- ○ A pinch of salt

INGREDIENTS (TOPPING)

- ○ 75g//2.64oz melted butter
- ○ 2 minced garlic cloves
- ○ 2 tsp chopped rosemary or thyme (optional)
- ○ 2 tsp chopped parsley (optional)
- ○ 100g//3.5oz cheddar/parmesan/cheese of your choice
- ○ A pinch of flaked rock salt

INSTRUCTIONS

1. Start by making your dough. Mix the yeast with the lukewarm water and the sugar in a jug. Cover the bowl with clingfilm and set it aside for 15 minutes or until a froth forms.

2. Beat the egg in a large bowl, then add the butter, flour, garlic, and salt to that same bowl and mix it well.

3. Add the frothy yeast and mix until it is smooth. If you do not have a dough-like consistency, add more water to make it less stiff or more flour to make it stiffer.

4. Turn your dough onto a floured surface and stretch and knead it for ten minutes.

5. Return the dough to the bowl and cover it with cling film. Leave it somewhere warm to rise for 30 minutes or so.

6. Preheat the oven to 180C//356F//gas mark 4. Line a baking tray with parchment paper.

7. Take the dough from the bowl and turn it over on itself a few times to knock the air out.

8. Separate the dough into small balls, no larger than a table tennis ball. Place these on a lined baking tray.

9 Score a line through the centre on each of the balls and set them aside.

10 To make your filling, combine the melted butter, garlic, and optional ingredients into one small bowl.

11 Brush the mixture over your dough balls until you have used it all. Sprinkle the cheese on top of the dough, and finally sprinkle with the rock salt.

12 Place in the centre of the oven and bake for 20-25 minutes or until the cheese is starting to crisp. Serve while still hot.

Baked Pies and Main Meals

Classic Chicken and Mushroom Pie

SERVES 4/5 PEOPLE
PREP TIME: 45 MINS | COOK TIME: 35 MINS | TOTAL TIME: 1 HR 20 MINS
NET CARBS PER ¼ PIE: 57G//2.1OZ | PROTEIN: 55G//1.94OZ |
FIBER: 1G//0.035OZ | FAT: 47G//1.65OZ | KCAL: 855

INGREDIENTS

- ⭕ 2 tbsp oil
- ⭕ 6 sliced chicken breasts
- ⭕ 1 diced onion
- ⭕ 250g//8.8oz sliced mushrooms
- ⭕ A pinch of salt/pepper
- ⭕ 1 tbsp thyme
- ⭕ 2 tbsp flour
- ⭕ 350ml//11.8floz chicken stock
- ⭕ 180ml//6floz milk
- ⭕ 500g//17.63oz fresh puff pastry
- ⭕ 1 beaten egg

INSTRUCTIONS

1   Heat the oil in a saucepan over a medium heat and add your sliced chicken. Cook until seared white.

2   Add the onion, mushrooms, salt and pepper, and thyme to the pan. Cook for a further five minutes stirring often. Add the flour and cook for another few minutes.

3   Add the chicken stock and remove the saucepan from the heat. While it is cooling, stir in the milk and return it to a low heat. Cover and simmer the entire mixture for 30 minutes.

4   Preheat the oven to 220C//428F//gas mark 7.

5   Roll out your pastry while the pan is cooking and line your pie tin with a brush of butter and parchment paper. Make sure your pastry is 1/5 an inch thick or more. You may use the extra pastry to decorate the pie lid.

6   Gently spoon the cooked mixture from the pan to the pie case. Place the lid on and glaze with the egg.

7   Put your pie in the oven and bake for thirty minutes or until golden brown and risen.

Vegetarian Shepherd's Pie

SERVES 4/5 PEOPLE
PREP TIME: 10 MINS | COOK TIME: 1 HR | TOTAL TIME: 1 HR 10 MINS
NET CARBS PER ¼ PIE: 66G//2.1OZ | PROTEIN: 16G//1.94OZ |
FIBER: 16G//0.035OZ | FAT: 15G//1.65OZ | KCAL: 530

INGREDIENTS

- 1 tbsp olive oil
- 1 large onion, peeled and chopped
- 2 large carrots, peeled and chopped
- 1 can chopped tomatoes (440g//15.5oz)
- 1 can lentils (400g//14.1oz)
- 1 vegetable stock cube
- 150ml//5.1floz boiling water
- 200ml//6.76floz red wine
- 900g//31.7oz potatoes, peeled and chopped
- 30g//1.05oz butter
- A pinch of salt and pepper
- 100g//3.5oz cheese of your choice
- 2 tbsp chopped rosemary or thyme (optional)
- 500g//17.6oz short crust pastry, ready to roll

INSTRUCTIONS

1 Put the oil in a frying pan and heat on a low heat. When it is hot enough to sizzle, add the onion. Gently heat the onions until they are caramelised/browned. Add the chopped carrots, the tomatoes, and the lentils.

2 In a separate jug, mix the stock cubes into the boiling water and add to the frying pan. Pour in the red wine and add in the optional rosemary or thyme. Allow ingredients to simmer.

3 Place the potatoes in a saucepan with some water and bring them to the boil for 15 minutes. Remove from the heat and drain, then mash in the butter. Add salt and pepper to taste.

4 Preheat your oven to 190C//374F//gas mark 5 and roll out your pastry to fit your pie tin. The pastry should be about ¼ inch thick.

5 Spoon your ingredients into the pie case, cover with mash, and bake for 20 minutes.

Old English Steak and Ale pie

SERVES 4/5 PEOPLE
PREP TIME: 25 MINS | COOK TIME: 1 HR 20 MINS | TOTAL TIME: 1 HR 45 MINS
NET CARBS PER ¼ PIE: 46G//1.6OZ | PROTEIN:58G//2.04OZ |
FIBER: 6G//0.21OZ | FAT: 54G//1.90OZ | KCAL: 923

INGREDIENTS

- 1 tbsp olive oil
- 900g//31.74oz raw steak, diced
- 2 large onions, diced
- 2 large carrots, chopped
- 150g//5.29oz sliced mushrooms
- 2 tsp thyme
- 400ml//13.5floz beef stock
- 400ml//13.5floz strong black ale
- 350g//12.3oz fresh puff pastry
- 25g//0.8ozg butter
- Salt and pepper to taste
- 1 beaten egg

INSTRUCTIONS

1 Heat the oil in a saucepan over a medium heat and place in the steak. Cook until it is seared on all sides.

2 Add in each of the vegetables and the thyme.

3 Add in the stock and ale and allow to simmer for 1 hour, covered and on a low heat.

4 While the mix is cooking, roll out your pastry. Line your pie tin with butter and parchment paper and place your pastry in the dish. Keep some for the lid.

5 Preheat your oven to 220C//428F//gas mark 7.

6 Season your pie mixture with salt and pepper before you remove it from the heat.

7 Gently spoon the mixture into your pie case and cover it with a pastry lid. Seal the pie closed with the egg. Brush the pie with the mix to glaze.

8 Cool for 30 minutes or until golden brown.

Country Cottage pie

SERVES 4/5 PEOPLE
PREP TIME: 25 MINS | COOK TIME: 30 MINS | TOTAL TIME: 55 MINS
NET CARBS PER ¼ PIE: 20G//0.7OZ | PROTEIN:16G//0.56OZ |
FIBER: 5G//0.17OZ | FAT: 35G//1.2OZ | KCAL: 658

INGREDIENTS

- ◯ 900g//31.74oz potatoes, peeled and diced
- ◯ 1 tbsp olive oil
- ◯ 1 large onion, finely diced
- ◯ 2 carrots, thinly sliced
- ◯ 1 small tin garden peas (150g//5.29oz)
- ◯ 1 celery stalk, diced
- ◯ 500g//17.6oz lean beef mince
- ◯ 2 bay leaves
- ◯ 1 tin chopped tomato (400g//14.10oz)
- ◯ 20g//0.70oz tomato puree
- ◯ 150ml//5.07floz beef stock
- ◯ A pinch of salt
- ◯ 30g//1.05oz butter

INSTRUCTIONS

| 1 | Place your potatoes in a pan of salted water and bring them to the boil. |

| 2 | Preheat oven to 180C//356F//gas mark 4. |

| 3 | Heat the oil in a frying pan over a medium heat. When the oil is hot, add the onion, carrots, peas, celery, and beef. Allow the beef to brown. |

| 4 | Add in the bay leaves, tomatoes, tomato puree, and the beef stock. Allow to simmer for 15 minutes. |

| 5 | Remove your potatoes from the heat, drain them, add in salt and butter and mash. |

| 6 | Remove bay leaves from the meat mixture and discard. Then place the mixture into an oven proof dish. |

| 7 | Spoon mash on top and place in the oven. Cook for 20 minutes or until golden brown. |

Succulent Shepherd's Pie

SERVES 4/5
PREP TIME: 20 MINS | COOK TIME: 45 MINS | TOTAL TIME: 1 HR 5 MINS
NET CARBS PER ¼ PIE: 52G//1.83OZ | PROTEIN:34G//1.19OZ |
FIBER: 6.7G//0.23OZ | FAT: 40G//1.41OZ | KCAL: 693

INGREDIENTS

○ 900g//31.74oz potatoes

○ 2 tbsp olive oil

○ 1 large, diced onion

○ 550g//19.4oz raw minced lamb

○ 250g// 8.8oz diced vegetables of your choice (carrots, peas, mange tout, green beans)

○ 100ml//3.38floz beef stock

○ 25g//0.88oz gravy browning

○ 2 tbsp Worcestershire sauce

○ Salt and pepper to taste

○ 60g//2.11oz salted butter

○ (Optional) 25g//0.88oz cheese

INSTRUCTIONS

1 Peel and chop your potatoes, place them in a pan with salted water. Bring them to the boil for 15-20 minutes.

2 Preheat your oven to 200C//392F//gas mark 6.

3 Place the oil into a frying pan and gently heat on a medium setting. Add in the onions.

4 Add the lamb to the pan and allow it to brown.

5 Add the diced vegetables to the pan and heat for a few minutes.

6 Mix your beef stock with your gravy browning and the Worcester sauce in a separate jug. Add it slowly to the mixture in the frying pan. Simmer for five minutes then turn the frying pan to a low heat.

7 Remove the potatoes from the heat and drain them. Put them back into the pot. Add salt and pepper to taste, and your butter. Mash the potato until it is smooth.

8 Spoon the frying pan contents into an oven proof dish and add the mashed potato as a pie lid. Optionally, you can add a sprinkle of cheese here for a crisper crust.

9 Place in the oven and cook for 30 minutes or until the mash has turned golden.

Baked Salmon

MAKES 1 PORTION
PREP TIME: 15 MINS | COOK TIME: 15 MINS | TOTAL TIME: 30 MINS
NET CARBS PER ¼ PIE: 52G//1.83OZ | PROTEIN:34G//1.19OZ |
FIBER: 6.7G//0.23OZ | FAT: 40G//1.41OZ | KCAL: 693

INGREDIENTS

- ○ 1 piece of salmon
- ○ A knob of butter
- ○ 1 half lemon
- ○ A pinch of salt
- ○ A sprinkle of dill
- ○ Optional substitutes for dill/ lemon include garlic, parsley, thyme, fennel seeds, rosemary, pesto, or other preferred herb/spice.
- ○ Optional substitutes for salmon include haddock, cod, hake, bass, or other fish of choice.

INSTRUCTIONS

1   Preheat the oven to 200C//392F//gas mark 6.

2   Select the salmon piece and prepare it by removing any bones or skin.

3   Place your piece of fish inside a square of cooking foil.

4   Place the knob of butter and the salt, lemon, and dill inside the foil.

5   Close the fish inside the foil so there are no gaps.

6   Place foiled fish onto a wire rack to cook, directly inside the oven.

7   Leave fish to bake for 10 minutes and serve.

Baked Chicken Parmigiana

MAKES 4 PORTIONS
PREP TIME: 15 MINS | COOK TIME: 15 MINS | TOTAL TIME: 30 MINS
NET CARBS PER PORTION: 22G//0.77OZ | PROTEIN:33G//1.16OZ |
FIBER: 1G//0.03OZ | FAT: 13G//0.45OZ | KCAL: 327

INGREDIENTS

- 100g//3.52oz flour
- 2 large beaten eggs
- 75g//2.64oz panko breadcrumbs
- 3 large chicken breasts
- 1 tbsp olive oil
- 2 diced garlic cloves
- 700ml//23.66floz passata sauce
- 1 tbsp sugar
- 1 tsp Italian herb seasoning/mixed herbs
- 70g//2.46oz grated Italian hard cheese/parmesan
- 1 ball mozzarella

INSTRUCTIONS

1   Add flour to one bowl, breadcrumbs to a second bowl, and place beaten eggs in a third.

2   Cut your chicken breasts in half along the width in a butterfly cut. Place between two sheets of clingfilm and bash with a meat hammer or a rolling pin. Bash the breast halves until they are flat.

3   Dip the chicken in flour, then in egg, then in breadcrumbs, leave to dry then repeat with a second coat. You do not need the flour the second time.

4   Heat the oil in a frying pan then add in the garlic and the passata sauce. Add in the sugar, mixed herbs, and season. Simmer for ten minutes.

5   While that is cooking, place the chicken under the grill to crisp for five minutes on each side.

6   Preheat your oven to 200C//392F//gas mark 6.

7 Put the chicken into an oven proof dish and spoon in the sauce. Make sure there is sauce underneath the chicken. Sprinkle on hard cheese and thinly slice the mozzarella ball and place the circles on top.

8 Bake for 20-25 minutes or until it is gooey and delicious. Serve immediately.

Baked Biscuits//Cookies

Dropped Scones/Biscuits

MAKES 8 SCONES
PREP TIME: 15 MINS | COOK TIME: 15 MINS | TOTAL TIME: 30 MINS
NET CARBS PER PORTION: 22G//0.77OZ | PROTEIN:33G//1.16OZ |
FIBER: 1G//0.03OZ | FAT: 13G//0.45OZ | KCAL: 327

INGREDIENTS

- ○ 55g//2oz butter
- ○ 30g//1.2oz sugar
- ○ 225g//8oz self-raising flour
- ○ A pinch of salt
- ○ 150ml//5floz whole milk

INSTRUCTIONS

1   Preheat your oven to 220C//428F//gas mark 7.

2   Cream the butter and sugar together in a large bowl.

3   Rub the flour into the butter and sugar mix and add the pinch of salt.

4   Add the milk a little at a time until the dough starts to come together.

5   Turn the dough onto a floured surface and roll to 2-inch thickness.

6   Cut out circles for your scones. You can use a cutter or a cup.

7   Place on a lined baking tray and brush with milk.

8   Place in the oven for 15-20 mins or until golden brown.

Traditional Scottish Shortbread Recipe

MAKES 20 INDIVIDUAL SHORTBREAD TRIANGLES
PREP TIME: 15 MINS | COOK TIME: 20 MINS | TOTAL TIME: 35 MINS

NET CARBS PER 2 BISCUITS: 16G//0.56OZ | PROTEIN: 2G//0.07OZ |
FIBER: 0.6G//0.021OZ | FAT: 4G//0.14OZ | KCAL: 156

INGREDIENTS

- ○ 100g butter, softened
- ○ 50g caster sugar plus dusting
- ○ 150g plain flour

INSTRUCTIONS

1 Preheat your oven to 170C//338F//gas mark 3 and line a baking tray.

2 Cream the butter and sugar together in a large mixing bowl.

3 Rub in the flour then press together into a dough.

4 Turn out the dough on a lightly floured surface.

5 Roll out shortbread dough to 1 inch thick.

6 Use a plate to mark circular biscuits and score with 4 lines through the centre.

7 Bake for 20 minutes or until golden.

8 Separate the biscuits when they are warm.

Chocolate Chip Cookies

MAKES 10 COOKIES
PREP TIME: 20 MINS | COOK TIME: 15 MINS | TOTAL TIME: 35 MINS
NET CARBS PER COOKIE: 16G//0.56OZ | PROTEIN: 3G//0.105OZ |
FIBER: 2G//0.070OZ | FAT: 16G//0.56OZ | KCAL: 308

INGREDIENTS

- ◯ 120g//4.23oz softened butter
- ◯ 75g//2.64oz light brown sugar
- ◯ 75g//2.64oz muscovado sugar
- ◯ 1 large egg
- ◯ 2 drops vanilla extract
- ◯ 180g//6.34oz plain flour
- ◯ 1 tsp bicarbonate of soda
- ◯ A pinch of salt
- ◯ 150g//5.3oz chocolate chips/chunks*

* You may use any kind of chocolate for this. Chocolate could be replaced with fudge.

INSTRUCTIONS

1 Preheat oven to 180C//356F//gas mark 4.

2 Cream the butter and sugars together until the mixture is smooth.

3 Beat in the egg and vanilla extract using a fork or metal spoon.

4 Sieve in the flour and fold it into the mixture, add the bicarbonate of soda.

5 Add the pinch of salt and the chocolate and mix well.

6 Prepare 4 baking sheets by lining them with parchment paper.

7 Scoop equal amounts of mixture onto the sheets. Space them out.

8 Place the cookie dough into the oven and bake for 15 minutes.

9 The cookies will spread out and turn golden brown.

Viennese Whirls

MAKES 10 BISCUITS
PREP TIME: 45 MINS | COOK TIME: 15 MINS | TOTAL TIME: 1 HR
NET CARBS PER 2 BISCUITS: 42G//1.48 OZ | PROTEIN: 2G//0.0705OZ |
FIBER: 1G//0.035OZ | FAT: 25G//0.88OZ | KCAL: 405

INGREDIENTS (BISCUITS)

- ○ 200g//7.05oz salted butter, softened
- ○ 50g//1.7oz icing sugar
- ○ 2 drops vanilla extract
- ○ 200g//7.05oz plain flour
- ○ 1 tbsp corn flour
- ○ 1 tsp baking powder

INGREDIENTS (FILLING)

- ○ 100g//3.52oz softened unsalted butter
- ○ 150g//5.29oz icing sugar
- ○ 30g//1.05oz jam of your choice (usually strawberry)

INSTRUCTIONS

1 Preheat your oven to 180C//356F//gas mark 4 and line two baking trays with parchment.

2 Mix the butter, vanilla extract, and icing sugar together in a large bowl using an electric whisk.

3 Sieve the flour, corn flour, and baking powder. Fold these dry ingredients into the mixture.

4 Put dough into a piping bag and pipe swirls onto the lined trays.

5 Bake for 15 minutes or until golden.

6 Remove from the oven and cool on a wire cooling rack for 20 minutes or more.

7 While cooling, add butter and icing sugar to a bowl and cream them together.

8 Each biscuit is then coated with jam, given a layer of cream, and stuck to another.

Ginger Snap Biscuits

MAKES 10 BISCUITS
PREP TIME: 15 MINS | COOK TIME: 35 MINS | TOTAL TIME: 50 MINS

NET CARBS PER BISCUIT: 5G//0.17 OZ | PROTEIN: 1G//0.035OZ |
FIBER: 1G//0.035OZ | FAT:5G//0.17OZ | KCAL: 120

INGREDIENTS

- ○ 150g//5.29oz softened butter
- ○ 75g//2.64oz soft brown sugar
- ○ 75g//2.64oz muscovado sugar
- ○ 2 tbsp golden syrup
- ○ 150g//5.29oz plain flour
- ○ 1 tbsp baking powder
- ○ 2 tbsp ground ginger
- ○ 1tbsp ground cinnamon

INSTRUCTIONS

1   Preheat the oven to 170C//338F//gas mark 3.

2   Line two baking trays with parchment paper.

3   Cream together the butter and the sugars in a large mixing bowl.

4   Add the syrup and beat until you have a smooth, silken consistency.

5   Gradually sieve in the flour, baking powder, and spices.

6   Fold the dry ingredients into the mixture slowly.

7   The mix should come to a dough stiff enough to roll into balls.

8   Portion out the mixture, roll into balls, then squash onto the lined trays.

9   Bake in the oven for 20 minutes or until golden brown.

10   Leave an extra 5-10 minutes for a crisper biscuit.

11   Allow to cool for 15-20 minutes and serve.

Country Oat Biscuits

MAKES 12 BISCUITS
PREP TIME: 15 MINS | COOK TIME: 15 MINS | TOTAL TIME: 30 MINS
NET CARBS PER BISCUIT: 17G//0.59 OZ | PROTEIN: 2G//0.070OZ |
FIBER: 1G//0.035OZ | FAT:7G//0.246OZ | KCAL: 140

INGREDIENTS

- ○ 75g//2.64oz wholemeal flour
- ○ 80g//2.82oz oats
- ○ 50g//1.76oz granulated sugar
- ○ 1 tsp baking powder
- ○ 75g//2.64oz butter
- ○ 1 tbsp golden syrup
- ○ 2 tbsp milk

INSTRUCTIONS

1 Heat up your oven to 180C//356F//gas mark 4.

2 Line two baking trays with parchment paper.

3 Sieve your flour into a large bowl and add in the oats and sugar.

4 Mix the baking powder in and stir well.

5 Heat a saucepan on a low heat and melt the butter, syrup, and milk.

6 Once the mixture is completely melted, add it to the dry ingredients.

7 Stir everything until it is coated.

8 Portion with a tablespoon and space out cookies on your baking trays.

9 Place into the oven and bake for 10-15 minutes, or until golden brown.

Empire Biscuits

MAKES 12 BISCUITS
PREP TIME: 1 HR | COOK TIME: 15 MINS | TOTAL TIME: 1 HR 15 MINS
NET CARBS PER BISCUIT: 59G//2.08OZ | PROTEIN: 2G//0.70OZ |
FAT: 7G//0.24OZ | FIBER: 1G//0.035OZ | KCAL: 305

INGREDIENTS

- 100g//3.5oz salted butter, softened
- 300g//10.58oz icing sugar
- 2 drops vanilla extract
- 180g//6.34oz plain flour
- 2 large eggs, yolks only
- 5 tbsp strawberry jam
- 50g//1.7oz tub of glacé cherries

INSTRUCTIONS

1 Cream the butter and 100g//3.5oz of the icing sugar together in a large bowl then stir in the vanilla extract.

2 Rub in the flour. Aim for a breadcrumb texture.

3 Beat the egg yolks and add them into the mixture. The mix should come together as a dough. If it is too dry, add a splash of milk. If it is too wet, add a little extra flour.

4   Tip the dough onto a lightly floured surface and knead for 2 minutes. Place it back into the bowl and cover with clingfilm. Put the bowl in the fridge to chill for half an hour, or until it is properly cold.

5   Remove the dough from the chill and preheat your oven to 180C//356F//gas mark 4.

6   Roll out the dough until it is the thickness of a pound/dollar coin.

7   Cut as many circular biscuits from the dough as you can, you should end up with 24 rounds.

8   Bake for 10-15 minutes or until golden brown.

9   Remove from the oven and allow to cool while you mix the remainder of your icing sugar with water.

10 To assemble your biscuits, coat one side in jam and sandwich together with a second biscuit. Icing sugar is then drizzled on top and a cherry is added. Remember not to add your icing sugar until the biscuits are cooled.

Baked Parmesan Tuiles

MAKES 10 TUILES
PREP TIME: 10 MINS | COOK TIME: 10 MINS | TOTAL TIME: 20 MINS
NET CARBS PER TUILE: 6G//0.21OZ | PROTEIN: 0G//0.00OZ |
FAT: 1G//0.035OZ | FIBER: 1G//0.035OZ | KCAL: 43

INGREDIENTS

- ○ 200g//7oz parmesan cheese or hard cheese equivalent
- ○ (Optional) 1 sprig rosemary, chopped

INSTRUCTIONS

1   Preheat your oven to 200C//392F//gas mark 6.

2   Grate the parmesan cheese on the finest part of your grater. If you have an electronic blender, reduce the parmesan to small particles by pulsing the cheese. If it gets too hot, you will cook it.

3   Line a baking tray with parchment paper.

4   Arrange the grated parmesan on the parchment paper in ten neat circles. You can shape the tuiles as you wish, but circles will impress your friends. Using a cheesecake mould can help. Sprinkle with chopped rosemary when prepared.

5   Place the tuiles into the oven and set a timer for ten minutes.

6   Remove from the oven and allow to cool. You should be able to pop the tuiles free of the parchment paper. They will resemble crisps.

Saltwater Crackers

MAKES 15 BISCUITS
PREP TIME: 25 MINS | COOK TIME: 15 MINS | TOTAL TIME: 40 MINS
NET CARBS PER BISCUIT: 9G//0.31OZ | PROTEIN: 1G//0.035OZ |
FAT: 2G//0.070OZ | FIBER: 0G//0OZ | KCAL: 60

INGREDIENTS

- ○ 200g//7oz plain flour
- ○ 1 teaspoon baking powder
- ○ 50g//1.76oz salted butter, softened
- ○ 20ml//0.67floz cold water
- ○ 30g//1oz Himalayan rock salt/flaked sea salt

INSTRUCTIONS

1   Preheat oven to 180C//356F//gas mark 4.

2   Mix the flour and baking powder together in a large bowl.

3   Rub in the butter, aiming for a breadcrumb consistency. If using a food processor, pulse the power on and off to avoid cooking the butter.

4   Use a dribble of water to bring the mixture together into a dough. You may not need all the water and you may need to add a little extra flour if it is too wet.

5   Turn the dough out onto a lightly floured surface.

6   Roll the dough until it is as thin as you can get it. Brush it with water and then sprinkle it with the salt. Make sure you press the salt into the dough, so it is not lost in the cooking process.

7   Bake in the oven for 15 minutes, remove and place on a wire rack to cool.

8   Once cooled, store in an airtight container for up to a fortnight.

Cakes and Desserts

Victoria Sandwich Cake

MAKES 6 PORTIONS OR ONE ROUND LOAF
PREP TIME: 30 MINS | COOK TIME: 25 MINS | TOTAL TIME: 55 MINS
NET CARBS PER PORTION: 50G//1.76OZ | PROTEIN: 5G//0.17OZ |
FAT: 31G//1.090OZ | FIBER: 0.5G//0.017OZ | KCAL: 500

INGREDIENTS

- ◯ 4 large eggs
- ◯ 225g//8oz softened butter
- ◯ 225g//8oz caster sugar
- ◯ 225g//8oz self-raising flour
- ◯ 1 tsp baking powder
- ◯ 100g//3.5oz strawberry or raspberry jam
- ◯ Clotted or whipped cream (optional)
- ◯ Icing sugar for dusting

INSTRUCTIONS

1 Preheat the oven to 180C//356F//gas mark 4 and line 2 cake tins with parchment paper. You can use one cake tin and cut the sponge in half, but two cake tins are better.

2 Using a hand mixer or a whisk, beat the eggs, butter, and sugar together in a bowl.

3 Gradually fold in the sieved flour and baking powder.

4 Divide the mix between the two lined cake tins and pop them in the oven for approximately 25 minutes.

5 Remove from the oven and place on a wire rack to cool. If you are using one cake tin and cutting the sponge in half, allow it to fully cool before you do so. Allowing cakes to cool inside the tins will make them less likely to break when you remove them.

6 Remove the cakes from their tins and slather the flat side of each with the jam. Sandwich the two pieces together.

7 You can either dust the cake with icing sugar to finish it or make up 50g//1.7oz icing sugar with a little water to drizzle it on top.

Carrot & Walnut Cake

MAKES 1 CAKE OR 8 PORTIONS
PREP TIME: 30 MINS | COOK TIME 35 MINS | TOTAL TIME: 1 HR 5 MINS
NET CARBS PER PORTION: 53G//1.8OZ | PROTEIN: 3.8G//0.13OZ |
FAT: 20.8G//0.70OZ | FIBER: 1.1G//0.038OZ | KCAL: 408

INGREDIENTS

- ◯ 300g//10.5oz self-raising flour
- ◯ 225g//8oz light brown sugar
- ◯ 1 tbsp baking powder
- ◯ 1 tsp ground ginger
- ◯ 1 tsp mixed spice
- ◯ 75g//2.6oz smashed walnuts
- ◯ 200g//7oz peeled and grated carrot
- ◯ 5 medium eggs, beaten
- ◯ 2 drops vanilla essence
- ◯ 50g//1.7oz softened butter
- ◯ 250g//8.8oz cream cheese (whole fat)
- ◯ 25g//0.88oz icing sugar

INSTRUCTIONS

1 Preheat the oven to 180C//356F//gas mark 4. Line two 8-inch cake tins with parchment paper and grease with a little butter to hold it in place.

2 Mix all the dry ingredients in a bowl, then add the walnuts, carrots, and eggs. The batter should be wet rather than stiff.

3 Divide the mixture evenly between the two cake tins and cook for 30-35 minutes, or until it is rounded and golden brown.

4 Remove from the oven and leave to cool on a wire rack until completely cold.

5 While it is cooling, mix the softened butter, cream cheese, vanilla essence and icing sugar in a bowl. This is your filling.

6 When the cake is cooled, smear filling on the two flat sides and sandwich together. Smear filling on top and around the edges of your cake, too.

Chocolate Cake

MAKES 12 PORTIONS
PREP TIME: 1 HR 30 MINS | COOK TIME 45 MINS | TOTAL TIME: 2 HRS 15 MINS
NET CARBS PER PORTION: 56G//1.97OZ | PROTEIN: 6.5G//0.22OZ |
FAT: 25G//0.88OZ | FIBER: 2.5G//0.088OZ | KCAL: 408

INGREDIENTS

- ○ 225g//8oz plain flour
- ○ 85g//3oz cocoa powder
- ○ 350g//12.34oz caster sugar
- ○ 2 tsp baking powder
- ○ 2 tsp bicarbonate of soda
- ○ 2 large eggs, beaten
- ○ 250ml//9floz whole milk
- ○ 125ml//4.22floz sunflower oil

INGREDIENTS (TOPPING)

- ○ 200g//7oz cooking chocolate
- ○ 200ml//7floz double cream
- ○ 250ml//9floz boiling water

INSTRUCTIONS

1 Preheat your oven to 180C//356F//gas mark 4 and line 2 8-inch cake tins.

2 Mix the dry ingredients in a large mixing bowl.

3 Stir in the beaten eggs, milk, and oil.

4 Divide the batter between the cake tins and bake for 35 mins.

5 Remove from oven and allow the cakes to cool on a wire rack.

6 Melt the chocolate and the cream together over the hot water on a low heat.

7 Let the cream and chocolate set for about an hour in the fridge.

8 Smear over the cake to sandwich together. Use this as a topping.

Marvellous Madeira Cake

MAKES 1 LOAF CAKE OR 8 SLICES
PREP TIME: 20 MINS | COOK TIME: 1 HR | TOTAL TIME: 1 HR 20 MINS

NET CARBS PER PORTION: 40G//1.41OZ | PROTEIN: 6G//0.21OZ |
FAT: 24G//0.084OZ | FIBER: 1.4G//0.49OZ | KCAL: 397

INGREDIENTS

- ○ 3 large eggs
- ○ 100g//3.5oz caster sugar
- ○ 75g//2.6oz soft brown sugar
- ○ 3 drops vanilla essence
- ○ The zest and juice of half a lemon
- ○ 200g//7oz self-raising flour
- ○ 50g//1.7oz ground almonds

INSTRUCTIONS

1 Use a 900g//31oz loaf tin, grease and line it with parchment paper. Preheat your oven to 170C//338F//gas mark 3.

2 Beat the sugars and the eggs in with whisk. A hand mixer would be best for this.

3 Add the vanilla and lemon zest and juice, then start folding in the dry ingredients. Add the almonds last.

4 Place the mixture into a lined cake tin and bake in the oven for an hour.

5 Remove from the oven when golden and spongey, then allow to cool for 20 minutes before slicing.

Ruby Red Velvet Cake

MAKES 8 PORTIONS OR ONE ROUND CAKE
PREP TIME: 1 HR 30 MINS | COOK TIME: 30 MINS | TOTAL TIME: 2 HOURS
NET CARBS PER PORTION: 36G//1.26OZ | PROTEIN:4G//0.14OZ |
FAT: 23G//0.81OZ | FIBER: 0.3G//0.010OZ | KCAL: 368

INGREDIENTS

- ◯ 300g//10.5oz self-raising flour
- ◯ 22g//0.77oz cocoa powder
- ◯ A teaspoon of baking powder
- ◯ A pinch of salt
- ◯ 115g//4oz unsalted butter, softened
- ◯ 350g//12.34oz caster sugar
- ◯ 2 large room temperature eggs
- ◯ 120ml//4floz vegetable oil
- ◯ 2 tsp red food colouring
- ◯ 1 tsp white wine vinegar
- ◯ 320ml//10.8floz whole milk

INGREDIENTS (TOPPING)

- ◯ 340g//12oz cream cheese (whole fat)
- ◯ 175g//6.17oz softened butter
- ◯ 360g//12.7oz icing sugar
- ◯ 2 tsp vanilla essence

INSTRUCTIONS

1 Preheat the oven to 180C//356F//gas mark 4. Line two 9-inch cake tins with parchment paper.

2 Whisk the flour, cocoa powder, baking powder and salt in a bowl, then sieve them together.

3 In a second bowl, cream 115g//4oz of the butter together with the caster sugar and beat in the eggs.

4 beat in the oil, the food colouring, the vinegar, and the milk.

5 Fold in the dry ingredients we set aside earlier.

6 Distribute the mixture between the tins evenly.

7 Place inside the oven and bake for 30 minutes.

8 Remove from the oven and leave to cool.

9 Mix the creamed cheese, leftover butter, icing sugar and vanilla for the frosting.

Coffee Cake

MAKES 1 ROUND CAKE OR 8 PORTIONS
PREP TIME: 20 MINS | COOK TIME 30 MINS | TOTAL TIME: 50 MINS
NET CARBS PER PORTION: 66G//2.32OZ | PROTEIN: 5G//0.17OZ |
FAT:30G//1.05OZ | FIBER: 1G//0.35OZ | KCAL: 559

INGREDIENTS

- ○ 170g//6oz unsalted butter, softened
- ○ 170g//6oz caster sugar
- ○ 170g//6oz self-raising flour
- ○ 3 large eggs, beaten.
- ○ 1 tbsp instant coffee, dissolved in 1 tbsp boiling water

INGREDIENTS (ICING)

- ○ 22g//0.77oz icing sugar
- ○ 100g//3.5oz unsalted butter, softened
- ○ 2 tbsp instant coffee, dissolved in 2 tbsp boiling water

INSTRUCTIONS

1 Preheat your oven to 180C//356F//gas mark 4. Line two 8-inch sandwich tins.

2 Whisk the butter and sugar until creamy and beat in the eggs, using a little flour with each egg. Add the rest of the flour and fold it in.

3 Fold in the coffee.

4 Divide the mixture between the two cake tins and place in the oven to bake for 30 minutes.

5 Remove from the oven and allow to cool on a wire rack.

6 While it is cooling, blend the icing sugar with the unsalted butter and the second lot of coffee, and mix together.

7 Smear on the flat sides of the two cakes and press the sponges together. You may use jam if you prefer.

8 Coat the cake in as much of the topping as you can and enjoy.

Baked New York Cheesecake

MAKES 16 PORTIONS
PREP TIME: 30 MINS | COOK TIME: 2 HR 25 MINS (PLUS OVERNIGHT
CHILLING TIME) | TOTAL TIME: 2 HRS 55 MINS
NET CARBS PER PORTION: 33G//1.16OZ | PROTEIN: 6G//0.21OZ |
FAT:18G//0.63OZ | FIBER: 1G//0.35OZ | KCAL: 320

INGREDIENTS (BASE)

- ○ 200g//7oz plain flour
- ○ 125g//4.5oz unsalted softened butter
- ○ 1 large beaten egg
- ○ 25g//0.88oz caster sugar

INGREDIENTS (CAKE)

- ○ 1200g//42oz creamed cheese, whole fat and softened
- ○ 350g//12oz caster sugar
- ○ 5 eggs plus 2 egg yolks, instructions on how to separate are here
- ○ 15g//0.17oz plain flour
- ○ 60ml//2floz double cream

INSTRUCTIONS

1 Preheat your oven to 200C//392F//gas mark 6 and grease and line a 25 cm diameter cake tin.

2 Combine all the ingredients for the base and mix well. Put the base mix into the tin and press it down to the bottom so that it is flat. Prick it with a knife a few times and place it in the oven to bake for about 15 minutes.

3 Remove it from the oven and let it cool. Turn your oven up to 240C//464F//gas mark 9.

4 Beat all the cheesecake ingredients together except for the cream. Add the cream all in one go and stop stirring as soon as it is mixed in.

5 When the base is cool, pour the mixture over the base and shake the pan so that it falls to the bottom.

6 Put into the oven and bake for 10 mins at 240C//464F//gas mark 9, then bring the temperature right down to 110C//230F//gas mark ¼.

7   Bake the cheesecake at this low temperature for about an hour.

8   Turn off the oven and leave the cake in there until it is completely cool.

9   Remove the baked New York cheesecake and chill overnight before eating.

Pineapple Upside Down Cake

MAKES 6 PORTIONS OR ONE ROUND CAKE
PREP TIME: 15 MINS | COOK TIME: 40 MINS | TOTAL TIME: 55 MINS
NET CARBS PER PORTION: 49G//1.7OZ | PROTEIN: 5G//0.17OZ |
FAT:23G//0.81OZ | FIBER: 1G//0.35OZ | KCAL: 407

INGREDIENTS (TOPPING)

- ○ 50g//1.7 oz softened unsalted butter
- ○ 50g//1.7oz soft brown sugar
- ○ 1 tin pineapple rings
- ○ 1 tub glacé cherries

INGREDIENTS

- ○ 100g//3.5oz softened unsalted butter
- ○ 100g//3.5oz caster sugar
- ○ 1 tsp vanilla essence
- ○ 2 large eggs
- ○ 100g//3.5oz self-raising flour
- ○ 1 tsp baking powder

INSTRUCTIONS

1   Preheat your oven to 180C//356F//gas mark 4 and grease and line a 20cm cake tin.

2   Mix the topping's butter and sugar together and use it to coat the inside of the cake tin. Cover the sticky mixture with the pineapple rings and place a cherry in the centre of each ring. It should take about 7 rings to cover your cake.

3   Cream the butter and sugar together in a bowl with the vanilla essence.

4   Beat in the 2 large eggs.

5   Fold in the sieved flour and baking powder.

6   Pour this batter into the cake tin, on top of the pineapple rings and cherries.

7   Place in the centre of your oven and bake for 35 mins or until golden brown.

8   Leave the cake to cool for about 15 minutes before turning it out onto a cooling rack. You should see the pineapple and cherries on the top.

Disclaimer

This book contains opinions and ideas of the author and is meant to teach the reader informative and helpful knowledge while due care should be taken by the user in the application of the information provided. The instructions and strategies are possibly not right for every reader and there is no guarantee that they work for everyone. Using this book and implementing the information/recipes therein contained is explicitly your own responsibility and risk. This work with all its contents, does not guarantee correctness, completion, quality or correctness of the provided information. Misinformation or misprints cannot be completely eliminated.